I0588441

LOST IN YOUR LOVE

WENDY LINDSTROM

OLIVERHEBERBOOKS

All rights reserved.

No part of this publication may be sold, copied, distributed, reproduced or transmitted in any form or by any means, mechanical or digital, including photocopying and recording or by any information storage and retrieval system without the prior written permission of both the publisher, Oliver Heber Books and the author, Wendy Lindstrom, except in the case of brief quotations embodied in critical articles and reviews.

PUBLISHER'S NOTE: This is a work of fiction. Names, characters, places, and incidents either are the product of the author's imagination or are used fictitiously. Any resemblance to actual persons, living or dead, business establishments, events, or locales is entirely coincidental.

Copyright © Wendy Lindstrom

Cover design by Erin Dameron-Hill

Published by Oliver-Heber Books

0 9 8 7 6 5 4 3 2 1

REVIEWS

From *New York Times* bestselling author Wendy Lindstrom comes a gripping novel about overcoming past wounds and the many ways we give and receive love.

"Riveting—a wonderful story. Couldn't put it down."—L. Benner

"A real page turner. This story has depth and heart, there are wonderful unexpected elements that will leave you breathless. You will not regret reading this one!"—Tammy Hooper

"Beautifully written. Much more than just a romance."—Old Book Barn Gazette

"Absorbing!"—Harriet Klausner

"The characters practically leapt from the pages, they seemed so alive."— Dafna Yee

PLEASE NOTE:

Lost in Your Love is the sweet and clean edition of Until I Found You book #10 in Wendy Lindstrom's award-winning and New York Times bestselling Grayson Brothers series. This means there are no open door love scenes in this book (Lost in Your Love).

If you prefer a more sensual read with open door love scenes, please feel free to return this book and get the sensual edition titled Until I Found You (it's the same book but with the love scenes included).

The different name (titles and series) for the sweet editions is simply to help readers differentiate the open door (sensual editions) from the closed door (sweet and clean editions) of the books to ensure the best reading experience.

CHAPTER ONE

NOVEMBER 1892

A frigid wind circled Gray Sullivan's neck as he leveled the barrel of his rifle and took aim. Slowly, he pulled the trigger. The rifle butt slammed his shoulder as the blast echoed through the frigid mountain air, but the buck he'd targeted darted through the pines unscathed. Gray stared at his rifle as if it had misfired, and yet he knew it had been his lack of desire that had caused the miss.

The truth was, he hadn't wanted to shoot the magnificent creature. The deer belonged here, and Gray was beginning to think he did too. The mountain silence soothed him, eased the shaky, erratic emotions that had set his teeth on edge each day on the job. His tolerance with labor disputes, picket lines, and violent protestors had dropped to zero. He could no longer be around his fellow agents without feeling irritated and provoked, so he'd agreed with his boss's suggestion to take a few days off before going undercover at the paper mill two miles down the mountain.

The solitude of the mountain forest appealed to Gray. He'd become a loner, a situation of his own making, which is what had drawn him to detective work for the Pinkerton Detective Agency. As an investigator, he could focus solely on his work, and travel and survive on his own with no encumbrances. At twenty-three years old, he'd already lost one family and gained another, and yet he felt disconnected, as if a piece of himself had broken off and was lost. He'd been searching for that piece with the same determination and devotion he used while searching for suspects, and yet it eluded him. His last hope was to find the answer here in the mountains of Maine.

Accepting it was futile to stay out in the biting cold, he slung his rifle across his back and headed in the direction of the cabin the agency had rented for him. Frigid air burned his lungs as his feet crunched through dried leaves and dead branches downed by hard winds from the previous night. The weather and dark sky overhead warned of a storm rolling in. Drawing the cold air deep into his lungs, he increased his pace, but as he stepped from the cold shadows of the trees and headed downstream, he stopped in stunned surprise.

At the edge of the stream, a woman stood hunched and shivering in the frigid wind. Slowly, painfully it seemed, she sank to her knees, revealing her stocking-clad thigh through a long, jagged tear in her skirt. He watched her dip trembling hands in the creek, then bring her cupped palms to her mouth. Her whole body quaked and she emitted a small gasp as she swallowed, her hands immediately clutching her throat as if it hurt her.

Instinctively, Gray surveyed the long expanse of rock-strewn creek bed above him, then checked downstream where the stream widened and gained momentum, but he saw no one. Methodically, he scanned the timberline and the high cliffs behind the woman, desperately hoping someone would appear and claim her, but the mountain remained eerily silent. She appeared to be alone, and in her exposed condition he knew she would be dead before nightfall.

Clenching his fists, he searched again. He did *not* want to get involved in whatever trouble had landed this woman on his path.

After the horrific mess at Homestead, and the four months following that he'd worked and tried to forget about the violence and unnecessary deaths of good men, Gray desperately needed a few days' respite.

But the harsh November wind battered the woman's body as she huddled on the stream bank.

With a groan of defeat, he knew another life would be lost if he didn't get involved.

There was a reason the woman was abandoned out here. His head said he didn't want to know. His gut agreed she'd be trouble. But his conscience conceded he was her only hope. It seemed there would be no escape from the world no matter how he tried to avoid it.

"Hello, miss!" he called out, his voice sounding loud in the silent wintery air.

His voice brought her head up. When she spotted him, her eyes widened in fright.

Her expression was a mere reflection of what must be in his own eyes, he thought, viewing her bloodied, bruised, and painfully swollen face.

Her gaze flicked to his rifle, and she struggled to her feet, splinting her side and holding her throat as she hobbled toward the trees.

"Wait," he yelled to her retreating back. "I'm a detective and I can help you." As a highly trained agent, he knew he was capable of protecting her. He'd hoped his declaration would convince the woman to trust him, but she hurried on, hunched and stumbling from her effort while he hesitated on the opposite bank, trying to decide how to help her without increasing her fear.

In a matter of seconds, he realized there wasn't a way, so he slung his rifle over his back and stepped into the water to cross the river. The icy jolt stopped him dead, but the shock brought clarity. The woman's injuries were not self-inflicted or sustained by any animal he could imagine. A person, almost certainly a man, had done that to her, and the wretch might still be lurking out here on the mountain.

With his senses keen and alert to danger, Gray sloshed across a narrow, rock-strewn area of the river. Clenching his teeth, he prayed the river wouldn't reach past his thighs because one slip could mean the difference between life or death—for both of them.

A hundred yards into the trees, he heard the woman panting. He found her lying partially concealed beneath a low-hanging pine bough, lying on her side and biting her fist, her nostrils flaring with each labored breath.

"I won't hurt you," he said, trying to gentle his voice from the intimidating baritone he'd acquired during his years of providing armed security, strike-breaking violent labor disputes, and tracking down criminals.

The woman panted and shivered, but said nothing.

"I only want to help you," he said, trying to quell the cold seeping into his bones. "I'll take you to your home or somewhere safe and warm." He lifted the rifle from his shoulder, intending to remove his jacket and offer it to her, but the terror in her eyes suddenly bordered on madness.

"I'm going to give you my jacket," he said softly, trying to reason with her. "It will keep you warm."

He placed the gun beside him, aiming the barrel away from them. He shrugged the jacket off his shoulders, but her gaze fastened on his gun. She tensed, glancing to either side of him as if searching for an escape route.

"It's too cold," he said, reading her pitiful thoughts of escape and trying to spare her the futile effort. In her advanced state of shock, he doubted she could even stand.

The pine-scented air sank icy teeth into his back as he knelt before her, offering the warmth of his jacket. She stiffened, came up on her elbow and edged away like a cornered animal.

He inched forward. "My name is Gray Sullivan. I'm a detective with the Pinkerton Agency, and you'll be safe with me."

Her chest heaved and her frantic wheezing mingled with the moaning wind that was slicing into them. He had to get her to the cabin before hypothermia claimed them both. Hoping to entice her with the warmth that lingered in his jacket, he leaned forward and draped it across her arm.

She gasped as if he'd struck her with a rock. Clutching her throat, she rolled to her knees and tried valiantly to gain her feet, but the effort proved too much. She shook so violently he could hear her teeth chatter. Then she fainted into the thick bed of dried pine needles.

Taking advantage of her inability to fight him, he plucked one of his mittens from his coat pocket and tugged it over her dirty stocking-clad foot. Somehow she'd lost one of her shoes. Then he wrapped her in the warm folds of his jacket. After pulling off his flannel shirt, he tied it around her legs, the only added protection he could give her until he got her back to the warmth of his cabin. Clad in his long underwear shirt and wet pants, Gray fought to keep his own teeth from chattering as he slung his rifle over his shoulder, then eased his arms beneath her. She wasn't heavy, but his bulky jacket, combined with his own violent shivering, made carrying her difficult.

As he made his way downriver, his feet and hands aching, he wondered what had befallen the beaten woman lying lifeless in his arms.

SHE CAME AWAKE SLOWLY to the smell of wood smoke, and deep, throbbing pain that racked her body.

A hand stroked her forehead, and she turned to it...desperate for anything that would ease the pain. Her lips parted and pressure built in her throat as she asked for help, but only a soft, disjointed gasp reached her ears followed by searing pain in her throat.

"Shhhh...you're burning up. Rest now..."

The voice was low, a man's voice, and his hands cool and gentle like a soothing river. She concentrated on relaxing beneath the tender stroke of his fingers, willing each rigid muscle to unlock its painful grip on her body. But something urgent pushed up from within her that stopped her from succumbing, that struggled hard to warn her, that told her to run for her life.

Her thoughts spun sideways and she fought to open her eyes, to resist the shadows that flickered at the edge of consciousness.

Something cold washed her face, and she licked her stinging, swollen lips.

She tried to ask why her lips were sore, but her question came forth as a raspy wheeze.

"I know it hurts. I'm sorry."

The man's voice drew her, compelled her to open her eyes. Wide, flannel-clad shoulders filled her gaze, and she felt a sudden frisson of fear skitter down her spine. She shrank away.

"You're safe here," he said, putting his hands on her arms to still her.

His large shoulders loomed over her, and she glanced at his face. A solid chin in need of a shave. Hard cheekbones. Proud nose. Green eyes that conveyed confidence and kindness though his mouth remained closed.

Who are you? she tried to ask, but only hoarse wheezing escaped. She raised a hand to her ravaged, aching throat, feeling as if she'd swallowed shards of glass.

Glancing beyond his shoulder at the fading light outside the window, she wondered where she was. Slowly, she surveyed her surroundings. She lay in a bed tucked beneath the window at one end of a cabin. To her right, a snapping woodstove was bracketed by two cushioned chairs and a shared tea table that held a large oil lantern. Beyond that, in the far right corner, stood an overflowing bookshelf, a small desk, and a table. To the left of that, a kitchen of sorts took up the other corner. As her gaze came full circle, she noticed a doorway off the main room but couldn't discern where it led. The last thing to catch her eye was the entrance door. It was solid oak and bolted with what must be two pounds of gleaming steel.

She glanced at the man hovering above her and felt an intense urge to leap from the bed and run for her life.

"Is there someone you can trust?" he asked.

His voice jolted her, but the intensity in his eyes kept her silent. Tingling with apprehension, she drew back, consumed by the need to get away from him. To get beyond that locked door.

"Miss," he said, forcing her to look at him, "I want to help you get home. I can contact a friend or family member if you give me a name and address of someone you trust."

Trust? Her mouth worked frantically, but no sound came, nor did a name or address. Whom could she trust?

He smiled and clasped her fingers. "Maybe you should start with your name."

She jerked her hand from his light grasp. Her name...her name was...she was...Confused, she shook her head, causing a nause-ating swirl of sensation that made her brace one hand on the wall in an effort to steady herself. She had to know her own name.

"Are you afraid to tell me?"

Panicked, she looked at her hand splayed on the wall. The broken fingernails and scraped knuckles didn't look familiar. Pain tore through her side as she sat up and peered into the mirror hanging on the wall opposite the bed.

Her own horrifying reflection rocked her world, and she

gasped in disbelief. That was not her face! Whoever she was, she couldn't be that monster in the mirror.

The man blocked her view. "You should look more like yourself in a couple of weeks when the swelling is down and your bruises are gone."

She searched his eyes, her own stinging from shock and unanswered questions.

Sadly, he shook his head. "I'm sorry, miss. I don't know what happened out there."

A series of inaudible squeaks came from her damaged throat, and she cringed in pain and shock. She couldn't talk! She couldn't remember and she couldn't talk!

"It'll come," he said, capturing her hands and cradling them between his hard palms as though to comfort her. "You'll feel better after you rest."

She pulled her hands free and huddled against the wall, hiding her bloodied fists in the folds of her blouse, fighting panic and waves of pain that cut through her body.

The man sighed and raked his hair back, leaving it furrowed like rich brown soil ready for planting. "I guess this bears repeating. I will not harm you in any way. I have no idea what happened out there, but whatever it was, I'm certain you're not safe. You need help, and I'm all you've got until you can remember who hurt you."

Someone did this to her? Her gaze riveted on his, then darted to the bolted door. Was it him? Was this part of a depraved game? Why couldn't she remember?

He trailed his finger through the air in front of her face, and she flinched away, watching warily to see what he was about. "I'm just checking your vision," he said, moving his finger toward her nose and away again. "Does your head ache?"

She tried to nod, but even the slight movement sickened her and started the black mist swirling in her head.

"Can you see clearly? Any double vision?"

Her head lolled as dizziness washed over her again.

"You need to lie back, miss." Trying to calm her, he softened his voice. "Maybe we can come up with a temporary name for you until you remember your own."

She leaned her head against the wall and peered at him through bleary slits.

"Do you know the first image that came to my mind when I saw you by the river?" he asked, not expecting a reply. "The weeping willows that grew along the creek I swam in as a boy. They were tall and graceful and also strong and resilient. They survived harsh winds and roughhousing of four young boys. So how does the name Willow sound, just until yours comes back to you?"

She couldn't answer.

"There's a storm rolling in and we might be here a while. For now, I will call you Willow until you can tell me your real name."

Her thoughts were growing jumbled and confused. Shadowed images of swaying treetops, hard breathing, and excruciating pain consumed her. Lightning flashed in her head and the world spun sideways. She gasped and raised her arms against the shadowed image that reached for her. Hands gripped her wrists, her throat, pushed her down...down...

"Easy, miss. You're safe here," Gray said, but he could see she was beyond rational thinking, that her fear was too fierce to be calmed.

To subdue her after what she must have already suffered was more than distasteful, but he worried her thrashing would cause more injury to herself. Heat rolled off her body in waves, making her actions admirable but pathetically feeble.

As gently as possible, he restrained her until she'd exhausted herself. Then he retrieved a sedative from his valise. From the bruises on her neck and the way she clutched her throat, he suspected she couldn't swallow a pill, so he crushed it into a powder and added it to a teaspoon of water. He hoped she could manage to swallow it. Even as he gave it to her, he questioned whether it was the right thing to do. He was uncertain of the extent of her injuries but knew she could cause her own death if she kept thrashing. The sedative seemed safer.

"Willow?" he called quietly, trying out the name to see if she would respond.

She licked her lips and struggled to look at him, but the fever and recent exertion had left her too weak to hold her head up.

He moved her hair away from her eyes. "It's okay now. No one will hurt you."

Whether his words calmed her or the fever claimed her, he couldn't tell, but her breathing slowed and her eyes drifted closed.

He tucked her beneath the blankets on his bed. Perspiration dotted her face, and he wiped it away with a cool cloth, careful not to punish her bruises or open the gash on her left cheek. The laceration probably needed stitches rather than the mesh of bandages and gauze he was using to mend it, but it was the best he could do for now. She needed a doctor, but the closest one was down the mountain. Even if he had a way to get her there, he doubted she could survive the ride. And he certainly couldn't leave her here alone to fetch a doctor.

From all appearances, someone was out there who wanted her dead. Until Willow could remember what happened to her and identify her assailant, she had to stay dead or risk them finishing the job.

So they were both left without a choice. Like it or not, Gray knew that until she remembered her name and what had happened to her, he and Willow were stuck with each other. But as soon as the woman's memory returned, he would carry her down the mountain and out of his life.

Retrieving a basin of cold water from the kitchen pump, he ruminated on the situation. An attempted murder with no motive, no known witness, and no suspect would be near impossible to solve, especially when the victim had no memory of the crime.

Perplexed, he carried the basin to the stove and warmed it from the kettle of hot water he kept there, then placed it beside the bed. After washing his hands, he returned to the bed where Willow was barely responsive to his touch. Her eyes were closed and her breathing slow and deep, so he began.

He lifted her scraped left hand. Work-roughened hands and fingers. Broken nails. No ring. Had she known her attacker?

Gently, he pulled back the blankets and unbuttoned her bloodstained blouse. Raised welts and bruises marred her neck and fever-blushed chest.

Seeing her like that, beaten and as vulnerable as a newborn, fueled his outrage with whoever hurt her. This woman was a survivor. He'd known that the moment he'd seen her standing unflinching in a wind that would have taken many men to their knees in a similar circumstance.

To violate her privacy was a trespass he regretted.

But to do nothing to help her was worse.

"Forgive me, Willow," he whispered. Doing his best to keep her covered with a blanket as he carefully removed her torn, dirty clothing, he closely inspected each piece for clues that might help him understand what had happened to her. Something shiny on her skirt caught his attention. For an instant, he thought it was a button, but on closer inspection it appeared to be a broken piece of gold chain about an inch long. One of the links was caught in the fabric of her skirt, and it was immediately evident the chain was not part of her ensemble or a decorative accent on her skirt. It was a broken section of chain that belonged to...something.

There was no indication she'd been wearing a necklace or bracelet, but her neck was so discolored with welts and bruising it was impossible to tell if a necklace had been pulled from around her neck. Could she have been assaulted by a thief in pursuit of her jewelry? Based on the poor quality and condition of her clothing, it seemed unlikely the woman would own a necklace of much value. But in Gray's line of work, he'd seen all manner of unlikely things, so he placed the section of chain links on the tea table.

Returning to the bed, he soaked a washcloth in the basin of warm water, hoping Willow would remain unconscious while he cleaned dirt and debris from her body and finished treating her abrasions.

To his surprise and great relief, she remained submissive and mostly unconscious while he checked her mouth and throat. Her tongue appeared a bit swollen, but there was no sign of blood. Her pupils had responded when he'd checked minutes earlier, and her breathing was slow with no signs of wheezing or gurgling. Her head, neck, and torso were spattered with blood and bruises.

As his mind raced with possibilities of what she might have suffered, his fists clenched. He didn't want to investigate further, but it was his job to do so. If she'd been attacked, and it appeared she had, he was the only witness to her injuries. Therefore, he needed to know the extent of her injuries and to try to piece together the story of how she'd come by them.

He tipped his head back, released a hard sigh, and prayed she'd just been the victim of an accident and not an assault.

Methodically, meticulously, he cleansed her body, gently smoothing the washcloth over her small shoulders, delicate collarbone, and elegant neck marred by bruises from large, angry hands. The telltale markings told him she'd been assaulted, and his gut twisted into a knot of rage.

Who are you, Willow?

Her slender arms lay slack at her sides, and her long fingers with ragged fingernails would have been little defense against her attacker.

Who would want to hurt you?

Her narrow hips and lean thighs revealed a woman who worked hard, her scraped, bloody knees a sure sign that she had struggled to survive.

Was it a lover perhaps?

He removed her stockings and the one shoe she'd been wearing, then cleaned a wide scrape across one slender ankle.

Whom did you trust that you shouldn't have?

He wiped the dirt off her calves and feet, his ministrations making her moan.

"I'm sorry," he whispered.

A curious tenderness rose up in him, and his face burned with shame for not wanting to get involved in this lady's trouble.

The salve he applied to her abrasions didn't evoke a response, nor did the gauze dressings, for which he was immensely thankful.

After he'd finished bathing her and treating her wounds, he worked as gently as possible to wrangle her arms into one of his flannel shirts. His gaze trailed Willow's jawline and elegant throat and drifted lower. The instant he realized where his gaze had landed, he closed the flannel shirt and buttoned it securely around her torso.

I'm sorry, Willow. However unintended on my part, you were undeserving of that violation.

He wondered if she would understand why he'd bathed and tended her battered body while she was unconscious, or if she would hate him for his trespass.

The only redeeming gift he could offer now was to brush her hair. Gently, he stroked away the pine needles and dried leaves while checking for any lacerations or telltale bumps.

When her lids fluttered, he touched her forehead. She was too hot. He checked her fingers and toes again for frostbite discoloration, then released a sigh of relief at their continued natural flush. For an hour, he sat beside her applying a cool compress to her heated cheeks and forehead, promising himself he would not get emotionally involved in this woman's life. He would take care of her and protect her, but her problems were hers alone.

After she'd settled and seemed cooler to his touch, he pulled on dry clothes, a dark jacket, and strapped on his pistol. He was fairly confident whoever hurt Willow had meant to kill her. Probably thought they had and were long gone. But he wasn't taking any chances.

And he had a feeling they wouldn't either.

CHAPTER TWO

Somewhere a door closed, the metallic thunk of a lock sounded, and slow footsteps approached. She struggled to open her eyes, but her lids felt weighted and too heavy.

The footsteps stopped beside the bed, and panic washed through her. She struggled to get up, to move away, to hide...

"Easy, Willow. Easy now."

His voice came to her like soft rain upon her face, cool, soothing, gentle. An image appeared in the mist, shifted, became a man's face. Green, compassion-filled eyes beckoned her, compelled her to trust him.

"Stay alive, Willow. Just stay alive," he crooned softly.

The stroke of his fingers through her hair startled her, then soothed her. Something cool floated across her face, and she felt a dribble of water on her tongue. She was so dry. She sucked the wet cloth into her mouth, needing more of the precious liquid, but it was so painful to swallow.

Another dribble of cool water wet her lips and slipped into her parched mouth. "Just a little for now," he said.

A cool cloth moved across her forehead, and she lifted her face in welcome. Fingers trailed over her scalp and along her jaw, gentle and soothing.

"Rest now," she heard him say, then his fingers trailed away. Everything within her focused on that loss. Slowly, painfully she reached, searched, and closed her fingers over his hand, the one stable thing in her fragmented world.

GRAY STARED at the delicate hand covering his own. Willow seemed to be groping for something to cling to, and he suddenly felt the urge to run from his own instincts to defend and protect. He was a sucker for the weak, the needy, the poor. Might as well stick a torch in his hand and call him the Statue of Liberty.

In an act of pure self-preservation, he pulled his hand free. He didn't want to offer Willow a safe harbor. He wanted her to awaken, to remember what happened, and go back to wherever she'd come from.

The absence of his hand made her brows pinch. He studied her face, observing that only the left side was badly injured. Though her right eye was also swollen, there was nothing else to conceal the fine line of her jaw or the elegant arch of her dark brows.

Who are you, Willow? Where do you belong? Do you have a family searching for you somewhere?

That possibility made him think of his own family and how he'd promised to reconnect with them months ago. He had spoken to his brother Leo just before being sent to Homestead, Pennsylvania, with three-hundred other Pinkerton men to break the strike at the Carnegie steel mill. Gray had promised to go to Crane Landing after that job, but the violent altercation had left three of his fellow agents and seven protestors dead, and Gray sick at heart. Too much had been lost that day, and Gray wished he could go back—all the way back to his childhood—and undo all the mistakes he'd made. Mistakes that had led him to that place at that moment, terrified he'd never see his family again, that he'd never have a chance to apologize to his parents or reconnect with his brothers. Everyone deserved a second chance, didn't they? But when he'd gotten that chance, when the bullets stopped flying and he could have gone home for a visit, he ran instead. He took another assignment, and another, until he'd found himself here on this mountain, alone. And empty.

"I'll do my best to give you a second chance if I can, Willow," he said, dabbing her forehead with a cold compress.

The roar of the wind and a loud thud against the side of the cabin startled him. In one swift move, he dove for his pistol and aimed at the door.

His heart thundered even as he realized the storm was picking up and it was likely the cause of the racket outside. Still, he knew he needed to be certain. From what he could see, the storm was going to blow long and hard and bury them in snow. If he had any hope of finding evidence that would lead him to Willow's attacker or get her back to her family, he needed to look now. It had already been twenty-four hours since he'd found her. He couldn't wait any longer.

He glanced at the silent, vulnerable woman who lay in his bed. Though he had no intention of getting personally involved, he knew he had a moral obligation to help her. Willow wasn't consciously aware of what had happened, but deep in her subconscious, buried beneath layers of fear, she knew who had hurt her. Someone had tried to kill her. Gray needed to know why.

He felt Willow's forehead, relieved to find it cool and dry. She seemed to be resting more comfortably, thanks to the sedative. He didn't see any new signs of bleeding, and she seemed to be breathing normally, so hopefully her injuries weren't life-threatening. She would likely sleep for a while, so he should be able to slip outside for a look around and get back before she woke again. As he pulled on his heavy jacket and holstered his pistol, he hesitated to leave the woman alone. But he knew he must, and so he slipped outside and locked the door behind him.

Outside, he stood in the biting wind, estimating if he hurried, he could hike upstream to where he'd found Willow, investigate the area, and get back within an hour, maybe less.

Still, the back of his neck tingled as he shielded himself between the tall, dense rows of firewood flanking his doorway and doubling as a wind block. The height of the woodpile allowed him to stand as he visually scouted the area, and he was suddenly glad the grueling physical pain of swinging an ax for hours had yielded a bit of cover for him, even if it hadn't eased his roiling conscience.

Refusing to slog through memories, Gray dragged in a mind-clearing breath, vowing silently that he would not fail the injured woman lying in his bed.

Approximately thirty yards of open, unprotected ground stood between him and the tree line. Gripping his pistol, he inched forward, took a deep breath, then shot from the cover of the woodpile. His feet barely skimmed the frozen grass as he sprinted toward the protection of the pines. Wind whistled past his ears, his senses bursting to life as blood pounded through him. His lungs and sinuses burned from the cold air as he dragged in deep, measured breaths, his legs pumping like a runaway locomotive down a mountain.

He expected to hear the sharp crack of a gun and feel the bite of a bullet, but he only heard the scurry of forest animals as he plunged into a cluster of pines. Silent and unmoving, he listened, ears straining, pistol ready. Gusts of frigid air chilled him. Tree limbs creaked. Wildlife rustled in the shadows. Something large moved to his right. He crouched and swung his pistol toward the sound. A bear? Or something else?

After a couple of minutes of scouting and listening, he felt certain he wasn't being watched. The trees offered moderate protection should he need it, but he suspected Willow's assailant was long gone.

As he hiked upstream, fat flakes of snow began to pelt his face and sting his eyes. Pulling his hat lower, he peered through the falling snow, scanning every tree or rock large enough to conceal a body, doing his best to survey his surroundings in the fading evening light.

The snowfall was picking up, and evidence would soon be buried. With determined steps, he increased his pace, wishing he were back in the cabin, alone, reading a book beside the crackling woodstove. That had been his plan when he'd come here. All he'd wanted was a few days of rest before having to return to a job that made him do things his conscience couldn't carry.

The unsettling thoughts dogged him as he hiked up a narrow path to the spot where he'd first found Willow.

Had it only been a day? To his exhausted body, it felt like a lifetime ago.

He scanned the area carefully, wondering how Willow had gotten here. Other than a few mud-packed trails that ended farther downhill, he couldn't determine her route in. If he could find her missing shoe, that might lead him to where she'd been attacked and possibly lead him to the wretch who assaulted her.

Whether the crime had been planned or had been spur-of-the-moment, criminals touched things, made mistakes, panicked if cornered. There were clues out here that told a story. He could feel it. And he was determined to find them.

Hours LATER, a low raspy moan startled Gray from his half-sleep and he jerked his pistol toward the door, heart pounding as his gaze flew through the cabin. A second moan brought him fully awake. He moved to Willow's side and placed the pistol on the floor beside him.

"Well, I'm sure glad to hear that," he said, feeling her forehead. Her eyes remained closed. He fished the washcloth from the basin and wiped her face. Another raspy moan came from her throat, and he smiled. "Sounds like you'll be able to talk after all."

As he gently bathed her face, wind and snow pummeled the cabin, caking the windows and turning the surrounding forest white.

He felt her forehead again. Tension tightened her face, and he stroked it away. "Easy, Willow. Easy," he said.

She paused as if listening for something, then let out a slow sigh and turned her cheek to his palm.

Surprised, he stroked her hair away from her bruised eyes and studied her swollen face. "Can you hear me?" he asked, gently cupping her jaw between his palms. "Can you hear what I'm saying?"

She sighed softly, like a sleepy lover snuggling deeper into the covers. The fear and anxiety that had filled her wheezy gasps earlier had disappeared. Did that mean she knew she could trust him, that he would protect her?

"Stay alive, Willow. Do you hear? Just stay alive and we'll sort this out," he said, tucking the blankets around her, leaving her arms outside them as she seemed to prefer. He felt her pulse thrum strong and steady against his fingers, then he settled back in his chair and stretched the knots from his shoulders.

Her fever seemed to have abated, and since her breathing wasn't labored and she wasn't coughing up blood, he assumed her congestion was from exposure to the weather.

For a long time, he studied the woman whose fingers had somehow trustingly intertwined with his. Despite his resolve to maintain his distance, to keep her problems out of his life, he felt himself slipping. This woman's vulnerability, her desperate need, had reached some deep, protected place within him. He wanted to take her to a hospital and turn her over to the authorities. But the raging storm outside and the unknown danger to her made it impossible.

Despite her physical weakness, he sensed a fierce strength in Willow that made her reach out and hang on. She desperately wanted to live.

And he was going to make sure she did.

THE SOUND of a horse trotting along the road caught Gray's attention. When the man on horseback slowed his mount, Gray knew he was about to get company. Dropping the load of firewood in his arms, he slipped his hand over the butt of his revolver and headed out to the road to meet his visitor.

"Good afternoon," he said, realizing the man was a police officer.

The thick-chested officer with deep-set eyes and a black mustache didn't return Gray's friendly greeting. "I'm looking for a missing woman," he said straightaway. "She's twenty-two years old, dark brown hair, average height, with brown eyes. Have you seen her?"

"Who is she?" Gray asked, skirting the direct question to avoid lying to an officer of the law.

"Name's Sophia Flynn. According to her parents, she didn't come home last night."

"Hmm..." Gray scratched his chin as if deep in thought. "Any chance she's with a beau?"

"Always a possibility, but her parents and the women she works with at the mill claim she doesn't have a suitor. Mind if I take a look inside?" the officer asked, giving a nod toward the cabin.

"You say she works at the mill?" Gray asked, purposely redirecting the conversation. "Because I can look into things there if you like."

"Do you work there?" the officer asked, suspicion thick in his voice.

"I will soon," Gray said. "I just came into town. I'm taking a few days to do some hunting before I start my investigation at the mill."

The officer's black eyebrows lifted. "What are you investigating? Are you a law officer?"

"I'm a personnel investigator. I'm here to try to improve working conditions for the employees." It wasn't his intended purpose, but if he could do anything to help the employees while doing his job as an undercover investigator, he would certainly try.

"Is that so?" The officer seemed genuinely interested. "My brother works at the mill, and conditions are in dire need of change."

"What's your brother's name?"

"Joseph Kline. He works as a machine tender, usually on one of the wire machines. It's hard, dangerous work," the officer said, "and the deplorable conditions are not just at Joe's job. The folks there are forced to work without proper lighting around machines that could crush or dismember them in the blink of an eye. It's already happened twice."

"I know how dangerous factory work can be, and I understand your agitation with the situation, Officer Kline. I'll introduce myself to your brother and see what I can do to improve things for him. And I'll certainly let you know if the missing girl should come knocking at my door," Gray said, knowing she wouldn't come knocking because she was already inside. Reaching up to shake the man's hand, he gave the officer a decisive nod and bid him a good day, hoping to send him on his way.

With a hard pump to Gray's hand, the officer said, "Much

obliged on both counts." With that, he tipped his hat and headed up the road presumably to the next residence.

Lowering his shoulders with a slow breath of relief, Gray headed back to his job of gathering firewood for the stove.

The fact that Sophia worked at the mill with unhappy employees, untenable working conditions, and suspected theft happening made Gray wonder if her assault was somehow connected.

Taking a long look up the mountain, he considered different scenarios that might have landed her here. The glistening evergreens pierced the sky where the mountain peaked, and the valley below seemed to cut across forever. This mountain held the answers. Gray just had to find them, and soon. If Willow's attacker decided to come back to assure himself that the evidence of his crime had been destroyed by wildlife, the man would realize Willow wasn't dead. Because animals would leave some trace of a body no matter how thorough they were at their task.

Not for the first time, Gray wondered if he should alert his agency and have them move Willow to another town farther away, but at the moment it wasn't an option because she was too injured to move. He considered the consequences of keeping her here, close to where he'd found her, but an inner voice told him to stay put, that the pieces of the puzzle were hidden on this mountain and in Willow's subconscious, and her life depended on him finding and piecing them together.

Dragging a hand over his eyes, he felt weary of the whole mess.

With an armload of firewood, he went inside where a missing girl—one Sophia Flynn—lay silent, the answers to her disappearance and injuries buried deep within her fear.

Maybe he could introduce information about her life one small fact at a time to see if one of those facts might trigger her memory. Would knowing her name spark her memory? Would it solve the mystery surrounding her? Maybe.

But if it didn't, if she learned her name but couldn't remember what happened to her or who assaulted her, she could be in more danger. Criminals didn't take kindly to their victims being able to identify them, and whoever assaulted Sophia wouldn't risk the possibility of her memory returning. To send her home to her parents, who might not be able to protect her, would put her, and perhaps her family, at great risk.

So, he couldn't, he *wouldn't* tell her.

That meant this wounded woman was his responsibility. Keeping her alive was his job. He'd learned the hard and painful lesson that trusting the wrong person could get someone hurt or killed. The only way to ensure Sophia Flynn's safety was to keep her hidden—and to lie to her.

She drifted in a hazy cloud, wondering if the man holding her hand was real.

"I'm glad you're awake," the man said.

His voice startled her, and she rubbed her eyes, wincing and gasping at the tenderness around them. The pain brought her fully awake, and she realized the man was sitting on the edge of her bed. He was handsome...and overwhelming. *Dominating* was suddenly the more appropriate word. She didn't know this place. Or this man. A warning whispered through her, chilled her, told her to beware.

As though he sensed her inclination to pull away, the man relaxed the pressure on her fingers but kept her hand in his. "Please don't," he said. "I've spent three days and nights looking after you. It wouldn't make any sense for me to undo all that hard work now, would it?"

Three days!

"I know you're frightened, Willow. It's understandable after what you must have suffered. But you're safe here. Do you understand?"

She only understood she was in a place she didn't recognize with a man she didn't know and in pain like she'd never before experienced. It hurt to move, but she was determined to get off her back and put some distance between them.

He helped her sit up and propped two bed pillows behind her.

She accepted his assistance, but shied when he raised his fingers to her face.

Sighing, he lowered his hand to the blankets. "I'll tell you what little I know about the circumstances surrounding your attack, but it's difficult when you shy away. Could you trust me enough to check your injuries?"

His eyes appealed to her, overpowered her with their intensity as his thick-fringed lashes blinked slowly, expectantly, willing her to answer.

Her gaze took in the empty cabin and the bolted door. She glanced outside the window where the wind howled and it seemed to be snowing sideways. Then she looked back at the man who claimed he'd taken care of her. Was he her captor or her rescuer? She was alone, injured, and totally at his mercy. Cornered, helpless, hopeless, and terrified, she knew she had to depend on him, but that didn't mean she had to trust him.

Hesitantly, she gave a small nod, hoping it would give her precious time to think, to try to remember...anything. Her heart hammered as she struggled for answers, but her thoughts were scattered and panicked. Why would someone want to kill her? Had she hurt someone? Stolen someone's husband? Exposed a criminal? Was she rich? Poor? Married? Single? What? She needed answers. She had to get on her feet and start searching for her life or she would lose her mind.

Closing her eyes, she tried for the millionth time to summon a memory, any sliver or fragment of what had happened to her. But the only image to surface was one of this man leaning over her, his hands gentle, his voice commanding her to stay alive when the darkness threatened to consume her. Otherwise, she could not recall a solitary scrap of her life outside this cabin.

"Are you all right, Willow?"

The sound of his voice snapped her eyes open and brought the reality of her situation into focus. Whether she could trust him or not was a moot point, so she simply gave him another nod to let him know she was willing to let him help her.

His shoulders relaxed as though he'd been holding his breath, awaiting her approval. "Thank you, Willow."

Another smile, softer, more intimate. Oh, he was handsome, this shepherd or jailer of hers. Her gaze stole upward, back to the green depths of his eyes, the eyes she'd seen in her dreams.

"How about something to eat?" he asked. "You haven't had more than a bit of water and a few teaspoons of broth since I found you. Your ribs are sticking out like fenceposts."

He'd seen her ribs? She looked at the rolled sleeves of a large flannel shirt that clothed her. Had he put this on her?

The gentle pressure of his finger beneath her chin brought her gaze back to his. "I'm sorry, Willow. There was no one else to do it."

Had the man just read her mind?

"Your blouse is ruined, but I washed and mended your skirt. My sewing skill is sadly lacking but I managed to stitch the fabric together enough to cover your legs."

Stunned, she watched him retrieve her skirt and show her his handiwork. The stitches were wide and the fabric bunched in several places, but he had indeed sewn her skirt.

"I assumed you would prefer wearing a badly sewn skirt to being wrapped up in a blanket, but for now I think the blanket will suffice. I made soup. A little broth might make you feel better."

She watched him ladle a small portion into a bowl from the kettle on the woodstove. It smelled delicious, and she suddenly felt famished. Her stomach growled, and she felt queasy.

He glanced at the table, then back at her. "Do you think you can walk?"

She nodded, then winced at the pain in her throat and her ribs as she moved her legs.

"You'd better wait for me," he said, placing the bowls on the table before returning to the bed. He uncovered her bare feet and frowned. "Wait a minute." He reached down and pulled a small crate from beneath the wooden bedframe. "These should work," he said, holding up a thick pair of men's socks he'd taken from the crate.

She flexed her bare toes and looked up at him.

"That's right," he said, kneeling to tug them over her feet. When he'd finished, he captured her ankles with his hands and winked at her. "You need some meat on these bones. My socks will probably fall right off you."

Before she could decide if she was offended by the warm fingers encircling her ankles, he released them, then sat beside her.

"We'll go easy, all right?"

She nodded, then stiffened when his arm slipped behind her.

"I see you're still afraid of me," he said softly. The disappointment in his voice tweaked her conscience, but the power in that muscled arm against her back was unnerving. "Have you changed your mind then?"

The man's voice was hypnotic. So deep, so intimate, so commanding. When she tucked her dirty hair behind her ears, her hands trembled, but she gave a negative shake of her head. She needed to get up, and that meant she had to accept his assistance.

"All right then. You're too weak to do this on your own. That means I'll have to support you. That's all I'm going to do, Willow. Nothing more. Understand?"

Chagrined, she kept her gaze lowered and nodded.

He helped her slide to the edge of the mattress where she paused with her legs draped over the side, head swimming.

"I'll count to three, and then I'll help you stand. Easy now."

She glanced at him, recognizing the words that had soothed her in the middle of her nightmares. The sudden movement made her head swim. Darkness swirled behind her eyes and she sagged against him, her head lolling against his chest. Fatigued and shaky, she leaned against him, hearing his strong, steady heartbeat beneath her ear, praying she wouldn't get sick all over him.

"Let me bring the soup to you," he said.

She shook her head, knowing she needed to get on her feet. After a moment, her head cleared and the shaking subsided. She placed her hands against his muscled chest to sit up.

"You'll probably get dizzy again when you stand. If you let me, I'll keep you upright until you can manage the few steps to the table."

Now that the initial wave of sickness had passed, she felt better. Encouraged, she adjusted her position so her feet touched the floor.

He stood in front of her, offering his hands.

She clasped them, knowing she would need his assistance.

"On three," he said. "One...two...three." Gently, he pulled her to her feet.

The second her weight shifted to her legs, her knees buckled. She grabbed a fistful of his shirt and clung to him while violent tremors racked her body. Even her teeth began to chatter as she fought to stay upright.

"I've got you, Willow."

He certainly did. Every inch of her shaking body was held firmly against his. One of his strong arms crossed her back, and his hand splayed over her hip to keep her steady. His other arm circled her beneath the shoulders and held her against his chest. Waves of dizziness washed over her, left her swaying. If he released her, she would drop at his feet like a rag rug.

"Hang on, Willow. It'll pass."

Sweat prickled her face and neck. Her head lolled forward, and she smelled the clean fabric of his shirt. His collar was open, and she heard the quick intake of his breath when her face touched his warm skin and the coarse hair of his chest. She tried to lift her head, to turn away, but she was too weak to do so. Her stomach clenched. She pinched her lips shut against the illness trying to project itself from her body. Finally, she gasped and raised shaking fingers to her mouth, sagging fully into his arms.

"I'm sorry," he said, then lifted her into his arms and carried her to the small room off the main cabin. Deftly, he lowered her to her knees beside a commode she had no time to appreciate before her stomach rebelled.

He knelt behind her on the floor and wrapped one arm gently around her waist, then used his free hand to hold her hair back as dry heaves wracked her body.

"I'm sorry, Willow. I should have known it would be too much for you."

Sweat burst from her pores and washed her with chills. Fire scorched her throat and ribs each time her stomach lurched. Her belly contracted with long, agonizing shudders that stole her breath. All the while, he held her up, saying he was sorry each time she moaned from the excruciating pain that wrenched her body. Even when she fought to keep the sound inside, he seemed to know. Tears streamed from her eyes and stung her cracked lips. It seemed an eternity before the heaves finally subsided. When the spasms stopped wrenching her stomach, she wilted against him, wasted. It was beyond her ability to even wipe her mouth.

Cradling her on his lap, he tenderly wiped the perspiration and tears from her face with his bare palm.

"I'm so sorry," he said.

She lay wasted in his arms, too weak to stop him from finger-combing her dirty hair. How could he stand to touch her? She was sweaty, smelled like used bed linens, and must look a fright. But he didn't seem to care at all. His fingers moved across her skull in slow gentle sweeps that soothed her. Who was this man? And what had torn her apart like this?

The answers escaped her as she lay there, selfishly absorbing the pleasure of his ministrations as her shaking subsided. Finally, when she could breathe without feeling sick, she tipped her head back and met his eyes.

His brows quirked, eyes questioning as she patted her chest with a limp hand. "It still hurts?" he asked as if trying to figure out what she was saying or asking.

She shook her head, mouthed the word 'who', then patted her chest again.

"Who?" His expression was puzzled. "Who hurt you? Who are you?"

She nodded, her gaze still locked with his.

His eyes darkened and he smoothed his fingers across her forehead. "I don't know the answer to either question, Willow. I found you by a stream three days ago. I went back and did a quick search of the area, but I couldn't find anything that might identify you or the person who hurt you. But I suspect you were assaulted then brought up the mountain and left for...well, I believe your attacker though you were dead."

Dead? Then someone did try to kill her? The idea was so horrifying it sent a violent shudder through her body.

"You're safe here," he said as if reading her mind. "I won't let anything happen to you."

So this man had rescued her, and brought her here, and kept her alive.

She reached up, tapped his chest twice.

His expression turned curious. "Me? My name?"

She nodded.

"Gray Sullivan."

Yes. That's right. She remembered now. The man's name in her dreams was Gray.

With a wobbly circular hand-gesture, she tried to ask if this was his home.

"Do I live here?" he asked. At her nod, he gave her a half-smile. "No. I'm just renting the place for a while."

She nodded, drifting in his gaze, feeling a bit of strength ebbing back into her body.

"I should get you back into bed while you're feeling better," he said.

Slowly, she shook her head and made a shoveling motion to her mouth.

"You want to eat?" he asked in surprise.

She nodded. It was the only way to get her strength back. And she really was hungry now that the nausea had passed.

"Well, if you think you can," he said doubtfully. "We'll give you some broth today, then maybe you'll be able to manage a few minutes on your feet tomorrow."

She gave a negative shake of her head.

"No?" he asked, one dark brow raised in question.

She made a shoveling motion toward her mouth as if she were eating, scrubbed at her hair, then pointed at the cast iron tub.

"You want to eat and take a bath?"

She pinched her nose and nodded.

He smiled down at her. "You don't smell, Willow."

She nodded to debate his comment.

He chuckled. "You don't. But I'll heat more water while you're eating if that will make you happy."

Her smile made her lip sting. Wincing, she touched her fingers to her mouth and realized her lip was bleeding.

"Your lips are chapped. I've been putting balm on them. They look much better today, but they aren't healed yet. You can apply more balm to your lips while I get you some soup."

To think he'd tended her so intimately made her flush.

"Willow, I need to point out that you're too weak to manage the tub alone," he said.

Alarm raced through her, and she tried to sit up. What a fool she was lying here in this stranger's arms like a trusting lamb on a butcher block.

His arms tightened gently around her. "Please stop," he commanded softly. "You can't even stand on your own. I just meant I'd have to help you in and out of the tub. I'll figure out a way to do it without compromising your modesty."

She met his eyes, silently letting him know that she had no intentions of trusting him. Or anybody.

He glanced at the tub, then back at her. "I'll find a way. You'll just have to trust me or do without a bath until you can manage it yourself." With that, he lifted her from the floor and carried her to the table.

CHAPTER THREE

The light clanking of a metal spoon against a bowl drew Gray's attention from the pot of water he was watching boil. Willow angled the bowl toward him, tipped it to show him she had eaten the small amount of chicken soup he'd given her, then measured an inch with her fingers.

"A little more then?"

She nodded.

He ladled in a small amount—mostly broth as he'd previously given her, since swallowing still seemed painful for her—and placed the bowl in front of her. As he turned back to the stove, she touched his arm. Surprised, he glanced down. She nodded toward the bowl, then back at him. Slowly, she placed her shaky palm over her heart, then gestured toward him as he read her lips.

Gray smiled. "You're welcome."

Despite the scabs and bruises on her face, her tentative smile was appealing. He was curious to see the woman who would emerge from beneath the swelling and bruises. Already her face had become more symmetrical. Only her left eye and cheek were swollen. Depending on the angle at which he viewed her, Willow's features could be quite intriguing.

"It's obvious you know how to communicate. Is there a reason you're not talking?"

She brought her hand to her throat and winced.

"It hurts too much?" he asked, suspecting he already knew the answer. Judging by the deep bruising around her throat, it didn't surprise him.

She nodded, but as he studied her, uncertainty filled her expression and made him realize he was staring at her, assessing her features for more than health reasons. Mentally chiding himself, he turned away. This woman did not need another reason to fear him. She needed to regain her strength and her memory and get back to her life. The sooner the better. For both of them.

Returning to the stove, he picked up two potholders and carried the heavy boiler pot to the bathroom. The tub would accommodate Willow quite comfortably, especially if the water were high enough for her to soak in. He had already added several buckets of cold water pumped from the kitchen faucet and carried to the bathroom. Now, he would warm the water to a comfortable temperature for her.

After accomplishing his task, he laid out a stack of bath towels and a washcloth. He placed some soap beside the tub, then picked up the empty pots and exited the bathroom.

After refilling the pots, he put more water on the stovetop to heat, then filled the woodstove. He stoked the fire while Willow finished her soup and watched him, her hand gripping the edge of the table as if to steady herself. In his estimation, she was ready to fall off the chair.

"Finished?" he asked, closing the stove door, then trying for her sake to appear nonchalant as he approached her.

She nodded and tried to pat her belly, but swayed dangerously on the chair.

He closed the distance in one long step and scooped her into his arms. Immediately, she tensed, her startled gaze flying to his.

For a moment, he thought she would try to wiggle free, but after her initial hesitation, she relaxed somewhat.

"Maybe you should rest for a while before you bathe," he suggested, moving toward the bed, knowing she needed to lie down.

She gripped his collar and shook her head, pointing at the bathroom.

He stopped. "Your bath can wait awhile, Willow. It's no trouble to heat more water later."

Again she shook her head.

"You're too weak to"

Her hard tug on his collar made him stare in surprise at the woman nearly fainting in his arms. Was there a temper behind that tug? Was this slip of woman who could barely sit up on her own really trying to demand his compliance?

Her head lolled back and she touched his cheek. "Please," she mouthed silently, and he surrendered right there. He didn't have the heart to deny her something so deeply desired, so he carried her into the bathroom and sat on the commode with her on his lap. She winced as he peeled the tape off her face, but she didn't make a sound. Not until he reached beneath her shirt.

She gasped, and his hand stilled instantly.

Of necessity, he had seen Willow's unclothed body while he'd given her sponge baths and changed her bandages. Were he to share that fact with her, the depth of her embarrassment would ruin what little ground they'd gained. He needed her to trust him.

The wariness in her eyes said she might have accepted his help but had no intention of trusting him. Considering what she'd been through, he couldn't blame her. She'd obviously trusted someone she shouldn't have and nearly paid for the mistake with her life. So who was it? A jealous suitor? Had she witnessed something she shouldn't have? What other motive could there be?

"Willow, I need to remove the binding from around your ribs, which means I'll need to lift your shirt. I don't have anything else to use, and you'll be more comfortable with the wrapping, at least for a few more days. But it's up to you."

For a tense moment, she studied his face as if trying to decide whether she could trust him. Then she gazed wistfully at the bath-water before nodding her assent.

He managed to unwrap her ribs with one hand, but she was so unstable it was like holding an infant with one hand. When she nearly slipped from his grasp, he tossed aside the wrapping and left her clothed in his shirt.

"You're going in like this," he said. Ignoring her raised brows, he dangled her feet above the tub. "How's the temperature?" he asked, dipping her toes. She released a loud sigh, and he lifted her away. "Too hot?"

Her eyes closed and her lips curved upward. Her head moved slowly from side to side, and he understood. With infinite slowness, he eased her into the tub, pausing at each scrape to see if the warm water was too much. She tensed a few times, and he paused while she absorbed the pain and decided whether to continue. They were both soaked by the time she was settled. Water dripped off the shirt he was wearing, and despite her wary look, he slipped it off and tossed it into a small handbasin between the commode and the tub.

"You can lay the shirt you're wearing over the edge of the tub after I leave," he told her. "Here's some soap and a washcloth and a couple of towels. If you need help, bang on the tub. Let me know when you're ready to get out."

Her eyes were closed and her head rested against the wall behind her. He did not like the pallor of her skin or the thought of leaving her alone. Especially when he was getting no response from her.

"Willow, if I don't hear splashing, I'm coming back in here."

Her eyes flew open, her left one still at half-mast from the swelling, but she gave him a small nod.

"Enjoy your bath," he said, then closed the door behind him.

———

WHILE WILLOW BATHED, Gray stripped the bed and changed the sheets, filled the woodbin, and washed out the bowls they had used for supper. Then he rummaged through his valise for a clean shirt for Willow and one for himself.

A solid thump in the bathroom sent his heart racing as he bolted into the small room.

Willow squeaked and hunched forward in an attempt to cover herself. That she wasn't unconscious or sprawled beside the tub was a miracle considering her shaky condition when he'd left her. But she was still upright and conscious, her eyes wary as she watched him gawk at her.

He couldn't help it. She'd removed the shirt she'd been wearing, and he could see how incredibly delicate she was. Hunched forward with her arms wrapped around her updrawn knees, her bare skin shimmering like a pearl, her shoulders couldn't have been wider than the length of his forearm, and they were beautifully sculpted and feminine. Her backbone peeped through wet strands of her hair, looking like small peaks of whipped cream laced with swirls of dark chocolate. Though he'd seen her unclothed as he'd bathed her, he was not prepared for the sweet allure of her modest pose or glistening wet body.

Her gaze remained wary, watchful.

"Ah...sorry." He backed toward the door and placed his hand on the casing, trying to act nonchalant when he really wanted to bolt from the room. "I thought you slipped. You're all right then?" he asked, feeling like an idiot for charging in on her and gawking like an adolescent.

Her nod was slow, tentative. She raised the cake of soap, showed it to him.

"Of course. I'm sorry. I'll let you bathe in peace." He spun on his heel and headed out to safer ground where he could breathe and marshal his common sense, but a loud thump on the tub turned him back.

She gripped the cake of soap, banged it on the side of the tub again, then beckoned him with it.

He swallowed to dispel the sudden dryness in his throat. He did not want to be in here. "You...you need help?" he asked.

She nodded and pointed feebly to the floor beside the tub.

Gray inhaled, flexed his fingers, and tried to mentally calm himself as if he were preparing to break a labor strike. But he wasn't confronting a group of angry, armed men. He was confronting his own response to the woman in his bathtub. *Just pull back and detach, Sullivan. No fear. No emotion. Just do the job.*

Releasing his breath, he knelt beside the tub, where Willow tried to hide her nakedness from him. "Ready to get out?" he asked, praying she'd say yes.

She fumbled for his hand, then raised it to her head, moving his fingers in her hair.

The woman was killing him.

Her cheek rested upon her bent knees, but there was no self-pity in her eyes. They flashed with determination, and he saw an honest glimpse of the woman inside. Willow's fierce struggle to manage on her own, to maintain her modesty, was admirable. That she would sacrifice her modesty to get her hair washed was heartbreaking. His own discomfort suddenly seemed insignificant, selfish. This woman needed his help. This was no time for base emotions. Resolved to his role as nursemaid, he handed her a dry cloth for her eyes, then dipped a glass into the tub to wet her hair. He lathered his palms and carefully massaged her head.

Her wheezy moan stilled his hands. "Does that hurt?"

Eyes closed, she slowly moved her head side to side.

The urge to bolt from the room was strong, but his conscience forced him to stay and help her. With resolve, he worked the soap through the length of her hair, then slowly, gently, massaged her skull. Tiny bumps sprinkled her shoulders, and she sighed so sweetly that his hands shook and his skin prickled with perspiration.

"I'll return in a moment," he said, gathering her hair and stacking it in a soapy pile between her shoulder blades. He slipped out of the bathroom and gulped a steadying breath. He'd never given a woman a bath before, much less washed her hair. If he'd have known Willow would moan like that, he would have run for his life.

He found a metal pitcher in the kitchen cupboard, worked the pump handle and filled it halfway with cold water, then added hot water from the steaming pot on the stove. When he returned to the bathroom with the pitcher of warm water, Willow's eyes were closed and a dreamy smile hovered on her lips.

Well, he was glad one of them was enjoying this. "Better cover your eyes," he suggested, wanting to rinse her hair and get her safely back into bed.

She turned her face to the damp cloth upon her knees.

He used the water glass and bathwater to remove most of the soap from her hair. Then he finished rinsing her hair with the pitcher of fresh, warm water.

"Can you lift your head for me?"

The effort made her whole body quake, but she raised her head, keeping her hands capped over the top of her scabbed knees for stability. His hands were not made for this sort of job and he struggled to secure the bulky towel around her hair.

"Can you stand?" he asked when it was finally secure.

Her nostrils flared and she lowered her towel-encased head back to her knees, giving a small, defeated shake.

He ached for her. Despite his own misgivings and the warning bells clanging in his head, he brushed the backs of his fingers along her wet jaw and encouraged her to look at him. "You managed longer than most would have in your condition."

She gazed intently into his eyes, delving too deeply for his comfort.

He looked away, laid a thick towel across his lap, then reached into the tub, soaking the dry shirt he'd just put on. Slipping his arms under her knees and around her back, he lifted her out and placed her on his lap. Averting his gaze in an attempt to protect her modesty, and his sanity, he draped a towel over her.

She drew her knees up, shivering, her teeth chattering while he struggled to cover her with a second towel. The instant it was around her, he got to his feet and carried her back to bed, wanting to tuck her beneath the covers and leave her there to dry. But procrastinating would just prolong his agony. He used the extra linen to dry her arms, then covered her with a blanket and adjusted it as he dried her legs. As discreetly as possible, he checked the scrapes on her knees and feet as he dried them. Focusing on her injuries sobered him, and he continued his assessment in a detached, professional manner.

Her abrasions were a healthy, healing pink as was the laceration on her cheek, but it was a deeper injury and still in need of attention. Keeping the blanket over her to keep her warm, he gathered the salve and gauze dressing from where he'd left them on the table. "This might be uncomfortable," he said, sitting down beside her.

She closed her eyes and turned her injured cheek toward him.

Delaying wouldn't lessen the pain, so he dabbed salve along the pink, wrinkled laceration. Willow's nostrils flared and she stiffened.

"I know...I'm sorry."

Seeing her hurting made him want to hold her and absorb her discomfort. Her wet lashes twitched as he covered the laceration with gauze, but he hesitated to press tape to her tender cheek. It still carried the red marks from the last dressing. Lifting the gauze, he inspected the laceration more thoroughly and could see it wasn't bleeding, so he decided to leave it uncovered for the evening.

He helped her sit up, then slipped her arms into the sleeves of his favorite blue flannel shirt, then pulled it around her and buttoned it to her neck. When she swayed on the bed, he could see she was faint with exhaustion. Deftly, he slid his hand up inside her shirt, hooked the top of the towel that was still wrapped around her, and tugged it loose. Her eyelids fluttered, but she didn't resist as he eased her back on the mattress. Still, he made sure to cover her thighs with the flannel shirt she was wearing before he removed the towel.

Willow's pride was surely in tatters by now, and he would not carelessly strip away what little remained.

SHE CAME AWAKE in a full-length stretch, wincing at the dull pain in her side, but enjoying the release in her tight muscles. The warmth of the bed made her burrow deeper beneath the blankets. Unwilling to leave her warm cocoon, she drifted in a pleasant half-sleep until the squeak of a chair brought her fully awake.

Gray was seated at the table across the room, writing in a note-book. With his elbow propped on the table, his forehead resting in his palm, he studied the page in front of him. Pen poised above the paper, a faraway look touched his eyes, as if his mind were somewhere else, as if he wished he were somewhere else.

It was the first time she had considered his life. Did he have a lady friend somewhere he longed to see? Or worse yet, a wife and family? Her own painful trauma had so preoccupied her, she'd given no thought to Gray or what he might be sacrificing to care for her. Because her mind was a hungry beast in relentless pursuit of answers, of any memory or scrap from her past that would satiate her need to know who she was or where she belonged. It gnawed at her insides, haunted her dreams, drove her to madness during her waking hours. But maybe knowing more about the man taking care of her would give the beast something to chew on. Maybe hearing Gray's story would take her mind off her own lost world.

The knowledge that she was likely putting him out was enough to rouse her to full awareness. She raised up on one elbow and pushed her hair off her face, determined to start pulling herself together. She would just ask him. If he did have a family or a lady friend who might be waiting for him, she would insist that he take her to the police and go back to his life. The police could find a safe place for her until her memory returned. Couldn't they? That made her wonder why Gray hadn't taken her to the authorities. She had so many questions, none of which her ravaged throat would allow her to ask.

He looked up, then his expression softening when she offered a tentative smile. "Feeling better?" he asked.

She nodded, although it wasn't completely true. The bath and soup broth had made her feel better, but she was still unbelievably weak and woozy, her balance overly sensitive to the slightest movement, and her throat felt ravaged. Swallowing was still excruciating.

She pointed to the table, to the book in front of him and drew a question mark in the air.

"This?" he asked, closing the book.

She nodded.

"It's nothing. Just doodling. Something to keep me occupied while you slept."

She watched him stash the book in the desk drawer and wondered why his expression had suddenly turned secretive. What did he write in that book that he was keeping from her? Was it something about her attack? A letter? Could this big, strapping man be penning a love letter to his lady? The thought made her pause, but the reality of Gray keeping secrets from her was unsettling. If he knew anything about her identity or the attack, it would be cruel of him to hide it from her.

She pointed again to the drawer, but he dismissed it with a wave of his hand. "It's just the notes and ramblings of a bored mind." He picked up a thin wooden case and approached the bed. "Do you play chess?"

Chess? Willow thought for a moment, then gave a slow nod. Apparently she had learned at some point in her past because she was certain she knew how to play. Interesting. What else did she know how to do that she hadn't yet remembered? Was she a mother? A wife?

Neither thought brought any illumination to the dark depths where her memories should be. Frustrated, she pushed the blankets off her legs and struggled to the edge of the mattress. Thankfully, Gray was too busy turning the stuffed armchairs toward each other to notice her trembling and weaving. After he'd placed the tea table between the chairs, he opened the chess set and arranged the playing pieces.

"Should we try to get you out of bed again?" he asked, turning back to her.

Before she could test her legs, he crossed to the bed and scooped her up in his arms. She gasped, her body stiffening as she met his eyes.

They stared at each other for a suspended heartbeat, but it was long enough for her to see him try to mask his disappointment. Her reaction had hurt his feelings. He had rescued her, fed her, clothed her, even bathed her, and still she didn't trust him.

But she couldn't let her guard down. Not even for this man.

It was no way to thank him, yet it was simply beyond her ability to fully trust him. Her memory loss and broken body left her too vulnerable. Until she regained her strength and her memory, her life was in constant jeopardy.

She pointed to the floor. If she could just manage a few steps it would be progress toward rebuilding her strength. She tried to wiggle from his arms but he held fast.

"You're too shaky." He crossed to the chair, settled her on the thick cushion, then retrieved the blanket from the bed. "Tomorrow we'll try. Tonight you rest."

Without a voice, she couldn't argue with him, but she wouldn't have had the wits to do so even if she could speak, because the way he gently tucked the blanket around her legs and feet sent a flutter through her belly.

"Choose your color. White or black?" he asked, taking the chair opposite her. His shoulders spanned the chair back, his dark hair blending with the autumn hues in his flannel shirt.

She pointed to the white pawn.

"White it is then," he said, turning the board until the white pieces were on her side. "Ladies first."

Hesitantly, she leaned forward, touched his left hand where it rested on his knee. He glanced up in apparent surprise. She tapped his bare ring finger, traced a circle around it, then drew a question mark on the back of his hand.

His expression turned curious as he studied her. "Are you asking if I'm married?"

Knowing she was prying, her face warmed, but she nodded.

"No, Willow," he said quietly, "I'm not married."

She touched her heart, pointed outside, then drew the hour-glass shape of a woman with her hands.

A smile tugged the corner of his mouth and his eyebrow quirked. "Do I have a woman out there somewhere?"

She nodded, placed her hand over her heart.

"That I love?"

Again she nodded.

His eyes darkened as they locked with hers, and she flushed from the intensity of his gaze. The way he studied her made her cringe. Her bruised face must look a fright. Suddenly, it dawned on her what he must be thinking and she flushed clear to her kneecaps. Had he really misunderstood her reason for asking? Did he think she was interested in him?

"No, Willow." His voice was low, desolate sounding to her ears. "There's no woman I share my heart with. There never has been."

For the first time since regaining consciousness, she was glad she couldn't speak. She had no idea what to say. The only word that came to mind was *why*? Why wouldn't a man as caring as Gray Sullivan share his heart with someone? He was too handsome, too charming, too gentle not to capture a lady's heart. Why then, was a man like him alone on this mountain?

Deciding she didn't want to know why, she lowered her gaze to the chessboard. She didn't want to get involved in his life when she couldn't even remember what her own was like. Maybe she didn't share her heart with anyone either. The thought made her ache. Was her life a reflection of the loneliness she saw in Gray's eyes? Had she been trying to lose herself in these mountains, too? Instinctively, she looked at him, and it seemed he was reading her own desolate thoughts.

She glanced away from his scrutinizing gaze and moved her pawn, plunking it down with a dull thud in the small wooden square, hoping to break the tense silence.

He said nothing as he moved his own pawn. She released her breath, thankful he was letting the conversation die. She reached for her knight, but his bronze fingers stole across the board and drew a lazy path across her knuckles. Her heart jumped and she glanced up.

The fire popped and a log thumped inside the stove. "How about you, Willow? Is there someone special in your life? Do you share your heart with another?"

Everything inside her felt as if it crashed into the pit of her stomach. She didn't know. She suspected there were people who loved each other so deeply nothing could keep their hearts from beating for one another. No matter what they faced, or what happened to them, they would always recognize the love within them. Not betrayal, not separation, not even memory loss could steal that assurance. But her heart had no memory of a love that great.

What on earth had happened to her? That question gnawed at her mind, like an animal in a trap, relentless and determined to free itself even at the cost of its own limb. She would give anything to know her name or any tidbit of her past.

Slowly she shrugged, then released the knight she held in her fingers. There was no knight or prince in her life, at least not that she could recall. Suddenly, she regretted asking Gray such a personal question. Though the intent had been good, the result had left her heart aching. Was she a lone pawn in life?

"Willow?"

Hesitant to meet his gaze, she fiddled with a stray piece of thread in the blanket covering her legs, and stole a glance across the chessboard. He sat with his elbows braced on his knees, his fingers laced between them. His shirtsleeves were turned up exposing muscled forearms that disappeared under the brown flannel covering his thick biceps. Of its own accord, her gaze moved upward, over his hard shoulders and whisker-shadowed jaw, until she was immersed in his green gaze.

"It's okay if you don't remember," he said. "Memory loss is an odd thing. You might start to remember bits and pieces, or it could all come flashing back at once. One never knows."

Oh, to even have one memory, one little spec of her life, would be a treasure. If she could just capture one tiny scrap of her past it would keep her sane. Maybe if she went back to where he'd found her, she would see something that would trigger her memory. The thought of going to that place frightened her, but it seemed the logical thing to do. The storm outside was a living monster at the moment, and she still couldn't walk unassisted, but she felt certain it would help to go to where he'd found her. It had to. So as soon as she could stand on her own without feeling dizzy, she was going to ask Gray to take her there.

"Your move, Willow."

She glanced at the board, but her mind was not on the game. There were so many questions she wanted to ask. Carelessly, she moved her bishop and sat back with a sigh, wishing she could talk, wishing she could hear the sound of her own voice and recognize it. But her throat felt broken.

"Are you tired?"

She slowly shook her head, careful not to upset her balance or strain her sore neck. She sat forward and pointed to the king, queen, and pawns. Then she pointed at him.

His brows furrowed, his expression perplexed. "I'm not sure what you're asking."

"Family?" she mouthed and pointed at him again.

"Do I have a family?"

She nodded.

He seemed to hesitate for a moment as if he wasn't sure, or perhaps it was a subject he didn't relish discussing. "Yes. My parents and younger sister live in Charleston. I have three brothers, two of them in Crane Landing. I plan to meet them there after I finish my job here."

She mouthed the word *when*?

He shrugged. "When am I going to meet them? Or when will I finish my job?"

She nodded and smiled, evoking a small chuckle from him.

"I don't know, Willow. I haven't started my job yet, and I don't know how long it will take to...well, how long I'll have to work here. Things have gotten...complicated."

Her smile faded and she nodded. She was the complication, crashing into his life like the unrelenting storm outside.

He touched her hand. "It's all right."

It didn't feel all right, but there was nothing she could do about their situation.

"Even if you weren't here, Willow, I'm basically snowbound." He gestured to the frosted windows and the mounting snow outside. "So let's focus on helping you heal and hopefully get your voice and your memory back."

She gave a small nod to let him know she shared his goal.

He captured her pawn. "That doesn't mean I'm going to go easy on you or give you any advantage here. I take my chess matches very seriously."

She smiled and lifted her chin to accept the challenge. As they moved their pieces and tried to check each other, she asked questions in her silent language. She had a deep curiosity about Gray and wanted to know about his siblings.

"You want to know more about my family?" he asked.

Again, she nodded.

He moved his knight and sat back. "Well, my sister, River, is sixteen with a wildly independent spirit. She has a kind, romantic heart, but is determined to blaze her own path in life. I fear for her and any man brave enough to court her."

The idea of Gray having a wild little sister made Willow smile. Leaning back in her chair, the chess game forgotten, she nodded for him to continue.

"My eldest brother, Leo, works at a shipbuilding company in

Crane Landing. He owns a schooner and runs merchandise down the East Coast, and also partners with my other older brother, Ashe, who owns a thriving merchant company with a vast fleet of merchant vessels. Apparently our younger brother, Cal, is in London, but that's really all I know about any of them. We haven't seen each other in many years."

She furrowed her brow, both surprised and intrigued by his comment.

"It's a long and complicated story," he said, sliding his rook forward three squares.

She gestured to the snow-spattered window as if to say they would be here a while. Gray had a family, and yet he seemed so alone. What about his parents, she wondered, pointing to the king and queen.

"My parents?"

She nodded, encouraging him to go on.

"That's an even longer story. Let's talk about you, Willow. Do you have any siblings?"

Her smile faded, and she released a sigh as if to say he knew very well that she didn't remember a single thing about her life.

CHAPTER FOUR

W illow stared listlessly out the window at snow-covered trees and a bleak winter sky. Nothing else was visible from where she sat on the bed, but she knew there was a world out there that belonged to her. Perhaps there was a grieving husband who was looking for her at this very minute. Maybe she even had children who needed their mommy to come home. Or maybe it was her own parents waiting for their daughter to come home. Or...maybe she was just a spinster with no life at all who had come to this mountain to disappear.

Since hearing about Gray's family, she couldn't seem to stop thinking about the possibility of having one of her own. Did she have any siblings? Her chest filled with warmth at the thought of a sister, a best friend, the one person who would love her no matter what. Surely she'd remember someone that special, wouldn't she?

With intense longing, she glanced at the bolted door. She knew it was to keep danger out, not her locked within, but she wanted to go home. To wherever that was. To whoever she was. She wanted to have a name, to belong somewhere or to someone. She felt so hopelessly lost, drifting with no direction or answers.

Frustrated, she slapped the wall.

"Willow?" She glanced up, embarrassed that Gray was watching her. "Are you all right?" he asked quietly.

No. I'm falling apart. She sighed and nodded.

He covered the pot of stew simmering on the stove then approached the bed. He offered his hands. "Would you like to get up for a while?"

She would like to get up for good, she thought, scooting to the edge of the mattress. But it still felt like she had a head full of water that sloshed around each time she moved. It made her woozy and nauseated and incapable of walking unassisted.

He offered his hands, but she grasped his muscled forearms instead. There was something unsettling about holding Gray's hands. The gentle strength in them when they touched and supported her felt too intimate.

Despite the polite distance he kept, there were moments when she felt something spark between them. When their gazes would meet as though each were searching for an identity in the other's eyes. But that was ridiculous. Gray knew who he was. He was probably just wondering whom he'd gotten saddled with.

Glancing at her fingers splayed on his forearms, Gray cupped her elbows in his palms, his fingers curving warmly up the backs of her arms. "I guess that'll work. On three," he said, counting slowly before gently pulling her up to face him.

The minute she was upright, her head swam and her knees quaked, but she stayed on her feet. The hot rush of nausea she expected didn't assail her this time...still, she sagged on Gray's arms like they were steel railings keeping her upright.

"Maybe you should wait another day," he suggested.

She leaned her forehead against his chest and shook her head. He felt so solid, like a lighthouse in her dark world. She breathed in the clean, woodsy smell of him, wishing she could trust him enough to let him hold her, to make her believe things would get better. But she couldn't afford to trust anyone. As soon as she regained her strength and was strong enough to travel, she was going in search of answers.

"You're shaking, Willow. Would you rather try after lunch?"

She lifted her chin and met his eyes, wishing he wouldn't look at her with such concern and tenderness, as if he would absorb her pain and give her the strength from his own body if he could do so. She didn't want his strength. She wanted her own unwilling body to respond to the commands her brain was sending to her legs. Nudging her toes against his foot, she tried to get him moving.

He glanced down in surprise, then back at her in obvious confusion.

She tried to tell him, worked so hard to push sound from her aching throat, but the pain was too great, and her words remained buried within her like her lost identity and her memory. Tears of frustration stung her eyes as she jiggled his arms.

"I'm sorry, Willow. I don't understand."

She stepped hard on his foot and pushed at his biceps.

His eyebrows raised. "Back up?" he asked, taking a step back.

She nodded.

He backed away with slow, measured steps as she followed along on trembling legs, her ribs aching with each shift of her body. When they approached the table, he guided her toward a chair, but she shook her head. Twenty steps was pathetic. She would take twenty more.

His expression softened. "Sit a minute, Willow. This is too much for you."

She squeezed his forearms, but her weak hands made no impression against the slate-hard muscles that shifted beneath her palms.

"You're going to fall," he said gently. His hair brushed her face as he tried to lower her onto the chair. She breathed in the fragrance of a fresh-bathed man, savored it, then slowly, deliberately bit his ear.

He reared back and clasped his offended extremity, staring at her as if she'd gone mad.

The loss of support caused her to pitch sideways, but his arm circled her waist and he hauled her against his body. Pain shot through her side and she bit her lip to keep from crying out. It wasn't his fault. If he realized he'd hurt her, he'd put her back in bed.

"What the devil are you doing, Willow?"

His expression was so bewildered she nearly smiled. She shouldn't have bitten him. Really. It was little thanks for every thing the man had done for her, but at his pace it would be weeks before she could walk on her own. And something told her she didn't have that kind of time. The sooner Gray understood their situation, the quicker she'd get back to her own life and leave him to his solitude.

She pointed at the bed to tell him she was done reclining on that mattress, but the words stuck in her broken throat. That's how it felt. Broken, as if something had cracked or snapped in the front of her throat that made swallowing painful and talking impossible.

"You want to lie down now?" His expression was such a mixture of exasperation and confusion that her shoulders sagged with guilt. She was making him as confused and frustrated as she felt. Unfortunately, she had no choice. There was only one way to regain her health. Food and exercise. So she pointed at the bed again and shook her head.

"What is it then?" The tone in his voice made her pause, but one look in his eyes told her it was concern rather than anger. "Where would you like me to put you?"

Be put? She stiffened. The thought of biting him again was suddenly appealing. It would be spiteful to wound him again, but she intended to stay on her feet as long as possible. If that meant putting a little pressure on his stocking-clad toes to get him moving, so be it.

When she wiggled her toes on his, Gray's eyebrows lifted. "What are you doing?" he asked, his voice low with intimate curiosity.

Heat surged to her face. Did he think she was flirting with him? She raised up on the balls of her feet to increase the weight on his toes and correct his misconception, but her legs weren't strong enough for balance. She pitched forward and crashed against his chest.

His arms closed around her and he staggered back two steps to keep them from tumbling to the floor. With his arms locked around her, he held her against him.

Only the steady thud of his heartbeat beneath her ear and the sound of stew bubbling in the pot on the stove could be heard. She held her breath, cowered against his tense body, praying she hadn't pushed him too far.

The silence was eerie, but not as frightening as the tone of his voice when he finally did speak. "Willow, we need to talk."

His continued kindness told her she shouldn't be afraid of him, but his tightly controlled tone alarmed her. With trepidation, she leaned back, forced herself to meet his gaze, then immediately wished she hadn't. His expression was no longer compassionate. His eyes had darkened to emerald sparks and two grim lines creased the sides of his mouth. Suddenly, she had no trouble imagining him, pistol in hand, facing an angry mob.

Fear crept along her spine, unnerved her. Moments like this reminded her that she was totally dependent on this man's mercy. Other than his name and his claim to be a lawman, she really knew nothing at all about Gray Sullivan. He could have lied about his job or even having a family.

He drew in a breath and let it out slowly. "I understand that you want to get back on your feet," he said, "but this is not the way to do it. At this rate, you'll kill both of us before supper."

Maybe he was right, she thought forlornly. But in her present condition she had little left to lose. He would either kill her or help her. At the moment, she didn't care which.

He must have sensed her defeat because the hardness in his eyes faded and his face relaxed. "You don't need to push yourself so hard."

She nodded, needing him to understand her desperation to regain some sort of independence. He had no idea how frightening it was to be so vulnerable and lost.

With light pressure beneath her chin, he tilted her face up and offered a forgiving smile. "Then spare us both some bruises and let me help you. You're turning out to be quite hardheaded, you know."

She searched his eyes to see if he was joking, but despite his smile, it appeared he meant what he said. Well, if he thought a little show of independence was a sign of stubbornness, he was in for a shock when she got her strength back. She was going to find her lost identity with or without his help.

"Willow? Although it's pleasant to have a woman in my arms again, I think my toes are getting numb."

Glancing down, she realized her feet were still perched on top of his. It must have been a subconscious reaction to the cold floor that made her seek the comfort of his wool-encased feet, but she was mortified.

Gray chuckled and gently tightened his arms around her. "I'm toying with you."

His warm laugh made her look up at him, and she found herself as mesmerized by him as she'd been the day a handsome young man waved at her from a loading dock. She had playfully curtsied to the boy, which had made him laugh, and she'd continued on her way to...to somewhere.

The sudden realization that she was remembering something made her squirm. She swayed precariously but didn't care if she had to crawl to the table. She needed to write a note.

Gray steadied her in his arms. "Where are you going?"

There was no time to use gestures he wouldn't understand so she simply hauled him along behind her as she wobbled. When she reached the table she leaned on it for support, and pretended to write on the table.

"You want to write something down?" he asked.

She nodded vigorously, cursing her sluggish brain for not thinking to do this earlier. As soon as he retrieved paper and a pen from the desk, she wrote frantically, then proudly passed the paper to him.

He squinted at the note and read out loud, "I remember a man." Gray looked up, uncertainty in his eyes.

She smiled.

"You remember a man?"

She nodded.

"The man who hurt you?"

She shook her head.

"Who then?"

She took the paper and wrote on it before he could misunderstand.

He read it and smiled. "You remember a man who waved to you from a loading dock?"

She smiled, feeling proud of herself and excited for the first time since waking up in the cabin.

"Do you remember who he was or where you were when you saw him?"

Her smile faded and she turned away, swamped by a tide of disappointment. She couldn't remember any of that.

Gray touched her shoulder. "It'll come, Willow."

She nodded but didn't believe him. It had been a week since he'd found her, and she still couldn't remember her own name.

The thought of living in a void for the rest of her life was terrifying. To live each day wondering if someone out there wanted her dead, or somewhere a man and child mourned her, or a mother waited, refusing to give up hope that her daughter was alive, was unbearable. To even think of those possibilities, of never knowing for sure wrung her heart.

With a steadying arm around her waist, Gray suggested she should lie down for a few minutes.

Gently, she clasped his chin and turned his face toward the bathroom.

"Oh, sorry." His chest deflated with a huge sigh. "I didn't think about that."

She let him help her into the room where he had so sweetly washed her hair a few nights past. As they'd been doing from the start, he waited for her to steady herself against the small sink stand. Panting from exertion while he hovered beside her, she struggled to stop the sloshing motion in her head. The bump on her skull and the swelling around her eyes had gone down considerably, but the dizziness still plagued her.

"I'll help you," he said quietly.

Her chin came up, further upsetting her balance, but she shook her head. The last several days of being helped on and off the commode had shredded her pride. The only thing worse would have been soiling herself and the bedding like an infant. Though Gray had shown compassion and managed to keep a professional detachment, he should not be her nursemaid. He was a man. A generous, handsome man who didn't deserve to be saddled with a woman who needed help with everything.

"Can you manage alone then?" he asked.

She averted her burning face and gave a slight nod to keep from upsetting her balance. After he left, she released a pent-up breath and collapsed onto the commode. Leaning her forehead onto her palms, she braced her elbows on her knees and waited until her dizziness ebbed. When her senses quit reeling, she wiggled Gray's long shirt from beneath her and relieved herself. Although her legs trembled and her head swam when she stood, she used the wall for support and managed to make her way to the door.

CHAPTER FIVE

It was late evening when Gray took out his journal and began to write.

Willow is quiet this evening, thoughtful, her mind somewhere beyond the confines of this small cabin. I have spoken to her twice, yet she seems not to hear me. Not even my journal writing can capture her attention or evoke her curiosity as it has the last several nights when she would steal glances at me, her gaze lingering on my journal. It intrigues her. But tonight, she is deep in her own thoughts, and I wonder if she is finally remembering.

She appears so fragile, so lonely tonight, sitting in the dark with her forehead leaned against the window glass, her eyes gazing out into the darkness, searching. How many nights have I done the same? Enough that I could tell her what she seeks is not out there. But she is not ready for this truth. She is still too frightened, too lost, too convinced that knowing her name will answer the question of who she is.

That, I have found, is something a person may never know.

Were Willow to discover my true thoughts, she would not trust me at all. My feelings are not hers to worry about though. She is trying to heal, to find herself and reclaim her life. To see her despair deepen each day, and feel my fondness for her growing, makes me want to bolt, to return her to her old life and break these bonds that are forming between us. This duty that was forced upon me by mere circumstance is becoming too personal. There is something special about this woman that reaches deep inside me. I have tried to remain aloof, a caretaker of sorts, but she draws me in with her quiet strength, wrings me out with the suffering she tries so hard to conceal.

I must locate the crime scene, but I don't know how far Willow might have traveled after the assault. Based on the condition in which I found her, I can't imagine it was far. Even if she only wandered a few yards from the scene, my search for evidence in a forest will be slow, painstaking work, especially after a delay of several days and hindered by snow. I must get back out there soon.

Time is pressing in on both of us. The clock is a harsh master when a job is involved. My investigation at the paper mill can't be put off much longer. But I can't leave Willow alone. Not yet.

Willow glanced up when she heard Gray close his secret book. She watched him put it in the drawer, then browse the novels on the shelf, his dark brows furrowed. His finger trailed the spines of several before he selected one and brought it with him to the padded armchair near the stove.

He sank deep into the cushions, long legs stretched out before him, looking so comfortable she had a sudden urge to curl up like a cat on his lap, to feel the gentle stroke of his hand and know she mattered to someone. To anyone. She was desperately lonely. That excruciating aching-to-the-marrow-of-her-bones lonely.

But as the minutes ticked by it seemed Gray preferred to keep his distance. She had noticed how he would pull away after any sort of involvement with her. She sighed, but he didn't look up, didn't offer her anything but the sight of his long, muscled body. It left her feeling oddly removed from herself. She remembered none of her romantic history, yet looking at Gray's powerful body sprawled before her, made her yearn for the comfort of his arms. Maybe it was simply a need to feel safe that elicited her desire to be held by him.

Her gaze shifted to Gray's chest where a patch of dark hair peeped from his open collar. He wore a shirt of forest green that rose and fell slowly as he breathed. For a time, she was content just to watch him, to let herself drift in the rhythm of his breathing.

"Are you all right, Willow?"

Startled, she met his eyes.

"You moaned. Is something wrong?"

Mortified, she shook her head and turned her hot face toward the window. She had to get out of this cabin.

"Close the curtain and come away from the window," he said. "It's unsafe even if it is dark where you're sitting. And it's a lot warmer over here near the stove."

Despite her embarrassment, she was desperate for company and a diversion from her troubling thoughts. Moving slowly, she closed the curtain then eased off the bed, Placing one hand on the arm of his chair, she stood, took three careful steps, and sat in the chair opposite him.

"You're getting steadier on your feet," he said.

She nodded, then pointed at the book in his hands and made a talking motion with her fingers.

"You want me to read to you?" he asked. When she nodded, he frowned at her. "Does your throat still hurt too much to talk?"

Releasing a hard sigh, she nodded, feeling as frustrated as he sounded. Her throat still felt raw, and when she coughed or even moaned, she felt a tearing pain deep in her throat. She worried that speaking would do more damage.

"Do you want some tea?"

She shook her head and pointed at his book.

He smiled. "It's *Huckleberry Finn.*"

She didn't care. Any diversion from her thoughts would be welcome. Since she couldn't remember her own identity, she would gladly become a character in a novel. At least a character in a book had a life, a purpose, and knew who they were.

She pulled a blanket around her and curled up in the chair opposite him.

"Have you ever read Mark Twain?" he asked.

She considered a moment, then shrugged.

"Well, you haven't read a book until you've read Mark Twain. Huck Finn lives life on his own terms, says what he thinks, and manages to get himself in all sorts of trouble." Gray glanced at her, a half-smile on his lips.

His uncustomary boyishness made her smile and ache to know more about him, the real man sitting across from her, not some storybook character.

Tentatively, she reached over and closed the book he'd begun to read. When he glanced up, his expression a mixture of curiosity and surprise. She took up the small pad and pen from the stand beside her chair and wrote *talk to me.*

―――――

HOURS LATER, Gray lay on his makeshift bed of chair cushions placed on the floor beside Willow's bed, wondering how he was going to dig up enough clues to learn her identity and find the wretch who'd hurt her. He was so deep in thought that Willow's wounded cry startled him.

"What is it?" he asked, leaning over the mattress, but he couldn't see her in the darkness.

Air whistled from her throat and she panted, then suddenly she was gouging his forearm with her ragged fingernails.

He sucked in his breath. "Easy, Willow." He slipped his hand over her clenching fingers. "You're all right. You're safe here." He stroked her trembling hand and slid his palm up her arm. "You're safe," he whispered.

Slowly, her fingers relaxed, and she grew still as if listening for something.

"You're safe, Willow. I'll protect you."

A rush of air left her lungs, and he felt her hand tremble. She slipped her palm over his forearm, but he was only certain she was awake when she squeezed his wrist.

"I'll light the lantern," he said, and started to move away, but she wouldn't release him. Her grip surprised him and made him hesitate. Kneeling at her bedside, he wondered what to do to ease her fear. "Do you not want me to light the lantern?" he asked.

He heard her shift on the mattress, then felt a light tug on his wrist. His heart thumped and he wished he could see her, but the moonless night left everything black. Not daring to move for fear of scaring her, he said, "I don't know what you need."

Her hand touched his chest, then she gave a tug on his shirt collar.

His heart hammered and he wondered if maybe she was dreaming. "Willow, are you awake?"

Capturing his hand, she brought it to her uninjured cheek where he felt her nod.

"Are you all right then?" he asked.

She gave a small negative movement of her head, and his heart cramped. Her jaw quivered and he realized she was crying, could feel the wetness of her tears on his fingers.

She patted the mattress, then gave a gentle tug on his arm.

"You want me to sit on your bed?" he asked softly.

She sat up slowly and painfully from the sound of her small sighs, then leaned against the wall and tugged on his hand.

Hoping he was reading her wordless commands correctly, he sat beside her and leaned his back against the wall.

She clutched his hand and released a long sigh.

He barely dared to breathe. She wasn't six inches from him. His palms were sweating. He didn't want her to need him like this. He didn't want any attachments between them.

"Are you upset because you're remembering?" he asked, praying her answer would be yes.

She brought his palm to her cheek and moved her head in a slight side-to-side motion. Then she tapped his hand twice.

"Two taps means No?" he asked.

Willow tapped his hand once and nodded her head.

"And one tap means Yes?"

She gave him one tap on the chest and nodded again.

"That'll work," he said, but wished he'd lit the lantern so he could see her. "Were you remembering what happened to you?"

She tapped his shoulder twice, but before Gray could ask another question, she tapped it again one time.

"No and yes?"

One tap.

He sighed. "You were remembering things but not clearly?"

One tap.

Whether she was dreaming or remembering fragments of what had happened to her wasn't a question either of them could answer. So he simply sat with her to offer whatever comfort she seemed to gain from his presence. As the silence lengthened, she began to wilt against him. Before long, her head was resting against his shoulder. In the silent night, he was glad she couldn't talk, that she couldn't share her secrets, or her fears, or what had terrified her so deeply she would seek comfort from a man she barely knew. They were strangers to each other, and that's how he wanted them to remain.

But as he sat there in the darkness, each breath he drew was filled with the fresh smell of Willow's hair. Her fingers, still wet with tears, had laced with his, and he grudgingly accepted the truth. Their lives were intertwined, and the path ahead of them was one they must hike together.

CHAPTER SIX

Gray watched the play of lantern light on Willow's hair as she wrote out question after question for him on the tablet. Her hair was still damp from her bath, and he admired the changing depths of color as it dried.

She was changing with each passing day, and the effect was testing his good intentions. Just twelve days ago, he could not have imagined the beauty of this woman's face. She'd merely been a wounded creature in need of aid, an intrusion in his life he hadn't wanted, a misfortunate individual who had tangled with the wrong person.

Now she had become a living, feeling human being that intrigued him beyond the point of good sense. Perhaps it was just the essence of mystery surrounding Willow that drew him. Maybe it was admiration for her incredible strength to survive. Perhaps it was simply the way she smiled at him, like she was doing now.

She handed him the tablet.

When he read her note asking why no one was looking for her, and he saw her pain-filled eyes, his heart cramped in sympathy. "We don't know that, Willow."

She pointed toward the door and lifted her palms as if saying no one had come knocking in search of her.

"Maybe your people just haven't thought to check this far up the mountain."

Slipping the tablet from his hand, she scribbled quickly and passed it back to him. *Go to the closest town and ask about me. Check the newspapers for any missing women.*

With a sigh and a chest full of dread, he said he would do so as soon as she was healthy enough to be left here alone, but he knew he wouldn't do it. When she gestured that she was fine, he shook his head. "You're not strong enough yet, but I'll go to town soon."

She plucked the pen from his hand and wrote *When?* at the corner of the tablet.

For a moment, her gaze seemed to bore into his eyes as if beseeching him to help her find answers. Her desperation was so evident it flooded him with guilt and sorrow. He ached to tell her the truth and relieve even a modicum of her heartache, and the heavy burden on his conscience, but he couldn't. For her sake.

When he didn't answer right away she pointed at him, then tapped her head as if to ask where his concentration had gone.

"Guess I was woolgathering."

She tipped her head, eyed him quizzically, and mouthed, "About what?"

About what kind of person would harm someone so full of life. About how he was going to ignore his desire to pull her into his arms.

Willow took back the pad, jotted another note, and handed it back. *I'd really like to know*, it read.

"You want to know what I was thinking?"

She nodded.

He couldn't remember the last time he had shared his private thoughts with anyone, but seeing Willow's look of expectation slowly fade as the silence stretched out beckoned him to try. She deserved an answer to a simple and sincere question. But how should he respond? If he spoke truthfully and told her he was thinking about her, would she misconstrue it or misread his intentions? He didn't know, but watching the light dim in her eyes, he knew there was only one way he could answer.

"I was thinking about you, Willow."

A flicker of surprise crossed her face. He experienced a sudden urge to link fingers with her hand resting on the arm of the chair. He shouldn't have started thinking about her hair. Shouldn't have studied her face or the depths of her eyes every time she looked at him during the past few days. But she was a mystery revealing itself one clue at a time. Her changing looks and developing personality intrigued him.

She leaned over, wrote on the pad, then turned it toward him so he could read it.

Her note and her expression wrenched his heart. "No. You're not a burden. I wasn't thinking that at all."

She tipped her head, compelling him to meet her eyes.

"Honestly," he said. "I was just thinking that your bruises are almost gone from around your eyes." He leaned to the side to peer at her left cheek. "There's just a smudge of yellow beneath your eye."

She ducked her head, her shy response creating a warm tug in his chest. She could be bold if she wanted something, but he sensed she was a shy creature by nature.

She fidgeted beneath his stare, and he gently captured her hand. "It's been almost two weeks since I found you, and I feel as if I've been watching a new woman emerge from beneath your bruises."

Her brows furrowed as if she were trying to decipher a hidden meaning in his comment.

"You have a fierce energy in you, Willow, a personality that's pulsing with life despite your injuries. You have an intelligence in your eyes that makes me wish you would talk and share your thoughts."

She touched her throat, her look sadly apologetic.

"I understand," he said, feeling selfish for encouraging her to talk. "It's enough to see you regaining your health and your beauty."

Though he hadn't meant to embarrass her, Willow's cheeks flushed. She touched her fingertips to the pink scar that slashed across her cheek.

"It doesn't matter, Willow. Not even a little."

THINKING about Gray kept Willow awake long after he had closed the book and made his bed on the floor beside her own. Until now, she hadn't considered their sleeping arrangements because she'd spent so much time in bed and had always been the first one to sleep, and the last one to rise. But as she studied him sprawled on the floor, she saw a man who made sacrifices without complaint.

The glow of the woodstove softened the angles of his face and dusted the tips of his lashes with gold. In sleep, Gray appeared more youthful, seemingly at peace with whatever demons plagued him and made him so serious during his waking hours. One arm rested outside the blanket and was folded across his chest, his fingers relaxed, his hand rising and falling with the rhythm of his breathing. That hand had touched her face with tenderness and washed her hair and supported her numerous times. But that same hand had written words in a journal each evening that he wouldn't share with her, and she couldn't help wondering if he was keeping something from her.

Frustrated, lonely, and desperate to understand the man she was so dependent on, she sat up. After waiting a moment for her head to clear and her legs to wake up, she slipped from the bed. She knew it was wrong to breach Gray's privacy, but if he knew something about her, anything at all that would help her remember, it would be just as wrong for him to withhold the information from her.

Carefully, she inched her way across the room, glancing at Gray's sleeping face. Her conscience rebelled, but her sense of survival demanded she investigate. Gripping the back of the chair, she guided herself into the deepening shadows of the room, slowly making her way to the table. If she could just get the journal and slip into the bathroom, she would skim his notes to see if he'd mentioned her. That's all. She wouldn't spend a minute more delving into his private notes.

Her fingertips grazed the table and glided across the surface as she skirted the chairs. The airy draw of the stovepipe moaned behind her. The ticking of the wall clock beat at half-time with her racing heart. Outside, the cold night was silent, motionless, as if holding its breath.

She touched the desk, trailed her fingers downward and pulled gently on the drawer. It gave a low, mournful creak as she eased it open. She tensed, held her breath and prayed the noise hadn't alerted Gray to her nocturnal prowling.

A quiet thump from the stove made her jump, but all else remained quiet. Slowly she reached inside the drawer, ran her fingertips over the leather surface of his journal...

"What are you doing, Willow?"

Gray's sleepy voice came from directly behind and so close to her ear, she released a startled squeak and sagged against the table.

He caught her waist to steady her. "Are you ill?"

She shook her head, her heart hammering against her sore ribcage. Desperate to disguise her prowling and prying, she imitated writing on her hand, then pointed to the drawer.

"You were looking for a pen?" he asked dubiously.

She nodded, tapped her finger against the hand she had written on.

"And stationery?"

Again, she nodded.

His brows furrowed. "It's the middle of the night."

She laid her cheek against her folded hands and feigned sleep, then opened her eyes and shook her head.

"You can't sleep," he said in weary conclusion. He raked his ruffled hair back and reached for the matches beside the lantern on the table. After it was glowing softly, he inspected her as though he needed to assure himself she was okay. Gently, he moved her aside and retrieved a pencil and sheaf of writing paper from the drawer.

Uncomfortable with him standing so close to her, she gestured to a badge of some sort lying in the drawer.

"It's mine," he said quietly, then handed her the pencil and paper.

"Tell—" Willow touched her throat, immediately regretting the impulse to speak.

"I think you need to see a doctor, Willow."

She frowned, pointed toward the badge, then scribbled a note on the top sheet of paper.

"It's late, and I'm too tired to talk." He remained quiet for a moment before pulling a chair out for her. "Don't stay up too long."

She caught his hand to stop him from leaving. "Gray—" She coughed and squeezed her eyes shut. Talking was too painful. She simply couldn't do it yet, so she wrote *please talk to me* on the paper and pushed it toward him.

"About what?" Before she could write, he placed his hand over hers. "It's late, Willow. You should be in bed." With that, he returned to his makeshift bed and turned his back to her.

Questions assailed her, but Gray had made it clear he wasn't interested in talking, so she sank onto the chair he'd pulled out for her, and began to write down all the questions she wanted to ask him tomorrow. When she finished her long list, she started another that consisted of answers and requests she could point to instead of having to use gestures every time she needed something or he asked her a question.

Then she began to sketch thin lines across a clean sheet of paper. The sight of Gray's broad back as he lay on his sleeping mat made it clear he didn't want to talk, so she focused on her sketching and shut him out as effectively as he was doing to her.

Feeling completely exiled by his refusal to talk to her, and deeply confused about her growing interest in him, she leaned back in the chair and continued to draw. How could he expect her to trust him when he wouldn't give her his in return? What sort of arrangement was that?

Curiously hurt, she sat at the table for a long time, her pencil trailing absently on the page as her mind wandered. An image began to appear on the page, pleasing her, then surprising her. Apparently, she could sketch quite well. In fact, the sketch was remarkably good. And having something to do to focus her chaotic thoughts was a balm to her nerves.

As the night deepened, visions flickered at the edges of her mind but she could not wrestle them down. Finally growing weary of the effort, she laid her head on her folded arms and drifted in murky images, too tired to sort them out or try to make sense of them. But she knew as soon as she was strong enough, she would leave this cabin and find a way to reclaim her life.

WILLOW IS SLEEPING in this morning after her late-night prowling. Her hair is spread across the pillow, her face delicate and beautiful. She is too innocent, too transparent to lie successfully to *a man who has spent his life as an undercover operative, living like a chameleon, changing my persona as easily as changing my shoes. She doesn't trust me.*

Last night she was searching for my journal.

As I linger over the sight of her in my bed I can no longer pretend an attraction doesn't exist. Nor can I feign disinterest in discovering the real woman hiding in Willow's subconscious. I am too intrigued by the drawing I found on the table this morning. It is a sketch of a man who appears shadowlike, his features unclear, but she has sketched him as if he's towering over her. And beneath the drawing is a pocket watch. Willow has finally begun to remember.

The sudden pounding on the door sent Gray's journal sliding across the table as he lunged for his gun. Willow vaulted up in bed, her face a mask of fear as her eyes searched for him. He motioned for her to go into the bathroom, and although her gait was still awkward and her balance tentative, she managed on her own.

"Hello there, is anyone home?" a male voice called from the other side of the door.

Gripping the door frame to the bathroom, Willow looked at Gray, but he had no idea who or what might meet him if he opened the door. So he shrugged in answer to her silent question.

Why hadn't he heard anyone approach? Had he been so absorbed in his journal, in his curiosity about Willow that he hadn't heard them? Could he have really been that negligent?

"Hellooo," the voice called again.

He gestured to Willow to close the bathroom door and stay out of sight.

Then he slowly opened the cabin door. He was met by a cold blast of air and his neighbor Ben, who had given him a ride from town out to the cabin when Gray first arrived. He hadn't recognized the man's voice.

"Was hoping you was in there," Ben said, then squatted to lace up one of his boots. "Right frigid out this morning."

"That it is," Gray said, wondering what had brought the man to his door.

As Ben stood, he tugged his worn hat lower over his ears, looking a bit sheepish. "I was wondering if you might need to hire a ride to town. Figured you might be running low on supplies."

"I could use your services tomorrow," Gray said, wanting to give Willow another day before leaving her alone for a few hours.

The man looked crestfallen and a little desperate. "I was hoping you might need a ride today."

That he was in urgent need of money was apparent, but Gray couldn't leave Willow yet. "Why don't I pay you today and have you take me into town tomorrow?"

A great relief seemed to wash over the man and his face brightened. "That would be right fine and much appreciated. You just say when to be here and I'll bring my wagon round for you."

Gray knew the man was a farmer with early morning chores, so he suggested that Ben pick him up after lunch so they could be back by mid-afternoon. Stepping outside and intentionally backing Ben up a step, Gray shut the door behind him. "I haven't met any other folks from around here but I see chimney smoke telling me we have neighbors."

"That big plume of smoke down yonder is from the paper mill," Ben said, gesturing in the direction of town just two miles down the mountain. "You'll know it if the wind shifts and carries that stench to your door."

Gray had smelled the sour stench when he'd arrived in town, and was greatly relieved the cabin was upwind of the plant.

"The Hawkins family lives up the road a ways. Family of eight with a busy sawmill. Below my place, close to the falls, is Twitchell's Grist Mill. Three brothers own and run the mill and live thereabouts with their families," Ben said, his gesture indicating they all lived in close proximity to the mill and to each other. "They're our closest neighbors, but I know most folks out this way if you want an introduction."

"That won't be necessary, at least not just yet," Gray said, "but how about you, Ben? Do you have a family?"

"Surely do," he said, his eyes beaming with pride. "My wife and I have three girls, eight, six, and four years old, and a son who turns a year old tomorrow."

"Sounds like you've got yourself a busy household," Gray said, hoping the money Ben would earn for taking him to town would buy whatever provisions the man's family needed.

A wide grin spread across Ben's face. "It certainly is, and a noisy one at that."

Despite numerous acres between mills and farms, Gray knew those farmers and mill owners seemed to communicate with one another and keep up on local gossip. "Since I'm new to the area, I'd be obliged if you have any news to share."

Ben's eyes widened and he leaned in as if to share a secret. "I hear a young woman in town recently disappeared. Officer Klein stopped by my farm to ask if we'd seen the girl. Apparently, there's nary a sign of where she might have run off to. Some think she stole away with a beau, others suspect she ran afoul of trouble. Don't know the girl myself, but it's a shame either way. Her parents must be devastated by her disappearance." He shook his head. "If anything ever happened to one of my girls, well, I'd go plum out of my mind."

Gray nodded. Just the thought of his little sister, River, disappearing without a trace wrenched his gut. "What was the woman's name?" he asked, already knowing the answer but hoping Ben might have more information.

"From what I hear it was Arthur and Elizabeth Flynn's daughter, Sophia. I don't know the family, but from what Lola Gorman says, Arthur and his daughter Sophia worked at the paper mill."

Ben shrugged. "Don't know much about them myself, but Mrs. Gorman says they're good folk."

"Who is Lola Gorman?"

"She owns the general store in town and knows all the gossip."

Gray smiled, knowing he'd just been handed a good source who could likely provide a wealth of information on the town and its inhabitants, and perhaps some insight into what might have happened to Sophia. Questions assailed him, but he kept them to himself. He would need to do some investigating in a way that wouldn't elicit too much interest.

Ben shoved his bare hands deeper into the pockets of his frayed coat. "I could shovel you out if you need a hand," he suggested, nodding to the drifts of snow congesting the cabin entrance and the drifted-in path that led out to where his horse stood, releasing frosty funnel clouds from his nostrils.

Gray wanted to help the man out, but he needed Ben to be on his way. And he hadn't shoveled because he wanted to keep access to the cabin as difficult as possible. He couldn't disguise the chimney smoke that signaled the cabin was occupied, but he could make it more difficult for someone to approach. The snow would slow a person down and make tracking them easier.

"Thank you for the offer, Ben, but I can manage," he said. He passed several bills to Ben. "If you have a horse I could rent when I need one, I'd be interested."

"I got plenty of mounts, sir. You just dash down the road when you need one and I'll have your mount saddled and ready to go in minutes," Ben said, with an eagerness that made Gray's heart twist in sympathy. He knew too well how it felt to be poor and desperate. The hard times had ended when Gordon and Pollyanna Drayton had taken in Gray and his baby sister, River, when he was eight years old, but he would never forget the pain of being cold, hungry, and scared.

CHAPTER SEVEN

"Have you ever put together a dissected puzzle?" Gray asked, watching Willow closely to see if his question might have sparked a memory. He'd been asking a variety of questions, dropping them into their conversations as casually as possible, but none of them had seemed to elicit any recall in Willow's mind. She remained a mystery...and a growing distraction.

She gave him a half-hearted shrug as if she might have done so but couldn't remember. He knew she was disappointed that their earlier visitor hadn't been someone looking for her.

"This one is of the eastern states," he said, gesturing to the puzzle. "My friend, Paul, who owns this cabin is a schoolmaster," he said, feeling guilty for concocting a story about how he'd come to be at the cabin, but it was imperative he keep the purpose of his work here a secret. "Paul brings his family here during the summer. That's why there's a shelf full of books and board games and such. He said he needs to keep his two boys occupied on rainy days and feels they might as well be learning something while they're playing."

Willow smiled as if she understood how two restless boys in a cabin could encourage one to provide multiple diversions.

"Would you like to put a puzzle together?" he asked, hoping to distract her while he was trying to piece together his own mental puzzle.

She nodded and made her way to the table where he was sitting.

To see her balance and strength so improved released the knot of worry that had been lodged between his shoulders. With the exception of her sore throat that still seemed to bother her, it appeared she was recovering fully from her injuries.

After she sat, she perused the odd-shaped puzzle pieces, then selected the one that represented the state of Maine and placed it in the top right corner.

Gray intentionally dallied as he looked over the wooden pieces that represented each of the eastern states, wanting to give Willow plenty of time to place a few more pieces of the puzzle. He needed to know if she knew her geography or if she'd just gotten lucky placing her first piece of the puzzle. He added the state of New York to act as if he were participating and make his observation of her less obvious.

Willow placed piece after piece in their proper place, making quick work of the puzzle, not only revealing her intelligence but eliciting Gray's curiosity. He wanted to know more about her, her life, and what could have brought her to such a tragic place. Could she really be the woman accused of theft?

She lifted her hands, palms up, as if to say, *Now what?*

"How about another puzzle?"

She shook her head, then pointed to the page of answers, phrases, and questions she'd been using since the night he'd caught her trying to find his journal.

"I'm bored," he read, then looked at her. "A game then?"

Another shake of her head.

"A book?"

She pointed to the door, then moved two of her fingers in a walking motion.

He laughed. "Are you saying you want to go outside for a walk?"

A smile bloomed on her face and she nodded.

"Not yet, Willow. You're not strong enough."

"Gray," she said, surprising him. She pressed her palm to her throat and coughed. "Outside, please."

He grinned. "You're talking, Willow."

She nodded and winced. "Still sore."

"I'm sure," he said. "But I'm really glad to hear you speak."

"Out. Please."

Back and forth they went, with her gesturing, pointing to her list of answers, then debating him on paper, and him saying *no* to her every request, until finally he said, "All right. We can go for a walk. Tomorrow when I return from town."

Her frown told him she wasn't pleased to be put off, but her nod of agreement allowed them to change the subject.

Leaning back in her chair, she released a hard sigh and did a slow visual survey of the cabin.

She looked so intent in her inspection it made him laugh. "Are you planning an escape?"

Ignoring him, she eased out of her chair and made her way to the sink where she worked the pump handle to dampen a linen cloth. Then she spent the next hour slowly dusting her way through the cabin.

He worried she was pushing her recovery too fast, that she might lose her balance and fall, but she moved with care and seemed to be aware of her limitations. Observing her, he could see she was much improved even from yesterday, so he left her to her wandering. Apparently, cleaning was her way of trying to regain her strength, and he had to admit, if only to himself, it was a smart idea. What worried him, though, was the more mobile she became, the more difficult it was going to be to keep her inside.

Later on, while Willow read, he washed their clothes in the tub, then hung them to dry over a rack he'd placed near the woodstove. Afterward, he did his best to create a meal out of the scant rations he had left. There was little doubt his trip to town tomorrow was necessary. He just hoped Willow would behave herself and remain safe while he was away.

Late that evening, after making a note of the supplies he needed, he tucked the list in his pocket, then stepped outside to get firewood for the stove. As he reached for a hefty piece of split birch, he heard the door creak behind him. He'd left it unlatched so he could nudge it open with his foot when carrying in firewood. Assuming the wind had blown the door open, he turned back, intending to pull it closed, but saw Willow stepping outside.

"Stay inside," he said, knowing she wasn't protected out in the open.

Snugging his large flannel shirt more securely around her shoulders, she surveyed the star-speckled night sky.

He slipped his hand behind her back as if to guide her back inside. "It's not safe out here."

"Please," she said, her voice ragged. "Two minutes."

He smiled. "It's nice to hear your voice."

She wrinkled her nose. "Sounds awful."

There was nothing awful about her, he thought, viewing her in the shadowed night. Golden light shone from the open doorway, illuminating her face and starlit eyes. Her chest lifted as she drew in a deep breath, then released it in a slow frosty funnel. The way she savored that simple breath of air on a wintery night captivated him. Instead of shrinking from the cold, she seemed to drink it in, to embrace it, to invite it to fill her body even as she shivered.

In all his travels and interactions with women, he'd never met one like her.

She gazed at him with questions in her eyes even as her body swayed toward him.

Their time together had conditioned his arms to catch her, to carry her, to comfort her, and he pulled her into the protective warmth of his embrace without a second thought. Her hair fell over her shoulders and down her back, the silken strands brushing his hands, tempting him to draw her closer. The firewood, the frigid night, the potential danger disappeared as he basked in the feel of her in his arms. Their eyes met and held. To drift in a moment when everything slowed and time seemed suspended was something he'd experienced during gun battles, but he'd never experienced that sentience with a woman. Until now.

It would be so easy to lower his mouth to hers, but he couldn't. He wouldn't. So he released her and stepped away. "Please go inside," he said, his own voice as ragged as hers sounded.

After she stepped inside, he blew out a hard breath and called himself a fool. The urge to deny something had transpired between them was strong, but he'd felt that connection in his gut. Whatever had just happened could not happen again. Willow was under his protection. It was his job to keep her safe, even from himself.

With that in mind, he turned back to the task of hauling in firewood. The pile had diminished significantly, and he would need to split more wood soon.

Once he'd filled the woodbins, he heated the last of the venison soup for their supper, then he tried to read, but his thoughts were scattered and he couldn't settle. Confusion over what had happened outside between them, and concern for her safety when he would leave her alone and unprotected tomorrow, gnawed a hole in him.

For a moment, he considered hiring Ben to pick up the items they needed, but immediately quashed the idea. Gray needed to get a few personal items for Willow without indicating he was shopping for a woman. He needed to nose around a bit to see if he could sniff out any clues as to Willow's identity and what might have happened to her.

The only thing he knew for certain was that he needed to dig up some answers. Which meant he had to leave Willow here. Alone.

———

AFTER A RESTLESS NIGHT of tossing on his makeshift bed, and eating a scant breakfast in the morning, Gray spent several minutes instructing Willow on how to hold and shoot his pistol. He hadn't loaded the gun because he wanted her to practice aiming and pulling the trigger, but her wobbly grip and lack of muzzle control terrified him. Multiple times he cautioned her to hold steady and not drop the barrel toward her lap. She balked and tried to refuse his lesson, but he wasn't leaving until he knew she could hold the gun and pull the trigger without shooting herself.

By the time he heard Ben pull his rig up out at the road, Gray was as frazzled as Willow. He loaded three bullets into the chamber and reminded her to stay inside with the door locked, and told her to not touch the gun unless someone tried to break in. With that, he carefully placed the gun on the coffee table, directing the muzzle away from the chair she was sitting in, then gave her shoulder a gentle squeeze. "I won't be long. Just stay inside and don't open the door to anyone."

She gave him a small, unconvincing nod. "Ask about me. In town." Her eyes squinted and she coughed. "Don't forget."

———

GRAY ENTERED Gorman's General Store and stopped inside the door. The interior seemed a bit dark after squinting against the glare of sunshine on snow, but as his eyes adjusted, he took in a vast array of goods. Barrels, crates, and tables were stacked high with clothing, men's hats, cigars, and other merchandise. Candles, soaps, fabrics, oils, canned goods, tea, sugar, and a sundry of baking products packed floor-to-ceiling shelving. Farm equipment, fishing rods, and other tools hung on the walls. Pots and pans of various sizes hung from ceiling hooks. At the back of the store, a woodstove and seating area was tucked in among more overflowing shelving.

As he made his way to a counter topped with jars of hard candies, pickles, and a tray of delicious smelling cinnamon buns, oak floorboards creaked beneath his boots. A stocky lady with graying hair twisted into a tidy bun introduced herself as Mrs. Gorman and asked if she could help him.

He replied using his undercover alias of Gray Alexander, and gave her the list of grocery items he needed.

"You must be new in town," she said, stepping around the counter.

Following her down an aisle, he said, "Yes, I'm here for a job."

"Are you seeking employment?" she asked, glancing back at him. "Farmwork is scarce this time of year, but you might find something at the paper mill here in town. Or perhaps one of the saw mills or the grist mill might need a hand."

"Thank you, Mrs. Gorman. I'm set for work, but if you could tell me a bit about Pine Ridge, I'd be much obliged."

As he'd hoped, she was happy to fill his ears with local happenings and gossip as she gathered the items he needed from overpacked shelves. "You'll find Pine Ridge is a town of honest, hardworking folk, which is why everyone is up in arms over the disappearance of Sophia Flynn."

"I heard about her from Officer Kline who stopped by my

place to ask if I'd seen her. Any idea what might have happened to the girl?" Gray asked, trying not to show too much interest.

The storekeeper's brows knit and she seemed distressed. "They're accusing her of running off with a young man, but I can't believe she would have done such a thing. I'd wager my bonnet on it."

"Did you know the girl?"

"She came in the store every week or so. She was a lovely girl. Quiet and polite. Never bought more than necessities and never asked for credit, not even when her family was in obvious need of assistance."

"Did she have a beau?"

Mrs. Gorman shook her head. "Not that I ever saw, nor have I heard anything to suggest she did. Honestly, I doubt she, or anyone working at the paper mill, would have time for such a pursuit. They work morning to night, six or seven days a week."

"Do any mill employees have an idea what might have happened to her?"

"The foreman said she came up missing during her shift. He suspected she was off in some dark corner sleeping, and had a couple of his employees search the mill and grounds for her. But they, and the local police, turned up nothing."

"Is the foreman a trustworthy man?"

Mrs. Gorman shrugged. "I don't know Mr. Wade well enough to say. He's always gruff when he comes in, so I leave him to his business and hurry him out the door when he's finished. That's simply an observation, mind you."

Gray gave her a reassuring nod. "Of course. Do you think the girl, Miss Flynn, might still be in the area?"

The woman shrugged. "I couldn't say, but I hope she's somewhere safe and that she didn't risk her reputation by running off with some young man. She such a pretty young gal with her dark hair and lovely smile, I wouldn't put it past a boy to encourage her to do so."

"Did Miss Flynn have a family?"

"She lived with her parents in mill housing. Her father, Arthur Flynn, works at the mill. Sophia's mother, Elizabeth, worked there until a few years ago. Now she takes in a bit of sewing and sells a few baked goods. In fact, she baked those cinnamon buns on the counter," Mrs. Gorman said, gesturing to the tray of puffy, glazed rolls. "They'll be gone within the hour, so if you have a mind to purchase any, you'd best do so quickly."

He had already considered purchasing a few of the delicious smelling buns, but now he would definitely buy some. If the woman in his cabin was Sophia Flynn, and it seemed very likely she was, then perhaps her mother's cinnamon buns would trigger her memory and help solve the mystery surrounding her assault. "I'll take a half dozen," he said. "Does Mrs. Flynn take special orders?" he asked, seeking a seemingly innocent way to learn more about Sophia's parents and garner more information about the woman in his care.

"I believe so, but you'll have to inquire with her directly."

"And where might I find the talented lady?"

Mrs. Gorman's eyes clouded. "She lives in the flats in housing provided by the mill. It's the only way many of the mill workers can keep a roof over their heads." The woman shuddered. "It's a dreadful place."

Gray's gut twisted in sympathy. Poverty was exhausting, grueling, and painful, but the worst part about deprivation was how it sucked the joy out of every moment of every day. To know Willow—*Sophia*—had endured that kind of life, wrenched his heart. Perhaps she'd run off trying to escape that life. But that seemed unlikely. When he'd found her, she'd been beaten, she had nothing of value in her possession, and she was terrified, which meant she might have been running away *from* someone, not *with* someone. The only way to know what had happened to Sophia was for her memory to return, or for Gray to figure out what happened during his investigation at the mill.

Mrs. Gorman wiped her hands on a brown bib apron she wore over her dress. "I believe that's everything on your list, Mr. Alexander. Will there be anything else then?"

"I need to purchase a coat, a hat, a pair of mittens, and a pair of warm boots for my nephew who is visiting me. And I suppose I should also fit him out with some long johns and a pair of dungarees," he added.

"How old is the boy?"

"Just turned fourteen," Gray said, the tale rolling off his tongue with ease. After years of working as an undercover operative, he had, of necessity, learned to improvise on his feet and create stories to fit any situation. Today, he was purchasing clothing for his young nephew. The storekeeper didn't need to know those clothes were for Willow.

"If he's an average size boy these should work," she said, pulling a pair of boots from the bottom shelf.

They looked too large for Willow. "He's a bit small for his age," Gray said, nodding toward a smaller pair of boots farther down the shelf. "Maybe that pair?"

"Of course," she said, then helped him select the remaining items on his list along with three wooden storage crates. They carried everything to the counter where she wrote his purchases in a book and added them up on her register.

At the last minute, he asked her for two small bags of hard candies and to wrap an additional half dozen cinnamon buns separately for him. Although his instruction seemed to elicit her curiosity, she rang up the candy and extra baked goods without prying. While she packed his supplies in the wooden crates and wrapped some of the items in paper tied with string, he casually queried her for more information about the town.

She noted several amenities he might have an interest in, such as the train depot, which he already knew about because he'd traveled to Pine Ridge by rail. For a town of eleven hundred people, he was surprised to learn it had two doctors, two churches, a meeting hall, a post office, a library, a small restaurant and bakery, a butcher shop, and three drinking establishments. "And there's the Pine Ridge Paper Mill, of course, which is the largest employer, though certainly not the fairest," Mrs. Gorman said, wrapping up the last package.

"You are a fount of knowledge, Mrs. Gorman, and I deeply appreciate your assistance," he said, giving her a warm smile as he picked up three of his packages. With a friendly wink at the blushing storekeeper, he headed outside to where Ben waited with the wagon.

It took three trips for Gray to load his crates and packages into the wagon, then he climbed onto the seat and handed Ben a bag of hard candies and a package of cinnamon buns. "A little something sweet for you and your family," he said.

Surprise lit Ben's eyes as he accepted the items. Lifting the package of cinnamon buns to his nose, he sniffed, then his eyes widened and a smile broke across his face. "It's been a long while since my family has had any sweets. My wife and kids will think it's Christmas."

"It's a small thank you for a big favor," Gray said. "I hadn't meant to keep you waiting outside in the cold so long."

"Don't bother me at all," Ben said, setting the bag and package of buns between them on the bench seat. "I'm grateful to have the work." He glanced at Gray with moist eyes. "Thank you, Mr. Alexander."

Gray clapped a hand over Ben's thin shoulder. "I'd like to think we're friends, Ben. Friends help each other out, and they don't call each other *mister*."

Ben dipped his head in a nod of acknowledgement. "I like the sound of that."

"Good because I need a friend I can trust."

Without hesitation, Ben looked at him, his eyes fierce with integrity. "Anything you need," he said, and Gray believed him. He'd met many men in his line of work, and Ben was one of very few he felt an immediate kinship with, that he intrinsically believed he could trust. Still, he proceeded with caution.

"I have a job to do at the paper mill and need to go to work right after Thanksgiving, which means I'll be away from my cabin each day. But I have a situation there that absolutely must not be revealed to anyone else. You would be the only person who knows the truth, and the one I'd depend on to help me."

"All right," Ben said.

"You couldn't even share this information with your wife. It could be dangerous if *anyone* were to find out."

"I understand." He looked at Gray. "If it's anything illegal, though, don't tell me about it because I couldn't help you with something like that."

"I'm glad to hear that because I would never ask such a thing."

"All right then," Ben said, giving a light flick of the reins to get the team moving. "Tell me what you have in mind."

As they headed to the butcher shop, Gray told Ben that his young nephew, Willy, was staying with him for a few weeks while the boy's parents were traveling. It soured Gray's stomach to mislead Ben, but until the circumstances surrounding Willow's assault were known, he wouldn't reveal her existence to anyone. So he simply asked Ben to keep an eye out for anyone nosing around the cabin, and to alert him immediately should such a thing happen. Although it didn't alleviate Gray's concern, Ben's quick agreement did provide a measure of relief.

After a brief stop at the butcher shop, they headed back up the mountain. During the ride, he asked Ben what he knew about the paper mill and the folks who worked there. Although Ben knew several of the employees, he couldn't provide much information other than his disgust at the dangerous and oppressive working conditions his friends had to endure at the hands of an over-bearing foreman and an absent owner who seemed to care only about production and profit.

"My farm doesn't provide much, especially at this time of year, but I'm grateful to work for myself," Ben said, halting the team when they'd reached the cabin.

"I understand completely," Gray said, stepping down from the wagon. He declined Ben's offer to help carry the crates and pack-ages to the door, then stacked the items so he could cart them to the door in three loads. Before he picked up the last load, he reached up to shake Ben's hand. "It's been a long time since I've had a friend. Thank you, Ben."

Ben shook Gray's hand. "I'm honored by your trust."

With that, the man bobbed his head in farewell, and drove his team and old wagon back down the road to where his farm and his family awaited the return of a good man.

As Gray turned toward the cabin and the woman waiting inside, he reminded himself to call her Willow. And he reminded himself that the only sure way to keep her safe was to lie to her.

CHAPTER EIGHT

Nearly three hours had passed since Gray left the cabin, and Willow's nerves were frayed. Every sound outside made her wonder if it was coming from the wind or an animal...or a person. To occupy herself, she did a bit of cleaning, but there was little to do, and so she sat and tried to read a book she'd plucked from the shelf. She was too tired to focus, so she leaned her head back and let her mind drift. Images flickered like a gutted candle behind her eyelids and drew her deeper into murky shadows of a midnight forest where something terrible lurked.

A loud thump startled her awake, and she glanced around the empty cabin in a panic. The sound had come from outside...near the door. Someone was there. With trembling hands, she picked up the pistol and pointed it toward the door just as it fired. Splinters of wood flew from the cabin wall. The repercussion from the pistol made the gun wobble in her grip, and she nearly dropped it.

"Willow! It's me!" She heard Gray shout through the door. "Put the gun down before you kill me."

The rush of relief made her weak, and she sagged back in her chair.

"Aim the muzzle away from the door," he shouted, clearly believing she might shoot him by accident.

Blowing out a steadying breath, she placed the pistol on the tea table and directed the muzzle toward the far wall.

"Is it safe to come in?" he asked, easing the door open a crack.

Too flushed with relief to speak, she watched him poke his head inside. When he saw the splintered door frame, he turned to her in disbelief. "You could have killed me."

He looked so shocked, a nervous giggle escaped her. "I'm sorry."

For a moment he simply looked at her as if he didn't know what to make of her reaction. "I called out twice."

"I didn't hear you."

"Obviously."

Struggling to get hold of her emotions, she stood on trembling legs. "Do you need help?"

"I can manage," he replied, carting in a large sack of potatoes. It took four trips for him to carry the crates and sacks inside. When he finished, he inspected where the bullet had struck. "The damage is superficial so I can patch it," he said, then grinned. "Next time aim right."

Relief washed over her. "I'm sorry."

"It's all right. I'm just glad you didn't blow the door off its hinges or shoot me."

A burble of laughter tumbled out and hurt her throat, but the levity felt good.

He winked at her. "What a beautiful sound. You have a nice laugh."

She touched her throat. "Still sore, but I can manage a few words now."

"That's good, but I'm going to miss your scribbled notes and trying to decipher your gestures."

Making a face at him, she turned away and began looking in

the crates to see what supplies he'd purchased. Now that swallowing was easier for her, she was ready for more than soup or stew.

"I bought boots for you," he said, coming up behind her. "And a hat, mittens, and a warm jacket. If you're going outside you'll need warm clothing."

She plucked the boots out of the crate closest to her. "Boys?" she asked, holding them up for inspection.

"I couldn't buy lady's garments without the storekeeper asking questions that I didn't want to answer," he said.

That confused her. "Didn't you ask if..." She pressed her fingertips to her tender throat. "...if anyone knew me?"

He glanced away from her. "I asked for any news in town, which a missing woman would surely be, but I didn't ask directly because we need to learn more about what happened to you before we ask questions that could put you in more danger."

Crestfallen, she gave him a nod to let him know she understood. She did, but she didn't like it. She *needed* to know who she was and what had happened to her. But it appeared those answers weren't forthcoming today."

"Would you like to take a short walk before supper?" he asked.

The thought of going outside made her smile.

He pointed to a crate on the floor. "All right, then. Get dressed while I take a look around to make sure it's safe out there. There are long johns and dungarees in that crate. They'll have to suffice because, for obvious reasons, I couldn't purchase lady's clothing for you. Get dressed while I take a look outside. I'll take my pistol with me so I know you won't shoot me when I come back." With that, he bolted out the door followed by her laughter.

When she pulled on the soft cotton long johns, her legs felt wrapped in a warm hug. The boy's britches felt foreign and too revealing, yet oddly liberating.

By the time Gray returned fifteen minutes later, she was dressed and waiting by the door.

For a moment, he eyed her in humorous appreciation.

She wrinkled her nose. "Not a word, Mr. Sullivan."

Grinning, he handed her a hard candy. "I brought us a treat and some supplies for our Thanksgiving dinner tomorrow," he said.

She glanced at him in surprise, the piece of candy clamped between her teeth.

"You remember what Thanksgiving is, don't you?"

She nodded because she felt blindsided by time. She remembered nothing from before she woke up in Gray's cabin, and little measure of how long she'd been in his care. Hours had blended into days, and she'd been too tired or in too much pain to care. But to realize tomorrow was a holiday jolted her. And it made her feel guilty. Gray should be with his family, and she should be...well, she didn't know exactly, but somehow knew she should be elsewhere.

"It's all right," he said, as if reading her mind. "I have no place I need to be, and hopefully we'll sort this out and get you safely home by Christmas. Or sooner if possible," he assured her. "But for today, let's just focus on getting you out for a walk."

Struggling to curb her anxiety, she turned toward the door.

"Wait a minute," he said, clasping her arm. When she faced him, he adjusted her scarf around her neck. His fingers brushed her jaw, sending streams of warmth through her, taking her back to the previous night when they'd stood in the dark and his touch had felt so...thrilling. This man had tended her wounds, carried her in his arms, even helped her in and out of the bath. She'd felt his tenderness, kindness, and caring touch but never the intimacy she'd felt in that moment with him under a night sky, or now as he tucked the end of her scarf in the collar of her jacket.

"There's still a good bit of snow outside so we're going to go slow and easy. I don't want all my hard work undone by your stubbornness." He winked at her, then escorted her outside.

Maintaining her balance while stepping through inches of snow was more challenging than she'd anticipated, but much easier in dungarees than in her skirt. Still, she wisely accepted Gray's assistance as they moved away from the cabin.

Around them towered dense forests broken by wide, snow-covered fields that offered sweeping views of distant peaks and valleys below, where rivers cut deep ravines.

Though it was cold outside, she enjoyed the fresh air, how it woke her lungs and stung her cheeks. She stopped and breathed in deeply and released a slow, frosty funnel of breath. Feeling an amazing sense of renewal, she bent over, reaching for her toes. Her ribs were tender, but the stretch seemed to unlock her legs and made her sigh with pleasure. It felt so good to be alive on such a glorious day.

That thought sobered her and she stood, suddenly overcome with emotion. She gazed at the forest where moose, deer, and other animals created trails that led deep into the woods and along stream banks like the one where Gray said he'd found her. To think she had almost died out here. If not for Gray, she would be dead right now, lying in a bed of frozen pine needles and maple leaves, her body covered with snow or torn asunder by some hungry mountain predator.

The wind suddenly felt cold, and she shivered, glancing behind her with unease. Who had wanted her dead? And why? Frustrated, she sagged against the scaly trunk of a towering black ash, and closed her eyes. If Gray's theory was right, she had been brought up here and left because her attacker likely thought she was dead. She imagined herself being carted up the mountain, willed her mind inward, to go back in time, to return to that day. Whom had she come here with? What had happened? Had she been attacked? Or had she simply fallen from a horse? Maybe it was that simple. Perhaps she was riding and something frightened her mount, caused it to panic, caused her to fall. Could that have been how she was injured?

She wanted to believe that, but her fear, and deep sense of dread, were real. She knew it was not a fall from a horse that had nearly killed her. Someone had hurt her and brought her up here with the sole purpose of disposing of her body. But why?

"Are you all right?" Gray asked, apparently sensing her distress.

She met his eyes. With her palm, she applied gentle pressure to her sore throat, and said, "Who would want me dead?"

Sadness washed his face. "I couldn't begin to imagine," he said, a mix of sorrow and disbelief in his voice. "Not the act, nor the reason, nor the beast who could do something so despicable, especially to you." He pulled her into a gentle hug. "But I vow to find and punish that person, Willow."

In his arms, that were so solid and safe, she fought the urge to burrow into him. Although she knew little about Gray Sullivan, she knew he was a man with a deep sense of integrity, and he would keep his word no matter the cost.

"Thank you," she said. "For everything." The painful tweak in her throat made her wince, but she felt he deserved a verbal acknowledgement for what he'd done for her.

He relaxed his arms and stepped back. "You don't need to thank me."

Their eyes met, and she saw a flash of something she couldn't identify. Was it guilt? Shame? Pity? Whatever it was, she didn't like it.

"Maybe we should head inside," he suggested. "I don't want you to catch a chill."

She shook her head and linked her arm with his. "A walk please," she said.

With a small nod, he turned them toward the cabin a short distance away.

She stopped him with a tug on his arm, then pointed the other direction. "Please."

Scowling, he released a frosty breath. "I think we've gone far enough for today, but I know you'll argue and resist until I give in, so we'll go a bit farther."

She rewarded him with a big smile. The cabin, for all its cozy appeal, could be stifling when one was locked inside. Not knowing when she would be able to get outside again, she intended to enjoy her brief respite as long as possible.

Using Gray's strong arm for support, she plodded through the snow one wobbly step at a time, willing her recovering body to embrace the exercise. A flash of red caught her eye, and she stopped, searching the tree line. When she spotted the cardinal, she smiled and glanced at Gray.

"There are two pairs of them out here," he said, gesturing in the direction of the cardinal. "You might see a blue jay or two as well."

She scanned the trees, hoping to see more wildlife. Although she heard the hammering of a woodpecker searching for a meal in a hollow tree somewhere in the distance, and the occasional chirp and tweet indicating other birds occupied the forest, only the cardinal presented itself.

They moved on, slowly and in silence, as if they were both on alert. Although Gray had scouted the area for several minutes before he'd taken her outside, he'd cautioned her to pay attention and tell him if she saw or heard anything. Knowing he was concerned put her on edge and had her glancing at shadows near the timberline and every divot in the snow that might have been made by a human.

When she paused and pointed to an area of scuffed snow, he said, "That's from a snowshoe hare."

"Or a coyote?" she asked.

He knelt and directed her attention to the back pair of tracks. "See how the back feet are shaped like snowshoes and they form a Y in the snow? The front tracks are circular. A coyote's tracks would have four toe prints and one lobe for each paw. No mistaking it as a snowshoe." He spent a few minutes explaining how to identify different types of tracks and where he'd seen them along stream banks and forest trails made by elk and white-tail deer.

"Do you hunt?" she asked, keeping her sentences short to spare her throat.

"I have, but I'd rather watch the animals than kill them."

Something in the way he said it, as if he truly valued the wildlife around them, made her deeply curious about him.

"How often are you here?" she asked, gesturing toward the cabin.

Dusting snow off his mittens, he stood. "It's my first visit." The change in his expression seemed to pull shades over his eyes, suggesting it wasn't a subject he wanted to discuss—which made her all the more curious. After a moment, he said, "I wanted to take some time away before going back to my job."

"Why?"

"I'd been working a lot of hours for a long time. I was tired," he said, as if to dismiss the subject.

"Why did you work so much?" she asked, really wanting to know.

"Willow, it's not important why I'm here, only that I am."

The importance of his presence couldn't be more obvious to her. "Didn't mean to pry," she said. She coughed once then swallowed, each act uncomfortable. "Please talk so I don't have to," she said, touching her throat and giving him a little smile that seemed to disarm him.

For a moment, they gazed at each other, small frosty puffs of breath being whisked away by a cold breeze that made her eyes water.

"All right," he said, "but I'll talk to you on the way *back* to the cabin." He hooked her hand in the crook of his elbow.

"Not yet," she said, giving his arm a small tug.

"Yes, Willow. This is enough for today." With that he took a decisive step forward that forced her to head back. "What do you want to know?"

"Everything," she said. It was the first time she'd heard him laugh, and the sound warmed her as if she'd just enjoyed a delicious cup of hot cocoa.

He gazed down at her with a smile on his face. "I like to sail," he said, surprising her, but then she realized sailing could be a solo pastime which seemed to suit a man like Gray.

"Why?" she asked, encouraging him to go on.

"Well, let's see." He tucked her more securely on his arm. "I like the sound of the ocean and the snapping of the sails and the cry of sea birds as I depart and return to the dock. When I'm out on the water it's...it's peaceful and I can think."

She glanced up at him. "About what?"

He shrugged. "I suppose I just let my thoughts drift like seaweed."

With her own thoughts such a tangled mess, she could easily envision how they could drift like seaweed in an undulating ocean.

"Where do you sail?" she asked.

"A few places, but mostly out of Charleston harbor." He was silent a moment, then said, "I haven't sailed in a long time."

"Why not?"

"I've been busy," he said, guiding her to the cabin door. "Now it's time for us to go in and for me to make supper."

Knowing he was done talking, she nodded resolutely, and said, "I can help."

"That's not necessary."

"Yes, it is. My cooking is better."

He glanced down at her. "Do you know this? Do you remember cooking?"

"No. I just know it will be better than yours."

His laughter filled the air and he gestured for her to proceed him inside.

CHAPTER NINE

After enjoying their Thanksgiving Day meal of roast turkey, mashed potatoes, canned beans, and cranberry jelly, Gray began to clear the table.

Willow slid her chair back and stood. "I'll help."

"Leave the turkey platter on the table," he said, worried it would be too heavy for her to manage. "I'll finish carving the meat for sandwiches, and use the carcass to make soup broth."

She looked at him. "What possessed a tough detective like you..." Her eyes squinted, and she touched her throat. "...to learn how to cook?"

"Necessity," he said, carrying their dishes to the sink. He put them in the dishpan of hot, soapy water he'd prepared before they ate, then turned and leaned back against the counter. "Meals aren't always available where I travel or when I have time to eat, so I paid a tavern cook to show me how to fry meat and boil potatoes. After that, I fumbled my way into making soups and stews. Can't say they're very tasty but it beats eating jerky and soda crackers."

Willow's warm laugh created an odd lightness in his chest and made him smile. "Your voice is sounding better and you're much steadier on your feet this evening."

"I'm feeling better," she said, giving her flat abdomen a pat. "A full meal is good medicine."

"I hope you saved room for a cinnamon bun because I purchased a half dozen for us."

Her eyes widened. "I think they're my favorite sweet." A smile bloomed on her lips. "Honestly, my mouth is watering." She touched her fingertips to her throat, but pleasure illuminated her face, pinking her cheeks and creating a sparkle in her eyes.

He couldn't look away. Her beauty drew him in like cold hands to a warm fire, and he had to fight the urge to pull her into his arms. It had been three weeks since he'd found her in the woods. Her bruises were gone, and the laceration on her cheek had closed and turned a healthy pink. Her balance was much better, and her strength seemed to be building quickly. If only her memory would return, too, he could take her back to her life—and get her out of his before he did something stupid. Because every day she was in his care revealed more about her, giving him glimpses into her private thoughts, her surprising sense of humor, her desire for companionship. She was becoming more than a job to him, and he couldn't let that happen.

He couldn't.

So he turned his attention to brewing a pot of coffee, then placed two fluffy cinnamon buns on a baking sheet and put them in the still-warm oven while they washed the dishes and stored the leftover food from their meal.

When the coffee finished brewing, he filled two cups and placed them on the table where Willow had just seated herself. Then he put the warm cinnamon buns on plates and placed one in front of her, watching closely for her reaction.

If the cinnamon buns evoked memories for her, she might remember her mother...and perhaps her own name and, hopefully, what had happened to her. If the treat didn't trigger her memory, no harm done.

The look of pure pleasure on her face when she took her first bite caused a simultaneous jolt in his brain and gut. He silently encouraged her to remember everything, and yet he felt a strange discomfort at the thought of losing her presence in his life.

"Absolute heaven," she said with a dreamy smile on her face. "It tastes like...home."

He waited, hoping and dreading that her memory would come flooding back like a spring freshet, but she took another bite of the cinnamon bun.

"What makes it taste like home?" he asked, wondering if a little nudge would help spark her memory.

She swallowed, then sipped her coffee as if considering his question. "It's warm and...comforting." Lifting one shoulder in a slight shrug, she said, "It's how I imagine home would feel."

It's the kind of home she deserved but not one she remembered, apparently. Feeling it was futile to press her, he turned his attention to his coffee and dessert.

"What was your home like?" she asked, cupping her palms around her cup.

One was a nightmare, the other heaven, but he wouldn't share that with her. "My parents were kind, our house was comfortable, and we had plenty to eat."

"And? That's all you have to say about it?" she asked with a hoarse laugh.

"What else do you want to know?"

"What was it like to grow up there?"

It was a life he didn't merit with parents who deserved far more than he gave them. "Well, we lived above my parents' bakery on King Street. I helped out each morning by washing dishes before I went to school. After school, I'd usually head down to the wharves on the Cooper River."

"That sounds like a wonderful place for..." Wincing, she took a sip of coffee, then continued, "...for a boy to spend his day."

"It was," he said, but they were bittersweet days because he missed his brothers.

"What did you do at the wharves?"

He filled his mouth with coffee, enjoying the warmth and robust taste for a moment before swallowing. "Sometimes I'd earn a few pennies helping local fishermen cart their catch off their boats, or assisting passengers with their luggage. Most days I'd just sit on the docks and watch all the activity."

"What happens at a wharf."

He laughed. "Everything of any importance happens there," he said. "I spent my afternoons watching huge ships drop anchor in the harbor, or farther out if the captain didn't want to tempt fate by trying to navigate through shifting sandbars. Large, powerful steamboats and an array of fishing craft were in constant motion negotiating their way in and out of port. Farmers brought their products to the dock for loading. Men moved all manner of freight to and from those vessels as passengers boarded or disembarked from them. The wharf was always alive with conversation, as the locals sought the latest news from the travelers and crewmen."

"How exciting," she said, her eyes filled with avid interest. "I'd like to see that."

"The ruckus can be a bit overwhelming at times."

"I'd risk it for a chance to see ships and the ocean."

The urge to take her there, to promise her something she desired caught him off guard, and he had to clamp his mouth closed to stop himself from making promises he couldn't keep. Leaning back in his chair, he released a hard breath and stretched his legs out beneath the table. "It was a good place for a boy to spend his day."

"Did you have friends to play with?"

"Sure, but most of my friends had chores after school."

"Didn't you?"

"My chores were done in the morning. Most of the work at

our bakery took place in the hours before dawn while I was sleeping, which is why I washed utensils, mixing bowls, and baking pans each morning before heading off to school. My parents would take turns napping and tending the bakery during the day. In the evenings, we would have supper together and maybe play a game or two. Then my sister and I would be sent off to bed. My parents would sleep for two or three hours, then start their workday again."

"Gracious, I didn't realize running a bakery was such hard work."

"That changed when my father took a job at a local factory. As soon as my parents could afford to stop supplying bread to the local markets, it significantly reduced their workload and allowed them to focus on selling pies and desserts like these cinnamon buns," he said, nodding to the remaining third on his plate. "Would you like the rest of it?" he asked. "I'm too full of turkey to finish dessert."

An impish grin tipped her lips as she pulled his plate in front of her. "Well, it would be sinful to waste it."

He hadn't seen this playful side of her, and it completely unarmed him. "What was your childhood like?" he asked, deeply intrigued and eager to know the child, the girl, the woman sitting across from him. The smile slipped from her face, and he immediately realized his blunder. "Ah, Willow, I wasn't thinking. I'm sorry."

"I know," she said, taking a sip of her coffee, "but I wish I could remember it."

"Of course you do," he said, reaching across the table to clasp her hand. "I hadn't meant to be insensitive."

She met his eyes. "Talking with me is surely difficult..." She took another sip of coffee presumably to soothe her throat. "... when I can't contribute to our conversations."

"I find it too easy to converse with you, but I suspect you're using this as an excuse to get me to talk about myself," he said, giving her a wink.

He could see her try and fail to smile. "I wish that were the case." She glanced toward the window, already dark in the winter evening. "Take me to the place where you found me."

It was something he needed to do to help him locate where she'd been assaulted or left in the woods, but she wasn't strong enough yet to make the short hike. "We'll go when you've been on your feet a bit longer."

"Is it far?"

"No, but it's uphill and there's still some snow on the ground."

For a moment, she seemed to mull over the situation, then said, "The snow is melting. I can make it with your help."

"We'll go in a couple of days," he said, feeling an urgency to do so, knowing the longer he waited to locate and investigate the area the more likely evidence would be lost. And he couldn't delay his investigation at the paper mill much longer, which meant Willow would be alone while he was away. He needed to get her solidly on her feet before he could do that. "Tomorrow we'll see how you manage a longer walk. If you hold up well, we can go the following day."

"All right," she said, her gaze drilling into him. "But I can't...I *won't*, wait any longer."

"Understood," he said, sharing her unspoken desperation to unravel the mystery of her life and the events that led her here.

———

As the night deepened, Willow sank into a fitful sleep where she found herself looking into a glistening lake and marveled at the way it created a mirror image of the colorful fall foliage and clear blue sky. She stared hard at the water, seeing her reflection but feeling as if she were looking at a stranger. Tears fell from her eyes and dropped into the water, sending out ripples that distorted her image.

Frustrated, she touched her reflection, hoping to feel a connection, but she was pulled beneath the water. Panicked, she fought to surface, but the more she struggled, the farther down she sank. The colorful trees faded until there was nothing but darkness and silence. She was trapped. Trapped in her own dark world, and for a moment she considered simply letting go. What was a life without a name, without a past, without memories and connections to loved ones? Would it matter if she simply disappeared?

The water above her erupted and two strong hands caught her arms and pulled her toward the surface. As she fought to hold on, she heard a voice call out to her, then felt herself being enfolded in warmth.

"It's all right, Willow. I'm right here."

Opening her eyes, she expected to see a blue sky above, but found herself in a man's arms in a dark room backlit by firelight.

"Are you awake now?" he asked.

It was Gray holding her, talking to her, comforting her, who'd reached into the dark depths to save her. He'd rescued her, healed her, and protected her, and in that moment she realized he was the only one who knew her. It wasn't her name or her past or where she'd come from that he saw, it was her essence, the core of her being that he connected with, because that's all she possessed. Lacing her fingers with his, the only sure and steady thing in her life, she leaned into his warmth and closed her eyes.

But the dream had upset her so much, she couldn't sleep.

So as soon as Gray was settled on his makeshift bed, she slipped from her own, saying she needed to use the bathroom. On her way past the table, she picked up the pad and pencil and took it with her. After closing the door, she lit the lantern and adjusted the wick to brighten the room. For a long while she stared at her reflection in the looking glass, then began to sketch the face she saw in the mirror, hoping the act would help her remember the woman looking back at her.

THE NEXT MORNING, dressed in her dungarees and bundled from head to toe for their walk, Willow waited while Gray did a thorough reconnaissance outside to ensure their safety.

He returned several minutes later looking all manly and handsome with his hair tousled and his cheeks ruddy from the wind. To stop herself from staring, she turned a circle for his inspection. "Will I pass as a boy?"

A slow smile spread across his face. "Not to me, but from a distance your disguise should work."

His smile created a joyful lightness in her belly. "Then let's go before I melt in here."

With a light laugh, he escorted her outside into the crisp winter air. They headed out behind the cabin and made their way down a small hill that took them to a deer path that led along a ridge. The wildlife trail dipped in and out of the forest, thrusting them into dappled shadows and bringing them back out to sunlight and a winter-blue sky.

Slowing to a stop, she took in the beauty of the deep ravine and winding river below. She inhaled the scent of pine and sighed with pleasure. "What a perfect day."

"Is this all it takes to make it a perfect day for you?"

She glanced up to see Gray smiling at her. "Well, this view, and escaping the confines of the cabin contribute significantly," she said.

"Hmm..." He rubbed his chin as if puzzled. "Could it be because you dislike my company?"

She laughed, enjoying this playful side of him. "I suggested no such thing," she said. "In fact, I find your company quite tolerable."

He arched an eyebrow. "Just tolerable?"

"Most days," she quipped, with a haughty lift of her nose.

His laughter washed over her, warmed her, delighted her. "I think I liked you better when you couldn't speak."

With a playful nudge against his side, she said, "Careful what you say. One hard shove could send you over the cliff."

"Then you'd be alone with no one to walk you back to the cabin when you get tired."

With a dramatic sigh, she said, "I suppose you're right. And I need..." she stopped, swallowed, then continued, "...someone to chop firewood, so consider your person safe for now."

"The relief is making my knees weak," he said, staggering back a step.

For a moment, she simply looked at him. The strong, serious detective who'd rescued her, who carried his duty like a shield to block personal connections, was lowering his guard. She'd seen his tenderness, his sense of humor, and even a hint of his passion one night beneath the stars when he was fetching firewood and she'd stepped outside behind him. In those moments, she felt connected to him, to his warmth and the wounds he carried.

"Have you reconsidered pushing me into the ravine?" he asked.

Instead of answering, she slipped her hand into the crook of his elbow and started them down the path they'd been walking. "I'm considering how lovely it is to be taking a walk...with someone who makes me laugh. What more does one need?"

"That's a good question," he said, snugging her hand between his elbow and ribs. "Is there anything you need, Willow?"

The sincerity in his voice surprised her. He was truly asking if she was in need of anything, so she considered his question as she took in the land around her. "I need to know who I am and where I fit in this world."

Slowing to a stop, he clasped her wrists and turned her to face him. "I know who you are. The woman standing right here in front of me loves nature. She's intelligent, creative, beautiful, and amazingly resilient. That's who you are."

"But where do I fit?"

"For now, you fit right here...with me."

"But that won't be forever," she said, feeling the weight of that truth heavy on her heart. "What happens when you leave?"

He slid his hands up her arms and gave them a gentle squeeze. "We'll figure it out. Let's just take one day at a time."

She nodded, accepting the situation, but knowing each new day brought her closer to him, and he would surely leave her when his job here was done. She couldn't let herself have feelings for him, but he was making that battle more difficult by the day.

CHAPTER TEN

W illow had no desire to learn how to use a weapon, but Gray was adamant about her learning to safely handle and fire his revolver before he went to work at the paper mill.

His manner whenever he mentioned the mill was strange, as if the place should hold some meaning for her. It was the same when he mentioned the general store and the storekeeper by name. But not one of those things was of any significance other than the fact that Gray had purchased their supplies at the store and he would be going to work at the mill in the morning.

"Are you with me, Willow?" he asked, giving her arm a little jiggle.

"Yes, but I'd rather be elsewhere," she said.

"I think you were." He grinned. "I'm right here, and I won't let anything happen to you."

"I'm not worried about me. If I shoot you, I'll be stuck here alone."

"Naw, we have neighbors down the road a ways."

"Is that why you brought us this far from the cabin?" she

asked, secretly pleased by the longer walk. "So they can't hear the gunshots?"

"They'll hear the shots but likely think it's a hunter. I'm just saying you could find help nearby if you needed it. But you won't if you pay attention now. Just take your time, follow my instructions, and you'll be an ace shot by suppertime."

She laughed at his gross exaggeration. "I'll be happy just to hit the target today."

"Well, you'll have to actually hold the revolver to do that." He placed the gun in her hand. "It's not loaded. Just get used to the weight and feel of it in your hand."

"It feels cold...like death," she said, trying to give it back to him.

"That's because you're thinking about it all wrong. This is simply a way to communicate your wishes, like you did with your hand gestures before you could speak."

"What am I supposed to communicate with a revolver?"

His expression grew serious. "Never point the muzzle toward anyone or anything unless you truly believe they intend to harm you. Pointing this at someone can simply mean you want them to stop."

"What if they don't stop?"

"Then they're either a foolish human being or a hungry animal intent on harming you. In either event, you might need this to stop them. And that's why we're practicing. Hopefully, you'll never need to use the revolver, but I can't go to work without knowing you can fire it and hit your intended target." A smile tilted his lips. "Now, quit stalling." With that, he positioned the gun in her hand, and corrected her grip.

"You showed me this the first time you left me alone in the cabin."

"Yes, I did, and you nearly shot me because you weren't gripping it correctly. I'm surprised you didn't shoot yourself in the leg."

"Me, too," she said, remembering how nervous she'd been and how her hands had shaken just touching the gun.

Once he seemed satisfied with her grip, he explained how to align the sights, and squeeze, not pull, the trigger. She repeated the process several times, then he told her to rest her arms.

After loading one bullet into the cylinder, he said, "All right, Willow, this is a live weapon now. That means you need to control your nerves so you can control the revolver. Are you ready?"

Releasing her pent up breath, she nodded. The only way to end the lesson was to hit the target and prove to him that she could handle the revolver safely and effectively. So she braced her feet and raised the revolver. Slowly, as he had instructed, she sighted the target, paused her ragged breathing, and squeezed the trigger. The revolver fired with an upward thrust in her grip. Fragments of wood flew from the high left side of the large dead tree stump she'd been aiming at. With a hard exhale, she lowered the weapon and looked at Gray.

"I'm pleasantly surprised," he said, eyebrows raised. "I didn't expect you to hit it."

She lifted her chin. "Why not? I did exactly as you instructed."

He laughed. "Yes, you did, and point taken. Let's see if you can do it again."

"I'd rather not," she said, passing the revolver back to him.

"I'd rather you did," he countered.

"All right, but on one condition. After I hit the target, we're done and you stop pestering me about this shooting business."

"If you can hit the target again, we can be finished with your lesson for the day."

"Then load another bullet and quit talking about it."

An amused grin tipped his lips as he slipped a single bullet into the cylinder, then carefully transferred it back to her. "Adjust your aim down a tad and to the right this time."

"Already planned to do so," she said, then adjusted her grip, sighted the target, and slowly squeezed the trigger. A second later, she grinned. "Lesson over," She lowered the muzzle and thrust the revolver at him. "Let's go for a walk."

"We already have. We walked out here."

She propped her hands on her hips. "I'm going for a walk. You can go with me or stay here."

He gawked as if she'd suddenly stomped on his foot.

"I'm healthy enough to take a longer walk. You've been putting me off long enough." She stopped and placed her palm on her throat, pausing for a moment. "I want to see where you found me."

"Willow, I don't like having you outside where you can be seen. It's not safe."

"We'll be in the woods, not walking the road. Even if someone sees me, they'll think I'm a boy," she said, gesturing to her dungarees and the knit cap pulled low over her head. "You know I'm right."

"I admit you look more like a lad than a woman, but it's safer for you inside."

"You need to find where I was left in the woods so you can search for evidence." She gave him a knowing look. "You said that. So let's go today."

Releasing a hard breath, he gave her a nod. "All right, but I need to stop at the cabin first. And if you get tired we're turning back."

She tugged on her mittens. "I won't get tired."

"We'll be walking uphill."

"I can manage." She grinned at him. "If not, you can carry me back."

His laughter warmed her clear to her cold toes.

At the cabin, she waited while he ducked inside. He returned a moment later with a rectangular leather case attached to a wide strap over his shoulder. For a moment, he visually looked her over head to toe as if to assure himself she was properly dressed for their outing. "Ready?" he asked, his cheeks ruddy from the chilly day.

With a nod, she followed him, wondering if she was truly ready for what might await her. As desperately as she longed for her memory to return, she feared what those memories might bring.

Gray tucked Willow's arm tight against his side to provide support and help her make the trek uphill. The snowmelt had left the stream bank soggy, making the walk more difficult for her, but she seemed to be enjoying herself.

When they finally rounded the bend and approached the place where he had first spotted her, she stopped, her body tense.

"Do you recognize this place?" he asked.

She nodded, turning a slow circle to see the entire area.

Slowly, her gaze traveled the fast-flowing stream bank and moved into the dark shadows of the forest. After a long moment, she sighed and rubbed her temples. Gray could see confusion in her eyes, as if memory fragments floated just outside her reach. She tilted her head as though listening closely for some sound, but all he could hear was the sound of whooshing water and the twitter of birds and scampering of wildlife in the dried under-brush of the forest. After several quiet moments she closed her eyes and swayed. Her chest rose and fell more rapidly, her nostrils flaring.

"Willow?" he called softly.

She didn't answer. He touched her wrist, and she gasped as

though he'd appeared out of thin air. Her gaze jerked to his, and she moved away.

He waited, watching her move toward a dense area of trees as though some unknown force was drawing her. Her eyes were fixed straight ahead, her steps slow.

Quietly, he followed her into the cold, dark shadows of the pines. She shivered and wrapped her arms around herself as she moved deeper into the woods.

He trailed behind, letting her wander and survey the landscape. Little things caught her attention. The reddish tips of sumac bushes, a large pine cone at the base of a tree, a clump of frozen maple leaves. He was beginning to wonder if she was remembering or simply wandering aimlessly when she came to a sudden stop.

"I can't remember what happened," she said, her shoulders slumping with disappointment.

"It's all right. Don't try to force it," he said. "I'm going to take a look around. Stay close, and if you spot anything that seems important, don't touch it. Just let me know you found something."

After indicating she understood, he began a horizontal line search along a steep embankment, reversing direction after twenty feet, moving east then west as he carefully made his way uphill in four-foot segments. Methodically, he scanned the area searching for evidence and clues. When Willow began to lag behind, he reminded her to stay close and to alert him if she found or remembered anything.

Nearly an hour had passed when he came across a woman's shoe partially hidden by broken branches and sodden, dead leaves. He could immediately see it was Willow's missing shoe, which confirmed her presence here. This was where she'd entered the forest. He was certain of it now. And he knew if there was any evidence to be found it would be in this area.

The rattle of a wagon passing on the road above drew his

attention to the top of the embankment a few feet farther up. He could hear horse hooves striking the dirt road, and surmised that Willow had likely been brought here in a conveyance and dumped over the steep bank.

As scenes of how she had come to be here played out in his mind, he fought to throttle his outrage. He needed a clear head to do his job. A hard nudge against his shoulder interrupted his dark thoughts.

"Is that my shoe?" Willow asked, pointing to the thin-soled, worn shoe partially buried in the leaves.

"I believe so, but leave it there for a moment," he said, opening one end of a leather box to expose the camera he'd brought with them. As he loaded a charged plate, he explained the importance of photographing a crime scene. Willow's interest seemed to grow as he photographed the shoe, then deepened as he examined the area around it. When he'd finished, he picked up the shoe and immediately noticed the broken laces, likely explaining why she'd lost it during her tumble down the hill.

She didn't seem to care that the shoe was worn thin and wet from lying in the sodden leaves. She held it tight to her abdomen as if reclaiming a piece of her life.

Knowing she needed a minute to gather herself, Gray continued to search for evidence, focusing on the area between where he'd found Willow's shoe and the road above. He was focusing so intently he didn't realize Willow had moved past him until she stopped suddenly in front of him.

"Look," she said, pointing at something on the ground in front of her.

It took a moment of searching before he saw a man's gold pocket watch with a broken chain lying a few feet from where he'd found Willow's shoe. The bit of chain that remained attached to the watch looked familiar. Then it hit him like a thunderclap. A few links of that chain had been snagged in Willow's skirt.

After photographing the watch, he picked it up and gave it to her. "Do you recognize the watch?" he asked.

She angled the item toward the light filtering down through the branches. "It seems familiar, but..." She shrugged, and Gray could see the defeat in her eyes.

"It's all right," he said gently. "It'll come to you, or we'll find the answers together."

Her brow furrowed as she gave one last inquisitive look at the watch before giving it to him.

With slumped shoulders, she turned away, then turned back just as suddenly. "Photograph me," she said, a strange lightness coming into her eyes.

"Do what?"

"Use your camera to photograph me, then put my picture in the newspaper. Surely someone will recognize me and know who I am."

The hope that filled her eyes slayed him. "What if the wrong person recognizes you?" he asked, hating to deflate her hope but knowing it was necessary.

"I'm willing to take that risk," she said. "Please, Gray, I simply can't go on this way."

Hearing her desperation, he feared she might do something rash like searching for answers herself. Knowing she could slip away from the cabin anytime he was at work, forced him into yet another lie. "All right," he said, lifting his camera. "Stand over there where the light is better."

While he knelt and inserted a plate into his camera, she moved away. "Is this all right?" she asked.

He looked up to see her standing stiffly in front of a staghorn sumac shrub. "That's fine," he replied, but when he stood and sighted her through the viewer, he knew he'd never forget the expression of bleak desperation on her face. It hurt to witness it, and he certainly didn't want to capture her like that because the image would haunt him forever. "Maybe you should smile a little," he suggested.

"Oh..." Her breath rushed out, and she fiddled with her hands as if unsure what to do with them.

"Maybe clasp your hands in front of you, and look a little less terrified. I wouldn't want anyone to think I'm holding you hostage."

"Oh, dear," she said, releasing a breathless laugh, a shy, slightly embarrassed smile lighting her beautiful face.

He photographed her at that exact moment and knew it was another image that would forever haunt him.

"Is that it, then?" she asked when he lowered his camera.

"Yes, but it could take weeks to get the plates developed," he said, knowing it would likely be much sooner, but using it as a delay tactic.

"That long?" she asked, disappointment thick in her voice. At his nod, her shoulders slumped and she released a long sigh.

"Tired?" he asked, wondering if the walk had been too much for her.

"I'm tired of living in a void," she said. "I'm tired of depending on your good will. And I'm tired of seeing a face in the mirror I can't recognize.

"I honestly can't imagine it, but I can understand your frustration. All we can do is keep searching for answers."

She seemed to hold her breath for a moment, then released it in a long, defeated sigh.

"Come on," he said, squatting down with his back to her. "Boarding all passengers. Your train leaves when my calves cramp from squatting. That's about five seconds from now."

Despite her misery, she smiled. She would not make this sweet man carry her all the way back to the cabin. If they didn't rush, she could make it on her own, especially since they would be hiking downhill. "I can walk," she said, tugging off his knit cap.

He rocked to his feet and faced her with wide eyes, an explosion of thick brown spikes sticking up from his head.

Unable to contain her laughter, she said, "You look like a wooly bear."

He reached out and captured her hands. "Well, you look beautiful," he countered. "The fresh air seems to be good for you."

Even through her mittens, she felt the strength in his hands, the hands that had brushed her hair off her face when she'd been too weak to do so. Images of him flashed through her mind, the smile on his lips when he was amused, his astonished expression when she revealed her temper, the way his eyes would darken when their gazes held too long.

An intense need to thank him rose up in her, but she had no words for what she felt. Her emotions were tangled and confused, as churned up as the gurgling stream cutting a winding path down the mountain. For the first time since she'd woken without a clue to her past, she realized she was making memories right here on the mountain. With Gray. With a man who would leave her behind once she recovered her memory or he solved the mystery of her.

"Everything all right?" he asked, dipping his head to look into her eyes.

At that moment, all she knew was she had to break whatever spell he was casting over her, to clear the cobwebs from her head. She was supposed to be learning about her past and what had happened to her up here. Not thinking about her future and wishing Gray would kiss her.

Willow woke to the aroma of fresh-brewed coffee and cinnamon. When she opened her eyes, Gray was seated at the table. "What a lovely smell to wake up to," she said, giving her body a good stretch before sitting up.

"I hope you don't mind coffee and cinnamon buns for breakfast again. I'll cook eggs tomorrow."

She smiled. "My mouth is watering in anticipation."

When she moved to the table, he placed a warm cinnamon bun and a cup of coffee in front of her. "I have to head to work soon."

"I know," she said, taking a bite of the warm bun. She savored it for a long moment as she chewed, her mind grasping for something just out of reach. Why did the smell and taste of these sweet buns fill her with such nostalgia and warmth? It wasn't just the heavenly taste of them. It was that they elicited something deeper, a sense of connection she'd been missing.

"That means you'll be here alone for a few hours," he said.

"I'll be fine," she said, taking another bite.

"You'll need to stay inside with the door locked until I return."

Chewing the sweet in her mouth, she gave him a nod to acknowledge she'd heard him.

"I can't put my job off any longer."

"I understand." She took a sip of coffee. "You needn't worry about me."

"But I will." He leaned back with a hard sigh. "Willow, you must stay inside and not answer the door for anyone for any reason. You have to understand how important it is that no one knows you're here."

"Or knows I'm alive," she added with a cheeky grin, hoping it would alleviate his concern.

"You can't afford to take this lightly."

"I'm well aware of the danger. I'll stay inside with the door locked and the revolver loaded. Now," she said, giving him a stern look, "go to work and let me finish my coffee and this delicious cinnamon bun in peace."

Rather than leaving the table, he smiled at her as if she amused him. "You have cinnamon on your chin."

She wiped her chin with a napkin.

"You missed it," he said, brushing the pad of his thumb across her chin.

His touch made her heart beat a little faster. Being holed up in the cabin with Gray, the only person she had in her lost world, was making her too dependent on him. Their forced intimacy was creating bonds, and in her case romantic inclinations, which would be painful to break. "Don't you need to leave?" she asked, desperate to get him out of the cabin.

"As soon as I check outside."

Popping the last bit of cinnamon bun into her mouth, and downing the last of her coffee, she said, "Then you should get going."

"I'll put the dishes in the sink," he said, reaching for her empty plate as she was laying her fork down. His warm fingers brushed the top of her hand, sending a jolt through her belly.

"I'll do it," she said, standing so quickly her chair scraped across the floorboards. "Just go."

Lifting his hands in surrender, he stepped back. "No need to rush me out the door."

Yes, there was a need to rush him out because the man was churning her up inside. "Go do your reconnaissance or whatever you do out there," she said, flapping her hand toward the door, "then go to work."

"Yes, ma'am," he said with a laugh. After pulling on his boots, buttoning himself in a thick wool coat, and tugging a wool hat over his head, he picked up his revolver and opened the door. "I'll return in fifteen minutes."

When she'd regained her breath and her good sense, she washed and rinsed their two plates and two cups and left them on a linen to dry. Then she freshened up in the bathroom, braided her hair, and hurried to dress. She'd just finished tying her boots when Gray returned carrying an armload of firewood.

After stoking the woodstove, he placed the revolver on a shelf by the door. "This is loaded," he said, "so don't touch it unless you absolutely have to."

"No worry there," she said, eyeing the gun with displeasure.

He crossed to where she stood watching him. "Stay inside."

"All right, but when you're in town and at work, don't forget to ask if anyone knows me. I mean if they know of a missing woman or, well, you know what I mean," she finished lamely.

For a moment, he simply looked at her, then he cupped her shoulders and gave them a gentle squeeze. "I'll return as soon as I'm able."

The instant the door closed behind him, she sagged against the table wishing his touch didn't make her belly flutter and her heart race.

CHAPTER ELEVEN

T he tall smokestacks of the Pine Ridge Paper Mill towered above a large compound of imposing brick walls, spewing sour-smelling smoke and obscuring the morning sunshine. The plant had been built on the banks of the Androscoggin River at the base of its grand waterfall that powered the mill and provided a means of transportation. It also helped circulate and treat the timber cut from the Maine mountain forests.

Gray could feel the oppressive atmosphere before he'd even set foot on the property. Outside in the muddy, rutted yard, he passed several men using teams of horses to haul logs to a loading dock at the far end of the complex, and more men and boys down at the river's edge using long metal hooks to sort a snarl of floating timber. Funnels of frosty air spewed from their mouths as they worked, but even in their threadbare clothing, they seemed oblivious to the frigid temperature.

With an empathetic shiver, Gray headed to the plant. The instant he stepped inside, he stopped in stunned surprise as the sheer scale and power of the machines assaulted his senses. Cranes and chains clanked overhead, steam hissed from vents, and the continuous thumping and clacking of machines echoed through the cavernous building. Weak, negligible light seeped in through dingy windows set high in the walls and washed the occupants with a gloomy stain. Everywhere he looked, poorly dressed men and boys labored at noisy machines, already looking beaten and exhausted in the early morning hour. To know these poor souls would still be here laboring long after Gray had left for the day twisted his gut in a knot of empathy.

Fumes burned his eyes as he surveyed the expansive buildings with open massive doors that connected one building to another and to another, far beyond the scope of his vision. He would walk every inch of the place and talk to as many employees as necessary to complete his investigation. First stop, though, was the office where he would find the men in charge of this prison. His years with the Pinkertons had taught him that those with the most power had the most to lose, and that's where his most likely suspects would be.

After asking directions of a young man who'd passed by, Gray headed toward the main offices in the north corner of the building. He opened a heavy wood door with multipaned glass to find himself face-to-face with a rugged-looking man wearing a white shirt, brown vest, and mile-deep scowl.

"Who the devil are you?" the man asked, using his squat body to block Gray's entrance. The man looked like a rusty old barrel with his ruddy complexion, round body, and a face that had seen better days.

Undeterred, Gray met the man's black gaze. "I'm Gray Alexander, the personnel inspector hired by your boss," he said, using his undercover alias. "And you are?" he asked with as much disdain as he'd been met with.

Surprise flashed across the man's whiskered face and he seemed taken aback. "I've heard nothing about this," he said, as if Gray were intentionally trying to mislead him.

Gray shrugged. "That's your problem. I'm here to do a job and I intend to do it."

"Not until I can confirm your story," the man said, continuing to stand in Gray's path.

"Then I suggest you call your boss now because I'm going to get started." With that, Gray stepped around the man and headed toward the first office, where a middle-aged man dressed in a worn black suitcoat sat peering intently at a ledger that lay open on his desk.

Upon Gray's approach, the man slammed the ledger closed and glared through wire-rimmed glasses perched low on his hawkish nose. "What is it?" he asked with a snarl, his features drawn tight in annoyance.

Gray nearly laughed at the absurdly rude greeting he'd encountered from both men. Still, he'd survived worse and wasn't to be deterred. Again, he introduced himself, using his title as personnel investigator.

"Why do we need a personnel investigator?" the man asked, bracing his forearms across the ledger in a protective manner that intrigued Gray.

"I'm here to see what I can do to improve productivity and increase profitability."

The man's relief was so apparent his narrow shoulders lowered as if he'd begun leaking air. "Well, that would surely be a welcome change," he said, pushing himself to his feet. He thrust out his boney hand. "Milton Fitch," he said. "I handle the accounting here."

Suspect number one. Gray camouflaged his suspicion with a warm grin. "May I impose upon you today to show me around the mill?" he asked, wanting the opportunity to talk with the man.

"Not possible," Milton said. "I've got more work than I can manage in a day, so you'll have to ask Silas Wade or Philo Holbrooke to show you around."

"Who is Silas Wade?" Gray asked.

"I am," said a churlish voice from the hallway. A second later, the scowling barrel of a man that had met Gray at the office door minutes earlier appeared. "I'm the foreman here, and it appears I'll be stuck with you until you've accomplished what you came for."

"I take it you spoke with Mr. Rathborne?"

The foreman ignored the direct question, reached into his vest pocket, then scowled as if he'd lost something. "What do you need?"

"I want to see the mill and talk to the employees," Gray said.

Wade arched one bushy eyebrow. "For what purpose?"

"That's my business, Mr. Wade." Gray turned toward the door. "Now, you can show me through the plant or I'll find my own way around." A hard snort came from behind him, and Gray glanced back at Silas Wade's scowling face. "The longer it takes me to do my job, the longer I'll be here."

"Then get going," Wade said, thrusting his whiskered chin toward the door, revealing two pink scratches on his neck partially covered by his rust-colored beard.

Suspect number two. Wade's obvious opposition to Gray's presence was enough to merit suspicion. But Gray made a mental note of what appeared to be another faint pink cut or scratch on Wade's neck, knowing men disguised all manner of sin beneath facial hair. He'd used a beard and mustache himself on more than one occasion as part of his disguise. If Silas Wade were trying to hide something, Gray would dig until he unearthed that bone.

Fifteen minutes into the tour, Gray had sized up Silas Wade as a gruff man who enjoyed wielding his power over the employees. Not one person would meet the foreman's eyes for more than a moment, and the younger boys on the floor seemed to shrink as if hoping to go unnoticed. That confirmed what Gray had already suspected, and now he knew just how to gain Wade's confidence.

"I'm impressed, Mr. Wade. You've got quite an operation here," Gray said, intentionally stroking the man's ego.

The foreman harrumphed and said, "The plant's running just fine without your meddling."

"It's not my intention to meddle, Mr. Wade. I'm simply doing a job I was hired to do. That doesn't mean anything needs to change."

The foreman cocked his head. "Is that so?"

Gray shrugged. "I can see you're a stern master running a tight ship. If there's nothing to be improved upon, then there's nothing for me to change."

That seemed to knock the chip off the man's wide shoulders. "This plant operates round the clock every day. There's no way to increase production without adding more hours to a day. If you can figure out how to do that, I'm all ears."

Surprised, Gray asked about the number of employees and length of their shifts.

"Three hundred twenty-seven employees working twelve-hour shifts," he said, continuing on with his step-scuff walk that seemed to strike fear into every person the foreman approached. Gray had immediately noticed Wade's awkward stride, the man's right toe scuffing the floor with each step as they walked through the plant. Gray was trained to notice such things, and also trained to pretend he hadn't. But he made a mental note of every detail and would add those details to his journal when he returned to the cabin.

The thought of Willow alone there sent a surge of concern through him. He ached to rush back and make sure she was safe, but it was imperative he keep his focus on the job at hand because he couldn't afford to miss anything. She had worked in this desolate place, and she might have been assaulted here. He needed to find answers to that question and to complete his task for the agency. That required a sharp mind, keen observation, and asking the right questions.

He had little time to ponder as Wade marched them through the plant like soldiers, pushing hard as if he wanted to put the tour and Gray firmly behind him. He studiously kept Gray from conversing with the workers, and spent more time asking questions than explaining the workings of the plant. Gray knew the man was digging for information, gauging the level of challenge he was facing. But Gray was good at the game and alleviated Wade's concerns at every turn, slowly lulling the man into a false sense of comradery. He needed to gain Wade's confidence, and that meant playing a part, however loathsome, to work his way around the man's guard.

Surprised to see two barefoot men working at a woodchip conveyor, Gray asked why they were barefoot.

With a flip of his pockmarked left hand, Wade said, "The floor gets too slippery for leather shoes." He turned away as if Gray had simply asked why the windows hadn't been cleaned. "Two years ago we converted our equipment and process for making paper. We use wood pulp now instead of rag fibers," Wade said, shouting to be heard over the noise of massive chippers and heavy rollers. "Our new Fourdrinier machines are the widest and fastest available," he said, gesturing toward three massive machines producing large continuous reels of paper. "We're producing nearly ninety thousand pounds of newsprint per day."

Gray released a low whistle, truly impressed. He'd done his research before coming to Pine Ridge for his undercover work, but standing beside the towering machines and seeing the vast enterprise in person was impressive. And deeply unsettling. These machines and this plant operated on the backs of exhausted, beaten-down laborers. That was a fact Gray couldn't avoid knowing as he looked into the weary eyes and observed the slumped shoulders of the people around him.

That thought plagued him as Wade expounded on how the moving-wire and cylinder-wire machines made newsprint and wrapped paper. Although Gray followed along with real interest in a complex process, he took in much more than the machines and processing that went into papermaking. He noticed the workers and the conditions and was intensely interested in the areas Silas Wade seemed to be avoiding. To test his suspicion that Wade was intentionally skirting some areas of the plant, Gray asked about them and was told it was a loading dock or an inventory room or a storage room. Perhaps those unseen regions were of no importance as Wade claimed, but Gray's instincts suggested otherwise. With or without the man's permission, Gray would investigate on his own later.

Just as they were entering the last in a long complex of buildings, they came upon a man who seemed surprisingly unaffected by their appearance. Whipcord thin and wearing a black felt hat, the man faced them with dead eyes. "Need something, Mr. Wade?"

Wade jutted his chin toward a long row of smaller machines where men, women, and even children were working.

"Numbers are up today," the man said before Wade could ask a question.

"Better be," Wade replied, then jerked his head toward Gray. "This is Gray Alexander, a personnel inspector hired by Rathborne." To Gray he said, "This is my assistant foreman Philo Holbrooke. Takes a lot to keep a place like this running," Wade said, arrogance fairly oozing from his thin mouth. "Philo is my eyes and ears on night shift."

Gray shook the man's cold hand and searched for any sign of emotion in Holbrooke's dark eyes. Finding none, Gray asked, "What do you do here?"

"Mostly observe and report any problems," Philo said flatly.

Gray instinctively knew it was a job Holbrooke did without

questioning orders. The man was a spy for Wade and didn't seem to feel any remorse or concern over his actions. In fact, the man seemed strangely devoid of any emotion, as if intentionally creating a screen to hide himself.

Suspect number three. Gray knew from experience as an operative it took effort and intelligence to create an alternate identity, one that might think and act opposite one's true nature. Was Philo Holbrooke truly the cold, emotional shell of a man he appeared to be, or was he using that facade to hide the mind and actions of a clever criminal?

Before Gray could get tangled in his musings, Wade steered him back in the direction they'd come. "We're done here, and I need to head back to the office now."

Gray stepped aside. "Go on without me. I need to talk to some of the workers now."

"About what?" Wade asked, seeming uncomfortable with the idea of Gray conversing with the laborers. "I just gave you all the information you need." When Gray didn't reply, Wade scowled. "These people need to be working not standing around talking with an investigator."

"Well, this investigator has been hired by your boss to do just that," Gray countered, then hoping to ease the antagonism he felt brewing with Wade, he said, "I'll keep my questions brief and meet you back in the office shortly." With that, he walked away and began stopping by random machines to ask questions about production and working conditions while hoping for more intimate details about the place and people who ran it. Although his approach was cautious and friendly with each worker he talked with, they were all looking over their shoulders, afraid to comment, even after Wade returned to the office.

After nearly an hour on the floor, threading his way through several buildings and receiving the same response that they just needed to work harder, Gray headed back into the building housing the Fourdrinier machines. Earlier, while he had been conversing with Wade and Holbrooke, an older man with hollow eyes and graying hair had seemed avidly interested in their discussion. The entire time Gray had been talking with Wade and Holbrooke, the man's gaze had darted between them and the machine he was running. That behavior was so inconsistent with every other worker who studiously avoided looking at them in their obvious desire to remain unnoticed that it had caught Gray's attention.

Now, when he approached, an odd hopefulness seemed to fill the man's hollow eyes.

After checking the equipment and adjusting a throttle of some sort, he met Gray several feet away from the clanking machine. Gray introduced himself and briefly explained why he was there, expressing his desire to help improve working conditions while improving productivity. The man's expression fell and he seemed so distraught that Gray was utterly baffled. "Is this a problem for you?" he asked.

"No sir. I just hoped you were here with news about Sophia."

Gray's gut contracted so hard he struggled to mask his surprise. "Are you referring to the girl accused of running off?" he forced himself to ask.

Surprise lit the man's tired eyes. "You know about her?"

"Only what Officer Kline revealed when he was out looking for her. Said she might have run off with a beau."

"She didn't run off," the man said. "She didn't have a fella."

"You know that for certain?" Gray asked.

The man nodded. "I do."

"You knew her well then?"

"Yes, sir. She's my daughter."

For one harsh moment, Gray's breath jammed in his chest. It took all his willpower not to tell the poor bereft man that his daughter was safe and sound at the cabin. But he couldn't do that because he knew the man's relief would be so obvious to others no matter how much Gray cautioned him to hide it, that it would compromise Sophia's safety. Of all the despicable things he'd been forced to do in his line of work, this was by far the most heinous cruelty.

He wanted to blurt out the truth and alleviate the man's torture.

But all he could do was his job.

So, he asked if Sophia had any close friends she might have gone off with.

Mr. Flynn shook his head. "She got on well with some of the women she worked with, but they rarely spent time together outside of work."

"Any particular reason?" Gray asked, deeply curious about Sophia's personal life.

"Most of the women are married and busy with their families. Sophia worked a lot of hours and spent the rest of her time helping her mother and me at home."

For several minutes, Gray talked with Sophia's father, who introduced himself as Arthur Flynn, about her disappearance. Mr. Flynn said he'd worked late that evening and assumed Sophia had gone home at the end of her shift. But he arrived home long after dark to learn from his wife, Elizabeth, that Sophia hadn't come home. He'd walked back to the mill in search of her, questioning every person in every department, none of whom had seen her. That's when Mr. Flynn went to Officer Kline who suggested that Sophia might have run off with a beau. Flynn's offense was so deep, Gray could see the anger churning in the man's eyes.

"Officer Kline waited until morning before he bothered to look for her," Mr. Flynn said, disgust thick in his voice. "I looked, though. I knocked on every door in town, waking people all night long, but no one..." His voice broke and he pursed his lips as if trying to hold back a storm of emotion. "Not one person had seen her since that morning."

Seeing the man struggle, weighed down by grief so heavy it nearly broke him, gouged a hole in Gray's chest...and in his conscience. Like river water smashing against its banks, Gray's mind scrambled for a way to alleviate the man's heartache without putting Sophia in more danger. Perhaps, if Mr. Flynn knew the truth, he could take time off and stay at the cabin while Gray was at the mill. The instant the thought crossed Gray's mind, he knew it wasn't an option. Even if he compensated Flynn for his time off, which the man surely needed but would likely reject, Gray instinctively knew that Silas Wade and whoever was responsible for assaulting Sophia would be too suspicious of Flynn's absence. That might encourage them to find out what Mr. Flynn was doing with his time away, and it might lead them to the cabin and to Sophia, which could put both her and her father in terrible danger.

So Gray offered the only reassurance he could. "Your daughter is missing, Mr. Flynn. That's terrifying, but it doesn't mean she's..." —he stopped himself from saying *dead*—"she could be safe and unharmed, just unable to communicate with you right now."

The man didn't look convinced.

"You have to concede it's a possibility, Mr. Flynn."

With a nod indicating he was simply resigned and not convinced, Mr. Flynn excused himself to check on the equipment he was running. Gray let him go because he couldn't think of another single thing to say that would give the man an ounce of comfort.

CHAPTER TWELVE

Each evening when Gray returned home from his job, Willow would meet him at the door with her heart pounding in anticipation and dread. Before he could finish his greeting, she would ask if he had learned anything about her identity. After six days of receiving a negative reply, and being confined to the cabin while Gray worked at the mill, she was too restless to stay inside another minute. The short jaunts they'd taken each evening in the dark, consisting of a few minutes spent outside behind the cabin, had done little to stave off the boredom, loneliness, and frustration that plagued her all week. "I want to take a long walk and get a tree," she said, reaching for the boots Gray had purchased for her.

"A tree?" he asked, one dark eyebrow lifting in a way that had become as familiar to her as the sound of his voice.

"Yes. Christmas is three weeks away, and I want to get a tree to decorate."

Both eyebrows lifted. "Where do you suggest we put it," he asked, glancing around their comfortable but small space.

"Depends on the size of the tree," she said, slipping off her shoe—the one they found where she'd been dumped in the woods.

They had cleaned and dried the shoe so she had a pair to wear inside, but it was heavily worn and not sufficient for outdoor wear. Gray had wanted to leave her shoe in the muddy condition in which they'd found it, saying it was evidence, but she'd felt an intense need to hold onto the one thing from her past that belonged to her. So she'd convinced him to clean and oil it for her, claiming she needed a pair of shoes to wear inside.

"What are you going to use for decorations?" he asked.

"I haven't decided yet," she said, pulling on one of the boy's boots he'd purchased for her. "Now, please stop asking questions and get dressed so we can go for a walk."

"As you wish, milady," he said, pushing himself to his feet.

His lighthearted quip made her laugh. All week he'd been quiet and contemplative, making notes in his journal, seeming distracted by something that deeply disturbed him. To see him smile and jest with her now was a relief. She'd feared he was growing tired of her and the situation he'd been saddled with, but perhaps he was just preoccupied with his new job. Whatever the case, she fully intended to enjoy a day outside.

As they stepped outside, and the first bracing breeze caressed her cheeks, she inhaled long and deep, drawing in the wintery scent of pine and crisp air. She held her breath for a moment, then released it in a long, frosty funnel. "What a beautiful day."

"Definitely beautiful," he said, but he was looking at her, not at the sparkling snow-covered world around them.

Their eyes met and held, making her a little breathless. Each day it was getting more difficult to see Gray as a detective keeping her safe, because he was becoming so much more than her protector.

"We should go," he said quietly.

With a nod, she turned and headed downhill.

"Willow?"

She stopped and looked back.

"If we go that way we'll have to drag the tree uphill to the cabin."

She grinned. "I don't mind. I won't be hauling it back."

He laughed. "I'm glad to see you still have your sense of humor after spending the week alone."

"What's humorous about you hauling the tree back?" she asked, captivated by the delight she saw in his eyes. That he enjoyed their play was wonderfully evident in the way his gaze drank her in. "Selecting the tree is my job. Carrying it back is yours."

"You know, the less you help the smaller the tree will be."

She laughed. She couldn't help herself. "If you're strong enough to carry me, you should have no trouble managing a tree my height and as round as a hoop skirt," she said, turning to head uphill.

"Is that so?" he asked, following along with a surprised belt of laughter. "Where do you propose to put it?"

Giving him a haughty lift of her nose, she said, "Wherever it looks best of course."

Snow had fallen the past two days and covered the ground in thick white fluff that swirled around their ankles as they followed a deer path. The sparkling blanket was so lovely she hated to disturb it.

"You seem to be walking better in those boots," he said, glancing down at her bulky leather footwear.

"That's because I'm wearing two pairs of your socks so my feet won't slip inside them."

"So that's where all my socks have gone," he said indignantly, as if she'd grossly trespassed upon his property.

"I need them to keep my feet warm and comfortable on our walk."

"Well, my feet are cold as a stone in these threadbare socks you left me."

Willow burst out laughing. "I know full well you're wearing thick, wool socks because I've been washing our garments each evening so your clothes are warm and dry for you each morning."

"I know you have," he said, taking her mitten-covered hand and tucking it into the crook of his elbow. "Thank you, but please don't overtax yourself and undo all your progress."

"I'm fit as a fiddle but on the brink of madness being trapped inside all day. I need chores to occupy my time. Must you work every day?" she asked, knowing he must but hoping he wouldn't.

"Unfortunately, yes."

"What do you do there?" she asked, stepping over a dried section of branch that had fallen across the path. At his silence, she glanced up to see a shadow drift over his eyes. "I suppose I shouldn't have asked," she said, feeling disheartened that he couldn't share that part of his life with her.

"It's all right. I can tell you that I'm investigating a situation at the mill," he said. "And I can tell you it's a cheerless place."

"How so?" she asked, brightening with interest.

"Well," he began, seeming to proceed with caution so as not to reveal details she shouldn't know, "it's a noisy, sour-smelling, gloomy place, but the workers I talk to seem like good, hard-working folks."

"Are you investigating anyone in particular?" she asked.

"No," Gray said, because everyone was a suspect until he learned what had happened to her. But he said, "I'm investigating a situation, not the people."

"Did you uncover anything this week?"

He grinned. "I can't tell you that, but I can tell you more about the mill." For several minutes, he parsed out tidbits of infor-mation, referring to the people as workers, foremen, clerks, repair-men, and machine tenders, describing his amazement at the size and power of the equipment, watching her closely to see if anything triggered a memory for her. But Willow's interest seemed to be that of someone listening to a story about a place they'd never been.

"How long will your investigation take?" she asked, letting him assist her up a small knoll.

"I don't know."

"What will happen after you finish your investigation?"

He sensed concern beneath her question, but he could only say he didn't know, because he didn't. If Willow didn't regain her memory on her own, he would be forced at some point to tell her everything he knew about her. And she would hate him for keeping it all from her.

Lost in his anguish, he nearly tripped over her when she stopped suddenly in front of him.

"That's the one," she said, pointing to a small fir at the edge of the path.

"That crooked little thing?" he asked with a laugh.

"Yes. It's perfect," she said, grinning up at him with such pleasure in her eyes it spread warmth through his chest.

"What happened to a tree as tall as you and as round as a hoop skirt?"

She grinned. "Fashion changes."

All he wanted to do in that moment was cup her rosy cheeks and kiss her. He'd traveled the country for his job, crossing paths with women who'd made it clear they would welcome his kiss, and he'd enjoyed intimate moments with some of them. But no matter how beautiful or alluring those women were, none had moved him like the one standing in front of him. For several intense seconds he fought the urge to draw her into his arms and show her how deeply she affected him, how desperately he was drawn to her, how hopelessly smitten he was with her.

"Is something the matter?" she asked, her smile fading to an expression of concern.

"No," he said, giving himself a mental shake. "I'm just

thinking that this tree seems to have no fashion sense at all. Or branches for that matter."

Stepping close to the tree that barely reached her shoulder, she began pointing out its merits. "Look at its shape," she said.

"It's crooked."

"It's unique, individual, special. You can tell by the shadow it casts," she said, using a small stick to trace the outline in the snow. "See how it creates a beautiful snow angel."

"I don't see anything but a crooked tree," he said, then suddenly felt himself shoved backwards. Winging his arms out to break his fall, he landed on his backside, shocked by the fact that she had intentionally pushed him. "What the devil?"

"Lie back and sweep your arms over the snow," she said, sitting down beside him as if nothing had happened.

"What?"

She gave him a hard nudge. "Lie on your back and make a snow angel, like this," she said, lying on her back and sweeping her arms up and down in the snow. A second later, she sat up and pointed to the snow behind her. "See the angel wings? That's a snow angel."

She was a snow angel, all pink-cheeked and dusted with snowflakes, and absolutely irresistible. To stop himself from kissing her, he flopped to his back and swept his arms across the snow, warning himself to cool off.

"Come on," she said, pushing to her feet, then reaching for his hand. "Now that you know how to do it, we'll make one together."

He didn't accept her assistance because he didn't trust himself not to pull her into his arms. Instead, he heaved himself to his feet and followed her up the path a few yards.

"All right," she said, standing in the path with her back to a small opening between pine trees. "Hold my hand, and when I count to three, we both sit and lie back in the snow to make our angel."

It seemed silly, like something a child would do, but she seemed so happy to be outside that he couldn't deny her.

When he clasped her hand, their mittens creating a thick cushion between them, she said, "On three. Ready?" At his nod, she counted, "One...two...three!" Together they sat and lay back, her gaze connecting with his as they looked at each other. "Sweep your arms but don't let go of my hand."

He never wanted to let go.

Lying there with her, snowflakes drifting down through the forest treetops to land on her flushed cheeks, was a moment he knew he would never forget. Her eyes sparkled and her lips tilted as she smiled at him. She had no idea how beautiful she was or how rare. Like her little tree, Willow was unique, individual, special. A one-of-a-kind beauty.

"What are you thinking?" she asked, her voice hushed, as if she didn't want to intrude upon the pristine solitude of the forest.

His every thought was filled with her, but he said, "I was thinking I could fall asleep right here."

"Better not," she said, pushing to her feet. "A bear might come along and make you his supper."

"Not if you drag me home with the tree."

With a joyful laugh, she moved a couple yards up the path. "Sleep at your own peril," she said, picking up a stick.

Watching her trail it through the snow, he sat up and got to his feet. "What are you doing?"

"I'm sketching," she said, appearing absorbed in her work.

He watched as she created outlines in the snow of a rabbit, a squirrel with a bushy tail, and a deer with antlers. "You have an amazing talent," he said, impressed at how easily and accurately she sketched.

"Apparently this is something I love to do," she said. "But I'm afraid I'm using up all your paper with my scribbling."

"I'll pick up more tomorrow after work," he said, making a mental note to stop at the store.

"You don't have to do that," she said. "I had meant to apologize, not suggest you purchase more paper."

"If having something to draw on brings you as much pleasure as sketching in the snow does, I'll purchase reams of paper for you. I'll even pick up canvas and paints if you like."

She laughed. "That won't be necessary. But now you have me wondering if I ever painted."

It struck him then, how unsettling it must be for her to not know such intimate details about herself. Silently, he vowed to do everything in his power to help her remember and recover those lost parts of herself.

"We should head back soon," he said, glancing at the sky and fading light.

With a long sigh, she said, "I suppose we must."

Using the small handsaw he'd brought with them, he cut down her crooked little tree and left it lying on its side on the path. "I'm sorry, but before we go, I need to cover this up," he said, scuffing his boots through the snow to obliterate the drawings she'd made. She said nothing as he kicked snow across the snow angels they'd made, but he could see the joy slipping from her expression.

"Cheer up, Willow," he said, pushing the cut end of the tree stump into her hand. "You get to haul your little tree home."

With a chirp of laughter, she tugged on the tree and made little progress. "I might need some assistance," she said, looking up at him with a smile that melted him.

To stop himself from pulling her into his arms, he gave her a playful wink and grabbed the tree trunk. "I've got it," he said, and headed downhill before he crossed a line that couldn't be uncrossed.

FORTY MINUTES later they arrived at the cabin. Willow went inside to make tea while Gray fashioned a tree stand out of scraps of wood. By the time he came inside, the tea was ready, and she had a corner cleared where she asked him to put the tree.

While they enjoyed their tea and warmed up from their brisk outing, she studied the small fir with its odd-shaped branches.

"Having second thoughts?" he asked.

"Not at all," she replied. "I'm just considering what we might have to use as decorations."

"Tell me what you need and I'll see what I can find in town tomorrow."

"You don't have to do that," she said, touched by his offer. "Truly, I'll come up with something."

"You could hang our wet socks on it."

She grinned. "I'll keep that in mind as a last resort."

"Is there anything at all you need in town?" he asked.

"More cinnamon buns."

He gave her a warm smile. "That's the first item on my list."

"It's the *only* item on mine."

His laughter filled the empty places where her memories should be. He was the only thing in her life. The only friend. The only joy. Feeling connected to him was normal. Being attracted to him was likely a result of their forced proximity. At least that's what she told herself because she couldn't allow it to be anything more than that. Because Gray, this man who filled her life, would eventually leave her. She understood and accepted that. What she couldn't accept was her inability to remain unaffected by him. Despite her best effort, it was utterly impossible. And so she camouflaged her feelings with humor and cautioned herself to consider him nothing more than her friend and protector.

"Will you please bring in the branches you cut off the tree?"

she asked, remembering that he'd needed to remove two of the lowest branches to attach the tree stand he'd made.

After he'd fetched the branches for her, she sat at the table and fashioned a wreath by shaping the pine branches and tying them with strips cut from her old blouse. Gray had washed it during her recovery, but it still bore the rusty stain of blood. Methodically, she cut away and discarded the stained and torn pieces of her blouse, the act of creating something beautiful with it bringing her a renewed sense of strength. She'd survived. She was alive and healthy and safe because of Gray.

But her heart was in significant danger because of that same man.

CHAPTER THIRTEEN

During Gray's second week at the mill, Silas Wade appeared to be avoiding him as intensely as Gray avoided Sophia's father. That was no easy feat when Arthur Flynn was often called to various areas of the plant in need of his exceptional skill in machine repair and maintenance. Still, Gray steered clear. To cross paths with Arthur Flynn again and see the agony in the man's eyes would have Gray blurting out the truth about Sophia. So he avoided the man, silently asking her father to forgive him, but the ticking clock in his head reminded him that every passing minute the man was suffering, and Sophia's attacker was free.

In every department, Gray noticed an undercurrent of deep discord among the workers. Some seemed as if they wanted to share their concerns with him while others would clam-up tight when he approached.

After three days of walking through the plant, observing the papermaking process and talking with the employees, Gray had ascertained which workers were most likely to share information. One woman named Dorothy Abner, who had worked as a rag sorter for years when paper had been made from pulverizing and chemically reducing rags to a gruel-like consistency, was now a picker working long hours removing clods of dirt from wood being fed into a woodchipper.

Raising her voice to be heard over the noisy equipment, she explained how the chips would be transferred to a steel vat and softened chemically with sulfite to create the wood pulp they now used for papermaking. With more than twenty years at Pine Ridge Paper Mill, Mrs. Abner, with her dark features and manly build, was a fount of knowledge. Because she was privy to all the gossip and knew every employee, she was more knowledgeable than most of management running the plant. Where other workers would duck their heads and try to avoid any interaction with their bosses, Dorothy Abner greeted them with a toothy smile that hid a brilliant mind. Gray cautioned himself not to let his admiration for the woman lower his guard. He needed to gather information, not provide it. And so he used his interest in her job to engage her in conversations throughout the week that yielded some surprising information.

Most of what she revealed simply reaffirmed his suspicion that he needed to dig deeper into Silas Wade and Philo Holbrooke, and that Sophia Flynn was a quiet, hardworking young woman who had labored as a clerk in the inventory department. Other gossip, not as interesting but still important, was about the unrest among employees and the whisper of an impending labor strike. Having barely survived the disastrous labor strike at Homestead, Pennsylvania, mere months ago, Gray dreaded the thought of these beaten-down employees embarking on a fool's mission, knowing the workers would lose more than they could ever hope to gain. Although he was here under the guise of a personnel inspector, he fully planned to suggest significant and desperately needed improvements to the owner when he presented his findings to the man.

With that in mind, Gray watched closely, listened carefully, and pushed his nose into those areas Silas Wade had studiously avoided showing him. The loading docks seemed to run like clockwork, with timber being brought in at one dock, then moved to the chipper and on through the process of being converted to wood pulp. The other docks were used mainly to receive supplies or to move reels of newsprint to wagons that would carry them to the railyard for delivery to large newspaper publishers in New York.

The entire plant was a beehive of activity around the clock, which is why it surprised Gray to find the inventory warehouse sparsely staffed and unusually quiet. It's also where Silas Wade seemed to spend a good amount of time, and where Gray's presence most seemed to irritate the man.

"What do you need now, Mr. Alexander?" Silas growled, reaching into his vest pocket, then scowling, an odd habit Gray had noted within an hour of meeting Wade. Now, nearing the end of his second week at the mill, he was deeply curious to know what Wade might be searching for. Had the man lost his wallet? Was he searching for a misplaced key or spectacles perhaps? Or was this just an odd habit of a peculiar man? People had unusual behaviors, some of them downright strange, but that didn't make them guilty of anything.

"How often do you do inventory?" Gray asked, surveying rows of metal racks stocked with reels of paper, tubs of sulfite for making wood pulp, crates of office supplies, custodial supplies and other items. At the far side of the vast room appeared to be a maintenance and repair area lined with workbenches and toolboxes and an enormous variety of tools that hung from pegs on the back wall.

Wade's scowl deepened. "I can't see how our inventory can possibly concern a personnel inspector," he snapped.

"Well, the employees who maintain this inventory concern me," Gray countered, "which means the management of such inventory is my concern."

Silas glared at him. "Holbrooke does it on night shift."

"How often?"

"Every month."

"Who orders your inventory?" Gray asked.

Wade's scowl deepened. "Depends on what we need," he said. "Now, I've got more important things to do than answer your questions." With that, Wade pivoted on his left heel and stalked off, his step-scuff-step-scuff gate growing distant as he disappeared into the maze of tall metal shelving.

Gray remained for a long time, mentally calculating the cost of the inventory and how easily a mismanaged inventory could kill a company's profit margin. Carrying too much inventory added unnecessary costs to the bottom line. Keeping too few of the necessary materials or parts on-hand could shut down production and result in canceled orders and lost sales. In his experience, most cases of embezzlement were the act of an accountant or clerk cooking the books. But Gray was beginning to suspect the drain on profits at this paper mill was directly tied to this area. And his most likely suspect was Philo Holbrooke, who managed the inventory.

He made a mental note to pay an early-morning visit to the mill so he could speak with Holbrooke, who would be finishing his shift at that time.

Catching up with one of the young stock hands wearing a tattered brown cap over a mop of black hair, Gray asked him how they tracked inventory. During their walk, he followed the skinny boy, who gestured with knobby knuckles and explained what little he knew about the items they stocked. Gray took his time looking and assessing how one might misappropriate that inventory for personal profit. As he followed the mop-haired boy named John, Gray did a slow walk-through of the repair and maintenance department and deemed it an unlikely target. After that, they visited the office area where Sophia had worked as a clerk.

"How many people work in this office?" he asked.

"Maybe two, but I'm not certain," John said. "I've only worked in inventory for a month and I'm still learning my way around."

"Whom did you replace?"

"Tony Beller," John said. "But he only worked here for a couple of months before they moved him to the loading docks, so he couldn't show me much about the job."

"Do you know who worked here before Tony?"

"I think it was Gus Thacker."

A niggling suspicion began to grow in Gray's gut. "How long did Gus work here?" he asked.

John shrugged. "Couldn't say, sir."

"Is Gus still employed here?" Gray asked.

Again the young man shrugged.

"All right, thank you, John. You can go back to your duties now. I'll show myself out when I finish up here."

"Yes, sir." The boy bobbed his head, pivoted on one worn boot heel, and disappeared down an aisle with his long-legged boot-clunking stride.

Alone in the windowless office with weak lighting and anemic white walls, Gray surveyed the room where Sophia had worked. How many hours had she spent each day sitting at the wooden table laboring over the ledgers strewn across the desk? As a Personnel Inspector, Gray was privy to employee records, and he knew the stingy amount Sophia and the other hardworking laborers were paid. Men in positions of power, like Silas Wade and Philo Holbrook, were paid a fair wage. But the employees doing the hard labor were paid a pittance and struggled just to survive. They had every reason to demand better pay and better working conditions. To think he'd stood on the opposite side of those strikes, protecting the assets of the wealthy industrialists who were oppressing these folks, shamed Gray so deeply it nauseated him. So did the thought of his future as a Pinkerton Detective. As an undercover operative and strike breaker, he was well compensated. But the fatter his wallet had grown, the more impoverished his conscience had become.

Blowing out a hard breath and giving himself a mental shake, he forced his attention back to the job at hand.

Several wooden crates filled with messy piles of what appeared to be inventory records were stacked four high and three wide in one corner of the office. Had Sophia made this mess? Or was this a result of her absence? Or perhaps the chaos was intentional, which would make sense if his suspicion about inventory theft was accurate. Lost or misplaced records made discovery of a crime far more difficult. Could Sophia have suspected as much? If she had, and she'd confronted the thief, it could have motivated that man to eliminate her as an obstacle.

The mere thought of what she'd suffered infuriated him. It took several deep breaths and a hard mental struggle for him to tamp it down. He needed to find proof of a crime and solid evidence against the person responsible. Until he had that, he had to focus on his investigation and not on his outrage.

Taking stock of the information he'd gathered, he noted when Sophia was last seen at the plant. He knew the day and time he'd found her in the woods and could judge, based on her condition and the frigid temperature, how long she could have survived had he not rescued her. With that information, he could narrow the window of time when she could have been dumped there. He knew how long it would take a horse and wagon to travel from the plant to where he'd found Sophia and her missing shoe. So, who would have been absent from the mill during that time?

He considered his three prime suspects, namely Silas Wade, Milton Fitch, and Philo Holbrook. Milton Fitch was a nervous, agitated man in a position to alter the books to fill his own pockets, but he hardly seemed capable of brutally beating a woman. Plus, any prolonged absence from his office where he spent nearly every minute of his day would surely have been noticed. That would be easy enough to confirm. Both Philo Holbrook and Silas Wade were in a position to manipulate inventory to their personal benefit, and either man was in a position to leave the mill for a period of time without subordinates daring to question them. Either there were two separate crimes happening at this plant, or there was one suspect guilty of both theft and attempted murder.

Whatever the case, Gray intended to continue investigating and piecing together details until he discovered the truth. Then he would corner the criminal. That moment of success had always brought him a deep sense of satisfaction. Now, the idea of facing the man responsible for assaulting Sophia made him worry that his sense of outrage would overrun his sense of duty. Even the thought of it had his hands curling into fists.

Needing to walk off his anger, he headed to the loading docks to talk with Tony Beller. Although the man had spent only a short time working in the inventory department, it was likely he'd worked with Sophia. Hopefully, Mr. Beller could shed some light on the murky mystery Gray was struggling to solve.

Willow eyed the crooked little pine tree that had sat in the corner unadorned all week. As she'd requested, Gray had purchased red and green ribbon, glue, and a spool of black thread at the general store. He'd brought the items home with him on Monday evening, along with a bundle of pencils and two large scratch pads for her. During their too-brief evening outings, she'd filled a small sack with pinecones, dried bark, pine twigs, and a large cluster of beautiful red winterberries. Each day while Gray had been at work, she'd made ornaments for their tree.

Now, standing by the table, Gray inspected her handmade decorations. "Willow, I'm honestly amazed that you could create something so nice from a bit of ribbon and forest debris. You have the hands and vision of an artist."

"Or I just needed something to keep my hands and mind occupied while you were at work all week. When we return from our walk, the decorations should be ready to hang on the tree," she said, wanting to give the glue a little longer to dry before moving them off the table.

"You've made your point," he said, reaching for his jacket. "I won't keep you waiting a moment longer, milady."

She laughed. "I like when you call me your lady."

"Well, it's either that or—"

"Don't say it," she said, giving him a playful shove toward the door.

Their laughter filled the air as they stepped outside. A thick blanket of snow spread out under a low winter sky.

"Looks as if we're in for more snow," he said, reaching for her hand as was his habit during their walks.

She was long past the need for his assistance but couldn't deny herself the pleasure of his touch or the intimacy they shared in those moments.

Inhaling a deep breath of crisp air and releasing it in happy burst, she said, "Let's walk for miles and miles today." The delight in his laughter sent a surge of joy through her. "Tell me more about your childhood," she said as they headed down a familiar deer path.

Glancing down at her, he asked, "What do you want to know?"

She thought for a moment, then asked, "What is one of your favorite memories?"

He was quiet so long she thought he might not answer, but she waited because there were times he seemed to need a moment to wrench open the compartment where he kept his private self. After another moment of him appearing to mentally dig into his past, a half-smile tilted his lips.

"I suppose one of my best memories would be the baseball game my father took me to when I was nine years old," he said, warmth lighting his eyes. "The Palmettos were challenging the Carolinas, and people came from miles around to watch. The pitchers from both teams wore out their arms trying to strike out the batters, sometimes successfully, but the batters used their skill to hit everything from singles to home runs. As the battle between teams escalated, the crowd and the noise grew wild. Men were shouting and laying wagers on the outcome. At one point, the game grew so intense the crowd surged forward in excitement and carried my father and me right onto the playing field."

"What?" Willow pressed her hand to her chest. She'd gotten so caught up in his story her heart was pounding in excitement.

He released a gust of laughter. "The players were as shocked as we were. The umpire blew his whistle and threw his hands in the air, halting play as he shouted at the crowd to get off the field. Then he spread his arms wide and stalked directly toward us while gesturing for us to move back." Again, Gray laughed. "The crowd was like a nervous group of cattle stumbling and tripping over each other as we all tried to back our way off the field."

Hands clasped in front of her chest, delighted laughter bubbled from her throat. "Did the game continue?" she asked, enthralled.

"After a few minutes, yes."

"It must have been wildly exciting to be at a game like that."

"It was. Especially as a boy. Being one of the players on the team is the only thing that could have topped that experience."

"I'm sure," she said, imagining the game and the excitement he must have experienced as a boy. "I have no experience with baseball, at least I don't think I have. But it seems like it would be a sporting good time."

"It is," he said, scuffing his foot through the snow near the base of a large pine.

"Are you looking for something?" she asked.

"Yes, I need to find a large pinecone."

"I'd have thought you'd be tired of hunting down items for my ornaments by now."

"It's not for an ornament." He glanced at her. "We need a large pinecone and a branch as straight as you can find."

"What are you going to do with those things?"

"I'm going to teach you how to play baseball."

She burst out laughing. "With a stick and a pinecone?"

"Exactly," he said, giving her a crooked grin. "Now, use those pretty brown eyes of yours to find what we need."

With a light laugh, she turned her attention to scouting for the items, but all she could think about was his offhand comment. He thought she had pretty eyes? Was he noticing things about her like she'd been noticing about him? Because she noticed everything about him. How his laugh enfolded her like a warm hug, or how his smile lifted her heart. Did he enjoy their conversations and playful banter as much as she did? Did he ever feel snared by the intimate tangle of their gazes?

"Found it," he said, startling her from her woolgathering. "I have our baseball." He held up a large pinecone and gently knocked snow from between the woody scales. "Just need to find our bat and we'll be set for your first lesson."

She wrinkled her nose. "I should warn you that you're setting yourself up for disappointment."

"You don't give yourself enough credit, Willow."

"Perhaps you give me too much?"

"This will work," he said, grasping a long branch partially buried in dried leaves beneath the snow. Giving the protruding end a hard tug, he pulled it out, broke off the skinny top, cleared the brittle spindle branches, and ended up with a branch as long and thick as Willow's arm. "Far from perfect but suitable."

"As my performance will be, I'm sure," she said.

He met her eyes, the smile fading from his own. "This isn't about performance, Willow. It's about feeling free to do what you want to do. But if you really don't want to do this, we don't have to."

"I do," she said. "Truly, I just don't know how."

"I'll show you," he said, closing the distance between them. After creating a circle in the snow and explaining it was home base, he showed her how to hold the stick-bat, then explained how to swing. Once he'd demonstrated, he passed their makeshift bat to her, adjusted her grip, then stepped behind her. "I'll help you get the feel of the swing," he said, circling his arms around her and closing his hands over hers. "Just bring the bat back and up, and then swing through to the other side." He drew the bat up toward her right shoulder, moved through the swing, then went through the motion two more times.

Feeling his body so close behind her, and the frosty warmth of his breath caressing her cheek, made her long to turn, to face him, to sink fully into his embrace.

"All right, Willow, I'll step away while you take a few swings on your own."

Her hands shook. Her body trembled. Her heart ached as she swung her makeshift bat.

"Pivot your hips when you swing," he said, watching her with a discerning eye.

She twisted her torso as she drew back, and she let it turn with her swing. All it did was upset her balance.

He caught her arm to steady her, then stepped behind her again and tapped one booted foot against hers. "Widen your stance." When she glanced over her shoulder, he said, "It's just the two of us out here. A wider stance will make you more stable so you don't fall on your face when you swing the bat." After she slid her right foot out a few inches, he stepped away. "Now, take another swing."

She did, and felt much steadier on her feet.

"Better. I think you're ready to try to hit something."

"I know one thing I could hit without missing," she said, garnering a burst of laughter from him.

"Naw, you need a bigger challenge," he said, backstepping until he was a few feet away from her. "Just watch the ball all the way to your bat." With that, he tossed the pinecone across the distance.

Without moving, Willow watched it drop to her feet.

"You're supposed to swing the bat."

"Oh, you said to watch it, not hit it."

He retrieved the cone from near her feet. When he stood, he gazed down at her. "This time, swing your bat and try to hit it."

"Right now?" she asked innocently.

He grinned and tenderly brushed her cheek with the backside of his glove. "You are such a surprise," he said, his voice filled with so much warmth it made her lose all focus. He saved her by moving back to his designated pitcher's mound, then showed her the pinecone. "Watch the ball. Swing the bat. Hit the ball." Then, in slow motion, he tossed it toward her.

She missed it completely.

"You took your eye off the ball."

Because she couldn't take her eyes off him. Gracious, she must pull herself together, and she couldn't do that with him crowding her each time he needed to retrieve the pinecone. Picking it up, she tossed it to him.

He caught it, showed it to her, then asked if she was ready.

Inhaling and releasing a settling breath, she gave him a nod.

He tossed the pinecone. She swung her bat. She heard the tick as the stick grazed the pinecone. "I hit it," she said in surprise.

"Well, you grazed it. You'll know when you hit it."

"You are a stern taskmaster," she said, playfully throwing the pinecone at him.

With a laugh, he sidestepped and caught it. "You have a good arm, Willow. Now, let's see if we can improve your batting average."

And so it went for several minutes while he tossed the pinecone and coached her, and she corrected her swing. Then finally, *whack!*

"I did it!" she said, releasing a laugh. "I actually hit it."

"You certainly did," he said, showing her the battered pinecone he'd plucked from the snow a couple of feet behind him. "Think you can do it again?"

"I'd like to try," she said, widening her stance, bat at the ready.

"Here it comes," he said, tossing the pinecone across the plate.

She missed it by a mile. Laughing, she tossed it back to him. "Apparently, that last hit was pure luck."

"Naw, you just took your eye off the ball. Watch it all the way to the bat," he said. After giving her a moment to reset, he tossed it again.

Whack!

"See?" he said, his expression lit with pleasure. "You can do it."

Overjoyed by her success, she readied herself for his next pitch. Amid solid hits, several strikes, and much laughter they played ball, forgetting for a while that danger lurked, that they had other lives waiting for them.

Willow was seeing a softer side of Gray that captivated her. She loved his laugh, the joy in his eyes, and the patience he displayed as he taught her how to play baseball. He would be a kind and patient father. The idea of him having children, of the possibility of those children being *their* children, shook her...and warmed her aching heart. Maybe her past would be forever lost, but could her future be filled with the promise of love and a family? Of a new and wonderful life? Or was she simply imagining the connection she felt with Gray.

To distract herself from such thoughts, she dropped her bat and walked to the pitcher's mound. "It's your turn to bat," she said, slipping the battered pinecone from his gloved hands.

"Are you tired?" he asked with concern.

"Not at all. I just want to try pitching."

"All right then," he said, moving to retrieve the bat.

She waited for him to get ready, then she tossed the pinecone.

"Um, you need to toss it across the plate, or at least get it in this vicinity," he said, using the bat to create a wide circle around himself.

His teasing made her laugh. "Noted," she said. "Now toss me the ball."

On her next toss, the ragged scales of the pinecone snagged on her mitten causing her to lob the cone high over his head. He jumped and took a wild swing at the pinecone, sending her into a fit of laughter that made her eyes water. When she caught her breath, she said, "I'll do better next time."

"Good because I don't think my back will hold up trying to hit your wild pitches."

Shoulders shaking from her laughter, it was all she could do to throw the pinecone to him. But it was close enough for him to strike with his bat and blast it to bits.

Grimacing, he glanced down at the pieces of pinecone scattered across the snow. "I think I just destroyed our ball."

"That's all right, I'll just toss snowballs," she said, scooping up snow and packing it into a lopsided blob. "Ready?"

"You expect me to hit that?" he asked in mock disdain.

"You either hit the snowball or it hits you," she said, throwing it at him.

With a quick pivot, and a short swing, he hit the snow blob, smashing it to pieces. "You need to improve your aim, my dear."

"I intend to," she said with a wicked little challenge in her voice. She packed another blob of snow, then wound up and let it fly.

It hit him on the shoulder. "You just walked the batter."

"Is that a bad thing?" she asked, scooping snow and packing another snowball.

"It is if you want to win the game."

"What if I don't want to win? What if I just want to taunt the batter?" she asked, lobbing the snowball and striking his chest.

A mischievous grin tilted his lips as he dropped the bat. "That could land you in big trouble," he said, slowly stalking her.

Giggling, she thrust her hands out to stop him, but he continued to move in. She squealed and backstepped, stumbling over her clunky boots and debris hidden beneath the snow. His arms swooped around her as they fell. She felt herself being hugged, turned, and cushioned as she landed atop him.

Their laughter filled the winter forest. Snowflakes drifted down around them like musical notes, creating a song only they could hear. Their eyes met like long lost lovers, their smiles softening as their lips found each other. Slow and sensuous, she sank into the kiss, her longing taking her deeper, closer to him, and to the truth that she had fallen in love with this man. He rolled her to her back and gazed down at her in wonder as he lowered his mouth to hers again.

The forest tucked them into its bosom, suspending time as two lost souls experienced their first taste of homecoming. Like mated loons returning to their snowy nest, they came together in a flowing, graceful dive, synchronizing their breaths and the movement of their mouths. With a soft moan, she arched her neck as he trailed kisses along the curve of her throat.

A twig snapped.

Then another cracking sound sent a painful bolt of awareness through Gray. In one move, he rolled to his back and drew his pistol, methodically scanning the forest for danger. For several seconds, he watched and listened before acknowledging the cause of the disturbance was a doe partially hidden in a cluster of pines a short distance from them. But what if it hadn't been a deer? What if it had been someone intent on hurting Willow? Disgusted with himself and his lack of restraint, he holstered his pistol and lunged to his feet.

Releasing a hard sigh, he helped Willow stand, then dusted her off with one of his gloves. "That should have never happened," he said, agitated with his lack of discipline. "I'm sorry."

"I'm not," she said, gazing up at him with her sparkling eyes and beautiful smile that tempted him relentlessly. "It seems I quite like kissing you."

The kiss went far beyond liking for him, and that was dangerous because he'd lost his mind and all sense of time while kissing her. He'd forgotten his duty and crossed a line. He couldn't let it happen again. "I got caught up in our game and made a mistake. It won't happen again. We should head back to the cabin now," he said, determined to break the spell they had unwittingly woven in the wintery wilderness. "I have firewood to split."

Her expression fell and every spark of joy died in her eyes, killing him inside. "Oh," she said quietly, then turned and walked away.

When he reached for her hand, she slipped it into her coat pocket and stepped away from him. Knowing his words had wounded her tore a ragged hole in his conscience, and he hated himself for doing it.

After seeing her safely inside the cabin, he began the laborious job of splitting firewood. For two hours he swung his axe, shedding his gloves, heavy coat, and wool hat, but unable to shed the image of her lush lips and the languid look in her eyes when they'd kissed. Still, he tried with all his might to drive her from his mind, working until sweat dripped from his forehead and his breathing became ragged. When he'd split enough firewood for two weeks, he put down his axe and wiped his forehead with his handkerchief, accepting the truth that nothing could eradicate her from his thoughts.

After stacking the firewood, he gathered his discarded clothing and went inside. To his surprise, Willow had decorated her little tree with her handmade ornaments. She'd threaded red winterberries into long strands and draped them around the tree. The pieces of evergreen she'd adorned with pine cones, dried leaves, and sprigs of winterberries were hung on the limbs with various lengths of thread. She'd also made small red and green bows out of ribbon and attached them throughout the branches. He couldn't believe how she'd managed to transform that crooked piece of wood and scraggly branches into a work of art. Nor could he believe how disappointed he felt that she hadn't waited for him, that she hadn't wanted to decorate the tree together. She'd seemed so excited about it earlier...before he'd crushed her joy beneath his self-loathing.

"The tree looks nice," he said, because he had no idea how to bridge the chasm he'd created between them.

She glanced at the tree, then at him. "I left bathwater for you," she said, returning her attention to her sketch pad.

There was so much he wanted to say, but nothing that would make a difference, so he simply thanked her, gathered clean clothes, and shut himself in the bathroom.

Willow was sitting at the table working on a sketch when Gray came out of the bathroom buttoning his shirt. The sight of his wet hair sticking out in all directions, as if he'd given it a good scrub with a towel after his bath and forgot to comb it, made her laugh.

He glanced at her with a question in his eyes. "Something funny?"

"I just heard your hair's desperate cry for a comb."

A slow grin tipped his mouth. "You heard it clear over there?"

"I did."

His smile softened. "Did you also hear the apology in my head?"

She sighed and leaned back in her chair. "You don't need to apologize. You did nothing wrong. Our play just got out of hand like you said. I'm the one who should apologize."

His eyebrows shot up. "For what?"

"For being forward and putting you in an awkward position," she said, her face heating from embarrassment.

"How so?" he asked, looking utterly confused.

Her behavior in the woods had left them both feeling uncomfortable, and she couldn't allow him to think he'd overstepped when she was the responsible party. "I shouldn't have kissed you."

"You didn't," he said, then tilted his head as if suddenly rethinking the moment. "Did you?"

"I'm not sure. Maybe." She shrugged because she honestly didn't know. "Does it matter?"

"Yes," he said, "because you're under my protection and I'm duty-bound to safeguard you, even from my own bad decisions. That means no kissing the person I'm protecting."

"Then let's agree that I kissed you, and your only bad decision was not combing your hair before leaving the bathroom."

"What?" A second later, he burst out laughing. "You astound

me, Willow. Honestly, I never know what to expect from you. I thought you were angry with me for calling our kiss a mistake."

"I wasn't angry. I was hurt because I thought you didn't like kissing me."

"Ah, Willow, nothing could be farther from the truth." He slipped his hand over hers where it rested on the table. "You are beautiful and very kissable."

She laughed. "For the record, so are you." Their gazes held, but she knew better than to linger there, so she pointed at his head. "Are you going to let your hair dry like that?"

His laughter filled the cabin...and her heart...and she knew they would be all right. It wasn't that he didn't like kissing her, it was simply that he felt he couldn't. So, she would be the one to initiate any future kissing. If she dared.

It was all she could think about while they played chess, and he beat her soundly three times.

"I sense your mind is elsewhere tonight," he said, gesturing to where her king lay toppled in defeat on the board.

"I was just contemplating why baseball is much more enjoyable than chess," she said, leaning back in the cushioned chair to indicate she was through playing for the evening. "Do you think we can try another ballgame on our next walk?"

"That depends. Do you think you can play without kissing me?"

Her jaw fell open and she stared at him. Of all the words to come out of his mouth, those were so unexpected and playful it completely unraveled her. Her mouth moved but the only sound to come out was a burble of laughter.

A mischievous grin tipped his lips. "Did I shock you?"

"Most definitely," she said, matching his smile with her own. "But I'm glad we can make light of our little...mishap."

Warmth filled his gaze. "Me, too." He stepped away from the

low table where they'd placed the gameboard. "I need to fill the stove and make some notes in my journal before bed."

"And you need to comb your hair," she added with a grin. He'd finger-combed it earlier, leaving it wonderfully messy, allowing her a glimpse of what he might have looked like as a devil-may-care youngster. How this man was still a bachelor was as big a mystery as her identity.

He gazed down at her with delight in his eyes. "This was a good day. Thank you for brightening our home with your little tree and your remarkable sense of humor." Then, with a playful wink, he left her to her thoughts about him, her life, and the possibility of experiencing another *mishap* with him.

CHAPTER FOURTEEN

At the end of his fourth week of investigation at the paper mill, Gray had determined that Milton Fitch was simply a nervous man who worked too hard and worried too much. So Gray had focused on Philo Holbrook and Silas Wade, creating multiple occasions to interact with each man and further study their behavior.

Philo appeared indifferent to Gray's probing questions and seemed to answer by rote with no emotion or apparent concern no matter how intrusive the question. In all Gray's travels and undercover operations, he'd never come across such a person. Was the man just an empty carcass, devoid of any emotion whatsoever, or was he a stone-cold killer?

Silas, on the other hand, seemed to exist in a constant state of agitation. Scuff-stepping his squat, barrel-like body through the plant, he barked orders at the workers, and ducked in and out of sight each time he spotted Gray heading his way. Undeterred, Gray had tracked him down relentlessly throughout the week, often finding him at the loading docks where reels of newsprint were being loaded on wagons to be taken to the railyard. But when Gray discovered Philo Holbrook was making one of those deliveries each week, he knew he'd stumbled upon something odd, and likely the area where company profits were being stolen.

Hoping to avoid both men, Gray came back on Saturday morning in search of evidence.

Oddly enough, when he started digging through the crates of paperwork in the inventory office where Sophia had worked, Silas showed up. The man was intent on driving him out of the office, claiming Gray had no authority to stick his nose into private mill business. Gray patiently explained that he was hired to interview their employees, inspect their production process, and investigate ways to improve mill profitability. That gave him latitude in all departments.

As if Silas realized his blustering and bullying would get him nowhere, he came back after lunch and changed tactics, trying to oust Gray from the office by suggesting they grab a beer at the Pine Ridge Tavern a few blocks from the plant.

It was Christmas Eve, and Gray had planned to head home early to take a walk with Willow. Unfortunately, his job had to come first, and Silas had just given him a perfect opportunity to casually interrogate him in a setting conducive to drunken revelations. Gray had pried loose many secrets in taverns across the country.

Leaning back in his chair, he stretched and released a loud yawn. "A mug of ale sounds good after sorting papers all morning." Getting to his feet, he said, "If Philo is still here, ask him to join us," Gray suggested, clapping a hand over Silas's meaty shoulder as he nudged him out the door. "I need to use the toilet first, so I'll meet you out front in a few minutes."

Silas seemed almost relieved by the suggestion, and headed toward the loading dock area without a backward glance. That gave Gray the time he needed to instruct the stock boy to have all the crates of papers, along with all the ledgers in the office, delivered to the general store in his name. It's where he'd been getting his mail, and Lola Gorman would hold the crates for him, along with another package already at the store waiting for him to pick up. The store was also where Ben dropped Gray off and picked him up each day, so Gray could load the crates into Ben's wagon and take them home with him today before Philo or Silas thought to destroy whatever evidence might be buried in them.

After assuring himself that the boy understood his instructions were to be carried out immediately, Gray headed out front and arrived just before Silas and Philo appeared.

During their walk to the tavern, neither of the men were talkative, but Gray had plenty of practice coaxing conversation from criminals who had something to hide. So he kept the subject light, spinning a couple of yarns about a farmer and his daughter that made Silas snort and got no reaction from Philo. Inside the small, dark tavern, as they settled at the bar, Gray continued talking about his past, all of it fabricated for the occasion. Silas sat with his elbows on the bar, his thick shoulders tense and hunched up around his ears, but as they finished their second mug, he seemed keenly interested in Gray's yarn about being on a train that was robbed. The truth was Gray had investigated the robbery and helped catch the criminals, but he didn't share any of that with Silas or Philo.

"Do either of you have plans for the holiday?" he forced himself to ask, fishing for personal information.

"This is my plan," Silas said, nodding toward his mug of ale. Philo gave a slight shake of his head.

"No wife waiting at home for you, then?" Gray asked.

Silas shook his head, then glanced at Gray. "You married?"

"Only to my job," he said, forcing a grin.

Silas grunted and bobbed his big head as if their bachelor status bonded them in some way.

By the time they ordered their fourth mug, Gray had hit his stride. Although Philo's bland expression remained fixed, and he stood with one elbow on the bar, he seemed to be listening to their conversation. Silas's relaxed manner indicated the alcohol was working and he was engaged in Gray's storytelling. The man sat with his back against the bar, legs splayed out, and his right hand sunk in his vest pocket. Every couple of seconds, the fabric of his vest pocket would pop out as if he were flicking his thumb against it.

Gray exchanged a glance with Philo, who seemed to notice it, too.

"Still haven't found your watch, then?" Philo asked, his monotone suggesting he couldn't care less one way or the other.

But Gray cared. Intensely. Because Silas had lost his *watch*. A pocket watch. A watch everyone had noticed because he'd carried it in his hand, flicking it open and snapping it closed while he walked through the plant terrorizing the workers. And when he'd lost that watch, they'd noticed that too because he continued to reach for it, continued his habit of flicking it open and closed, continued to be agitated by its absence. Gray would bet his life it was the same watch he'd found where Sophia had been beaten and left for dead.

"Give me another one," Silas told the bartender, turning to face the bar.

All of the man's peculiar quirks Gray had noted over the course of his investigation settled into place, creating a horrifying story.

Silas had assaulted Sophia.

That big brute had swung his fist into Sophia's beautiful face and wrapped his thick fingers around her slender throat, intent on choking the life from the most perfect person Gray had ever known.

Rage detonated inside him like a blast in a coal mine, shaking his bones, obscuring his vision. He gripped the bar to stop his hands from reaching for Silas's thick throat—the throat that had carried two red marks when they'd first met. Had those scratches come from Sophia's fingernails when she'd fought for her life?

Gut roiling and fists clenched, Gray struggled to breathe, to gain control, to hold back the torrent he wanted to unleash on Silas Wade. He ached to make Wade experience what he'd done to Sophia, to make the wretch beg for his life, but that would only land Gray behind bars where Wade deserved to be.

It wasn't the first time in his undercover work Gray had to tamp down his emotions to finish a job, but this was the most intense battle he'd ever waged to pull himself together and not blow his cover or the operation. To put the thieving beast in a cage where he belonged, Gray needed to find real evidence, and that meant he must find the resolve to interrogate Silas rather than throttle the man.

Taking a deep drink of his ale, then releasing a slow, measured breath, Gray focused on his job. He had to do his job. For Willow's sake.

But it was simply beyond his ability at the moment. Releasing a hard breath to relieve the pressure in his chest, he set his mug on the bar. "I've got to head home," he said, needing to leave.

"What's the rush?" Silas asked, but didn't seem to care if Gray stayed or left, only to know where Gray was going.

Shoving his hands into his pockets to keep from reaching for Silas's thick throat, Gray said, "I've been invited to supper at a friend's house and I'd best not be late." With that, he pushed himself away from the bar, and left the tavern before his rage exploded in a violent blast that would bring down the whole place.

WHEN GRAY ARRIVED HOME, Willow noticed he seemed tense and distracted. She watched him carry in several crates filled with papers and leather books, and a couple other of crates holding canned goods and other household staples. On his last trip, he brought in a smaller sealed crate he asked her not to open, and two wrapped packages, one emitting the aroma of baked chicken, and the other the lovely scent of cinnamon.

As soon as he placed the packages on the table, she leaned down and sniffed. "Smells like this might be our supper," she said, her stomach growling in anticipation. "And this is a package of cinnamon buns?"

The frown he'd been wearing slipped away. "Yes, and I purchased a dozen of them for you," he replied, apparently pleased by her obvious delight.

"These will certainly brighten our holiday," she said. "Do you have time for one now?" she asked, gesturing to the package of baked goods.

"I need to put these things away first, but it will only take a few minutes."

"While you do that, I'll brew some tea," she said, and set about doing just that.

Twenty minutes later, Gray had stored the items, and she had made the tea. As she placed two cups on the table, she glanced at the crates of papers he'd moved to a corner near the table. "What's all that?" she asked, taking a seat.

"Papers from the mill that I need to sort through," he said, taking a seat at the table where she'd set a plate for him.

"Maybe I can help," she said, unwrapping the cinnamon buns. "I'd love to have something to do."

For a moment, he seemed to consider her offer, studying her as if mentally weighing a problem, then gave a small nod. "All right. We can sort through them together."

She couldn't stop her smile. The thought of having something interesting to occupy her mind was a relief. And it elicited her curiosity. "What are the papers for?"

"They're documents from the inventory department at the paper mill. Purchase orders, receipts for goods and materials from suppliers, stock requisition forms and transfer sheets, and other documents used to manage the inventory. I need to compare those documents to the ledgers to see if anything was missed or overlooked."

"Do you think there's a problem?" she asked, intrigued by the potential mystery.

Sighing, he settled back on his chair. "Unfortunately, I do. But I can't make an accusation without proof to back it up, so that's why I need to sort through that mountain of papers." By the scowl on his face, it was the last thing he wanted to do.

"If you show me what to do, I can look through the papers while you're at the mill."

He shook his head. "I don't want you looking at them when I'm not here."

"Why not?" she asked, baffled by his response.

"Because it might—you might—miss something."

"Not if you're clear about what you want me to look for. I'll be very careful."

He slipped his hand over hers. "I know you will, but there's a reason we need to go through those things together."

"All right," she said, drawing her hand away. "We have some time before supper if you want to start now." When he hesitated, she added, "It sounds as if you need this done quickly. The sooner we start, the sooner we finish."

"You make a valid point," he said, getting to his feet. "If you'll clear the table, I'll get the ledgers."

While she moved the packages and their plates to the kitchen counter and poured them a second cup of tea, he piled several stacks of papers and four thick ledgers on the table. There had to be hundreds of documents in just those few stacks, and suddenly, she could understand how he might feel daunted by the task of sorting through them. But she felt a thrum of excitement at having something productive to do, a task that might help Gray in his work, and one they could do together.

They worked in tandem with her giving him numbers, dates, and amounts for receipts, requisition sheets, purchase orders, and other documents, and Gray confirming the entry was made correctly in one of the ledgers. The documents he couldn't confirm were placed in a separate pile. But after two hours, they'd barely made a dent in the mess of papers on the table.

With a groan, he leaned back in his chair. "This is going to take weeks to accomplish without more help."

"It won't if you let me work through these documents while you're at the mill."

"No, Willow." Pushing to his feet, he glanced at her, a glint of hardness in his eyes she'd never before seen. "I need to go out for a bit. Leave the papers in the crate, and I'll be back shortly."

"All right, but must you go out on Christmas Eve?"

"There's a man I need to see. I won't be long. If you put the potatoes on to boil, we can have supper when I get back." Crossing the room, he pulled on his coat and hat, then checked his revolver before putting it back on the shelf for her use should she need it. "I'll return soon," he said, opening the door. "Lock up behind me."

With that, he was gone, and Willow stood a little stunned at his abrupt departure. Then she heard him call through the door.

"Willow, lock the door!"

Hurrying to do so, she threw the bolt and was rewarded with a solid clunk.

"Are you still by the door?"

She laughed a little. "Yes, and apparently so are you."

He laughed too. "I have a surprise for you when I get back."

"I'm intrigued," she said. "Maybe you should stay and give it to me now."

He laughed again. "I won't be long," he said.

She listened for a moment and heard nothing, so she hurried to the bathroom and peered out the small window. He was already on the road heading toward town at a jog. Questions about who he was going to see and for what purpose circled her thoughts as she peeled potatoes and put them on the stove to cook.

When she returned to the table, her tea was cold, but she sat with the cup in her hands to stop herself from rifling through the papers. Gray had asked her not to look at them without him. But why? What harm could come from such a mundane task as sorting and comparing documents to ledgers? It made no sense to her, but she had agreed to his request and would honor her promise.

Moving to the kitchen, she dumped her tea in the sink, checked the pot of potatoes that had begun to boil, then unwrapped the baked chicken, put it in a roasting pan, and slipped it into the oven to heat.

After setting the table, she freshened up in the bathroom and braided her hair. She was reading near the woodstove when she heard Gray call out and his key turn the lock, signaling his return.

GRAY FELT MUCH LIGHTER when he returned to the cabin. Knowing he'd picked the right man for the job of ferreting out anomalies in the inventory ledgers, and that the man could work fast, lifted a weight off Gray's shoulders. As soon as he had the evidence he needed to put Silas Wade in prison, Gray would hunt down the wretch and drag him there himself. Until that proof was in Gray's hands, however, he needed to bank his fury and wait. The only way to keep his mind off Wade was to focus on Willow. So, after they'd eaten their supper, he asked if she would like to open the gift he'd gotten her.

Surprise lit her eyes and arched her dark eyebrows. "A gift? For me?"

He smiled, pleased by her surprise. "Care to guess what's in the crate?" he asked, gesturing to the wooden box on the floor.

"I haven't a clue," she said with a laugh. When he pulled the package from the crate and set it on the table, she said, "I still haven't a clue what it is."

"You'll know when you unwrap it," he said, enjoying the anticipation on her face as she pulled away the paper.

"What a gorgeous box," she said, but he quickly realized she didn't understand what she was looking at.

"It's a music box," he said, lifting the intricately carved wooden top to reveal a large metal disc with tiny rectangular holes punched in it. "The holes in this metal disc engage with the teeth of a gear. This thing here is a musical comb," he explained, pointing out the long, cylindrical arm extending from the center of the disc to the edge of the box. "It has tiny metal tines that are plucked by those punched holes and it makes the music."

"Does it work?" she asked.

"Of course," he said with a laugh. "Just gently wind the hand crank on the side of the box, and the music will play."

Tentatively, she gave the handle a rotation. The disc made a quarter turn, creating a few notes before stalling.

"Maybe wind it a bit more," he suggested.

She gave the hand crank six full rotations, then stood with mouth agape as the sound of a hundred tiny bells ringing in song filled the cabin like twinkling stars in a night sky. It was a joyful sound that brought tears to her eyes. Appearing enthralled, she didn't say a word until the last tinkling note played and the disc stopped rotating. "I've never heard such a beautiful sound in my life," she whispered.

He had. It was the sound of her laughter.

She wound the hand crank and listened again until every last note and resonating vibration had ceased, then she threw her arms around his neck and kissed his cheek. "Thank you," she whispered, then eased back to meet his eyes. "The music box is beautiful, and the thought behind your gift has filled my heart to overflowing. But it's too much, Gray. This is an heirloom gift you give to the woman you love."

"There's no other woman in my life, Willow."

"Then perhaps you should save the music box until there is," she said. "After everything you've done for me, I can't deny you the pleasure of giving this beautiful gift to the woman who becomes your wife. It would make a magnificent engagement gift."

"Perhaps, but I'm giving it to you."

"Gray, I encourage you to reconsider. This is too special to be given to just anyone."

"You're not just anyone, Willow, and the music box isn't special to me. I received it from the owner of a mining company that had its payroll stolen. I tracked down the robbers and returned the payroll to the owner of the mining company, who was so grateful he insisted I accept the exorbitantly expensive music box in addition to my pay." It was a treasure Gray hadn't been able to fully appreciate until now. Seeing the amazement and joy in Willow's eyes made him glad to give it to her. "I have no use for it, and it pleases me deeply to give it to you."

"I really shouldn't accept this, but it's so beautiful I'm not sure I can resist," she said softly.

"Then don't." Reaching for the hand crank on the box, he gave it a few easy turns. The sound of musical, tinkling bells filled the cabin and brought a wide smile to her beautiful face. "Dance with me," he said.

She laughed and executed a playful twirl. "This is perfect for a waltz,' she said, beginning the steps.

"You remember how to waltz and the name of the dance. That's good," he said, wondering if any of her other memories were returning.

"Apparently, I do." Gracing him with a wide smile, she dipped a curtsey. "I believe you asked for a dance, sir?"

"I did, but I should warn you that I might step on your toes."

"Not to worry. I'm wearing your thick socks."

Laughter rolled up from his belly as he reached for her hand. "On three?" he asked, moving his free hand to her waist. At her nod, he counted, "One-two-three, one-two-three," and off they went, waltzing between the table and chairs, bumping against the edge of the bed, taking a thrilling twirl through the bathroom and back out again, their laughter a joyful companion to the music. Stopping only long enough to wind the music box, they danced until they were breathless with exertion, with laughter, with joy.

"This music makes me feel as if I'm floating," she exclaimed.

"You're light as dandelion fluff," he said, pulling her closer, knowing he shouldn't. But this woman, with her pain, her humor, her tenderness, and strength, had removed his armor piece by piece. Now he was unarmed and vulnerable, his heart wrenched open like a plundered treasure chest. But she hadn't taken anything from him. She was filling his life with treasures, her smile, her laughter, moments that carried him away and made him forget, made him feel, deeply and passionately. She made him care, made him want *more*.

"Thank you," she whispered, gazing into his eyes. "You've brought music to my life and filled my empty world with sunlight and laughter. I don't want the music to end."

He knew she wasn't talking about the music box. She was talking about them. "Maybe it doesn't have to." The words were out of his mouth before he could wrestle them into submission, because his heart refused to be silenced by duty another minute.

"Do you think it's possible?" she asked softly. "For the two of us to keep playing our song when you no longer have to be my protector?"

"I'll always protect you," he said, knowing he would always lay his life on the line for her.

"But someday, it won't be your job. You'll just be a man I met on a walk one day."

The idea of it made him smile. "And you'll just be a lovely lady who caught my eye, and I can court you properly."

"I would like that very much."

As their breathing settled, their bodies moved closer. With her face tilted up, he simply lowered his mouth to hers. He couldn't stop himself. Couldn't deny the truth any longer. He'd fallen in love with her.

He held her against his chest, his heart beating for her and for the life they were dreaming of. He'd never considered the possibility of love, of a family of his own. But he was holding that dream in his arms, and she was real. As he gazed into her eyes, he wondered if such a life was possible for him, or if it was a wishful fantasy of a lost man.

"I have a gift for you, too," she said, slipping from his embrace. She knelt down and searched under the bed, then pulled out what appeared to be a booklet bound with ribbon on one side. "This is for you," she said, placing it in his hands.

Intrigued, he opened the booklet to find pages filled with Willow's sketches. They were intricate, beautiful sketches of the wildlife they'd encountered on their walks. She'd sketched deer grazing on twigs in the forest and lying on the stream bank, an owl peering from the cavity of an aging sycamore, a pileated woodpecker excavating bark from a dead spruce, a fox with its white chest, black legs, and white-tipped tail, trotting across a snowy field, and a fluffy cottontail nibbling bark from a birch tree. Willow had captured moments between the two of them, too. She'd sketched them playing chess, his fingers positioned on a pawn, creases between his eyebrows as if contemplating the move. She'd sketched them lying in the snowy forest making snow-angels like children, and playing baseball with a battered pinecone and a crooked stick, their shared joy evident in their expressions. This was their story, and she'd captured it in lifelike sketches.

Moved beyond words, he knew no matter how many years he lived, this would be the most beautiful gift he would ever receive.

"Willow, this is..." He shook his head, struggling to find words.

"You deserve more," she said, "but it's all I have to give."

He cupped her face. "This is a treasure. This is a gift you give to the man you love."

"Then I've given it to the right person," she whispered, stunning him, thrilling him, terrifying him. "You don't have to say anything," she said with a little laugh. "I know we can't have this conversation until your job is finished." Placing her palm against his cheek, she whispered, "I hope it's soon."

Then she walked away, preventing him from making confessions and promises he wasn't at liberty to make. Not yet. But when that day came, when he finally shed the shackles of his job, he would tell her everything. And if she could forgive him, he would promise her the world.

CHAPTER FIFTEEN

After a breakfast of hot coffee, fried potatoes, and warm cinnamon buns, Willow took a leisurely bath. When she came out, she was surprised to see that Gray had packed the papers and ledgers back into the crates.

"I thought we were going to work through some of those today," she said, feeling a little disappointed.

"I've asked someone else to handle this task," he said. "In fact, he'll be here in a few minutes to pick up the crates." Sighing, he finger-combed his hair back, a habit she'd noted when something weighed on his mind. "I'd planned to put the crates outside, but it's snowing. These documents can't get ruined, so I'll have to keep them inside until he arrives."

"I don't mind," she said, not understanding why it should upset him.

"I don't want him to know you're here," he said. "You'll need to stay in the bathroom while we take the crates out."

"Won't they get wet in his wagon?" she asked.

"He's borrowing a wagon from the mill. They all have tarps in them. I just don't have one here to protect the papers until he gets here."

"All right. I'll stay in the bathroom," she said, "but I wish you would have just let me sort through the papers. I enjoyed it."

"It's a job I need done immediately and privately."

"I could have done that," she said, not understanding his resistance.

"Not without me here," he replied, with a finality that put an end to their discussion.

Feeling a chill in the air, she went to the woodstove to stoke the fire. She'd just closed the door when a light knock at the door startled her.

"He's here," Gray whispered, jerking his chin toward the bathroom.

Poker in hand, she moved quietly across the room and slipped into the bathroom. But she didn't close and lock the door as Gray had instructed. She left a small gap, hoping to see the mystery man.

She heard Gray's footsteps on the wood plank flooring, then the sound of the lock being turned. A second later, a loud bang sounded along with a hard grunt, followed by scuffling feet and thudding bodies moving deeper into the room.

"Where is she?" a man bellowed.

That voice....

Fear punched through her like ice water bursting through a dam. She remembered the feel of a man's hard knuckles slamming into her face, the swirling blackness that sucked her down, the grip of his fingers as they closed like a vice around her throat. Moments of her life flashed in her head like fireworks—pain, fear, desperation as she fought to survive, the futile effort and slow slipping away even as she fought to hang on, then the resigned surrender. She remembered everything...

She was Sophia Flynn, and she'd been attacked by...*him*. Silas Wade. Her boss.

The crack of pistol fire snapped her head up as if he'd struck her in the face. But the man was attacking Gray who'd rescued her, nursed her back to health, who was risking his life to protect her even now.

Outraged, she gripped the iron poker in her hand and rushed to Gray's defense. Silas raised his arm to block the iron rod she swung at him. It struck his forearm with a hard thud, and he howled in pain and outrage. Splinting his arm against his side, he aimed his revolver at her and warned Gray not to take another step. "I'll shoot her," he said between clenched teeth. "You know I will."

Blood dribbled from Gray's mouth, and horror filled his eyes as he looked at her. "Why did you come out?" he asked.

"Because I recognized his voice and knew why he'd come here. I'm not leaving you alone with this beast," she said, trying to hide the poker behind her.

"Drop it, Miss Flynn, or that poker will be the last thing you touch." She had no doubt he would pull the trigger and end her life, so she released her grip. The sound of iron clanking on the floorboards seemed to satisfy him. "Get over here."

Before she could obey, Gray pulled her behind him. "Touch her, and I'll kill you."

Silas scoffed. "I'll shoot you dead before you take two steps."

"What do you want?" Gray demanded.

"Miss Flynn, of course."

"You'll have to go through me first," Gray said, and she knew this brave, beautiful man was about to sacrifice his life for her.

"I have your watch!" she blurted, desperately seeking a way to distract Wade. "It's your pocket watch. I found it where you...left me in the woods."

"Get it," he snapped.

Gray caught her arm to keep her behind him.

Silas pulled the trigger with a resounding crack, and stuffing exploded from the chair just inches from Gray's legs. "Next one will hit its mark. Now, get the watch!" Silas snapped.

She knew Wade would kill them. Either way, he wouldn't leave without making sure they were dead. She had to do something, anything to distract him. Giving Gray a small shove from behind that rocked him forward, she darted away before he could grab her arm and stop her. Hurrying to the desk, she rifled through the drawer until she found the pocket watch with the broken chain. As she slipped her hand around the cold metal, an idea came to her.

Turning, she took a couple of steps and stopped by the table. "I'm not getting within ten feet of you," she said to Silas. Then, glancing at Gray, praying he would understand her silent message, she said, "I'll toss it to you on the count of three."

"Bring it over here!" Silas snapped.

"One," she said, glancing at Gray who gave her a slight nod.

Silas growled low in his throat, letting her know he was out of patience. "Bring the watch to me right now, Miss Flynn."

"Two," she said, ignoring his command. This was it. "Three!" She threw the watch over Silas's head, forcing him to look up.

It was the distraction they needed, and Gray didn't waste a second. He drove his athletic body into Silas's round torso, propelling him into the door, forcing a hard grunt from Silas as his head bounced off the oak panels. The men crashed to the floor, and Silas howled with outrage and pain, bucking and twisting to free himself, trying to angle his pistol toward Gray who wrenched Silas's injured arm behind his back.

She stepped on Silas's hand to lock the pistol against the floor. When he tried to yank it free, she shifted her weight and heard his knuckles crack. As he cussed and vowed to kill her, she knelt on his forearm and wrenched the weapon from his hand, which was no easy feat while trying to keep the muzzle aimed away from them. After passing the pistol to Gray, she pushed to her feet and stepped away.

"There are handcuffs in my duffel bag under the bed," Gray told her, controlling Silas with one knee planted on the man's back and the pistol pressed to the base of his skull.

Even with what looked like a broken forearm and a gun against his head, Wade continued to struggle.

While she rifled through the duffle bag for the cuffs, Gray fought to control Wade who was growling, cursing, and thrashing, kicking his boots against the door. When she found the cuffs, it took both of them to control Silas long enough to cuff him.

Wade kicked and fought to get to his feet. Another tussle ensued, and after getting kicked a second time, Gray backhanded Wade's mottled face and grabbed a fistful of the man's shirt. He gave him a hard shake. "Kick me again, and I'll shoot you in your black heart. Believe me, Wade, it's taking every bit of my restraint not to kill you. If you kick me again, I'll do it."

The fury blazing from Gray's eyes seemed to convince Wade to stop struggling. Taking advantage of the momentary pause, she pulled the laces open on one of Wade's boots and yanked it off his foot. He started to struggle, then stopped abruptly as if he knew Gray was at the edge of his tolerance. She stripped the other boot, then pulled the laces from them.

Gray tied Wade's ankles with the laces, but she could see they wouldn't contain the man's strong thrashing legs. Without restraints, it was going to be a battle to prevent him from running, especially when Gray went for help.

That's when she remembered her leftover spools of ribbon. Pushing to her feet, she tossed Wade's boots outside as far as she could throw them, then fetched her ribbon. Seeing what she was about to do, Gray pressed the revolver to Wade's temple. "Move one inch or hurt her in any way, and it will be the last thing you do."

The man laughed. "You think shoelaces and some pretty ribbon can hold me?"

"Not for long," Gray said, "but a revolver and a man willing to use it can."

Despite Wade's growl and murderous glare, he didn't move.

Weaving the cheerful red and green ribbon in a figure eight around his ankles, Willow continued until she'd used every inch of ribbon, wrapping it as tightly as he'd wrapped his brutal fingers around her neck. When she finished, she looked at Gray. "How are you going to deliver this Christmas package to the police?"

He glanced at his watch. "In a wagon that will arrive any minute."

"The devil you are," Wade said, tucking his legs and rolling to his knees as if preparing to bolt.

Gray reached down and hauled Wade to his feet. "You want to wait outside? Fine with me." With that, he gave Wade a shove that sent him hopping out the door. Before Gray followed Wade outside, he swept her into a hard hug and pressed a kiss to her forehead. "Stay inside and lock the door."

Knowing a debate would only distract him, she closed and bolted the door behind him. Alone, she melted against the door, remembering everything that man had done to her.

Wade was her boss, the man in charge, the man who was supposed to protect the assets of the mill and the people who worked there. Instead, he stole company property, terrorized the workers, and attempted to kill her when she discovered his theft. Staring into his black eyes today had left no doubt of his intent and that he would have gladly killed Gray had they not outsmarted the beast.

A hard thump outside followed by the clunking sound of a woodpile falling over startled her. If Silas had freed his legs, he might hurt Gray, or run off and disappear in the forest.

Grabbing the pistol from the corner shelf, she checked the

chamber to make sure it was loaded and ready to fire, then opened the door.

To her surprise, Silas was still tied hand and foot, and was lying in the snow, groaning beneath a pile of firewood.

Gray was standing a few feet away shaking his head in disgust. "I warned you to stop kicking the woodpile," he said to Wade. "You are a fool of immense proportions."

"I'm freezing and need a doctor," Silas bellowed, anger mottling his ruddy complexion.

The man was wearing a heavy coat, and Willow knew whatever injury he'd sustained in their scuffle wasn't life threatening. It could wait to be treated until after he was in police custody.

"You did this!" he hissed, glaring at her.

"If you believe your predicament is my fault, you're not only a murderous crook, you're also an insane one. I have no sympathy for you, Mr. Wade. You've brought all of this on yourself," she said, meeting his angry stare without flinching.

"I agree with her," Gray said, reaching down to lift a thick piece of firewood off Silas's bound legs.

The wretch glared at her. "I should have buried you in the woods where I dumped your body."

"Well, Mr. Wade, it appears you've buried yourself instead," she said, allowing herself a bit of satisfaction to see the tyrant on his back. Then, she stepped inside and closed the door, unable to hear another word without cramming her boot heel in his foul mouth.

A few minutes later, she heard the rattle of a wagon pulling up out front. When she opened the door, she saw Milton Fitch sitting on the wagon seat, reins in hand, eyes wide as he took in the scene.

Feeling as stunned as he appeared to be, she glanced at Gray. "This is the man you went to see last night?"

"Yes. I asked him to come by this morning for the papers. I

suspect he's a little shocked to find his boss trussed like a holiday turkey. You'll need to come with us. It'll be a cold ride, so bring a heavy blanket and the pocket watch with you."

She wanted to tell him that her name was Sophia, but he was already striding briskly to the wagon.

Rushing inside, she dressed quickly and tucked the watch in her pocket. Then, she hurried outside to the wagon and handed Gray his heavy coat, hat, and gloves. After he'd pulled them on, he helped her onto the seat and tucked her in beside a man she'd seen at the plant but had never spoken to. Then Gray hopped into the back of the wagon where he'd dumped Wade, who was cussing and struggling and threatening all of them.

At Gray's command, Milton Fitch got the team underway. He glanced over at her, gave her a nervous head-bob as a greeting, and didn't say a single word all the way to town.

NEARLY THIRTY MINUTES LATER, Gray knocked on Officer Kline's door. He apologized for disturbing him and his family on a holiday, but as soon as Kline learned the reason for their visit, and that it was Silas Wade trussed up in the back of the wagon, he pulled on his boots and coat.

"No need to apologize," Kline said, closing the door behind him. "Putting that brute behind bars will be a gift for the whole town." He glanced at Gray. "My brother said things have improved since you've been at the mill."

"Not enough, I'm afraid," Gray replied as both men climbed into the back of the wagon where Silas Wade sat glaring at them. It seemed Wade had run out of steam, and judging by the grimace on his face, he was feeling a good bit of pain from his injured arm. Gray couldn't work up a single ounce of sympathy for the man, and it appeared Officer Kline was of the same mind.

They arrived at the police station a couple of minutes later. Officer Kline warned Wade of dire consequences should he give him any trouble, then he cut the bonds from around Wade's ankles and escorted him straight into a jail cell. After sending Milton Fitch for the doctor and to fetch Sophia's parents, Officer Kline listened to Sophia's story about discovering missing inventory.

"When I found Mr. Wade alone in the shipping bay, I shared my concerns with him," she said, continuing with a somber expression. "I thought he would be pleased with my discovery and eager to find the culprit, but he...he grabbed my arms and slammed me against the wall," she said with raised eyebrows, as if the man's unexpected reaction still surprised her. "He said if I told anyone about it, he would slit my throat."

"What did you do then?" Officer Kline asked.

"I screamed." For a moment, she seemed to be searching for words. "I knew by the look on his face that he meant every word. I tried to free myself, but he struck my head with his fist. The over-head lights exploded and my vision filled with shards of sparkling glass. Then he hit me again, and the world tipped on its side, then everything went black."

Gray clenched his fists, knowing there was more to come, dreading that Sophia was forced to relive the assault.

"I remember waking up feeling painfully cold," she said, continuing in a monotone voice, as if seeing the assault play out in her mind. "My teeth were chattering and there was a loud ringing in my left ear. It felt as if the whole world rocked beneath me. It nauseated me. I braced my hands beside me and realized I was lying under a tarp on something hard. It took a moment to understand I was in a wagon that was moving...and another moment to realize I'd been put there by Mr. Wade."

When she paused and drew a trembling breath, Gray stroked her shoulder. He couldn't help himself.

"What happened then, Miss Flynn?" Officer Kline asked quietly.

"I tried to crawl out of the wagon, but..." Her mouth quivered slightly and she seemed to be struggling for words. "Mr. Wade saw me trying to escape." She looked at Officer Kline. "He stopped the wagon and threw me on the ground. When I tried to get up, he kicked me in the side. Then he put his hands around my throat, and...I knew he was going to kill me." As her gaze drifted into the distance, her eyes dulled. "I fought, but he was so strong." Her voice dwindled to a whisper. "I could smell ink on his clothing and ale on his breath. His fingers tightened around my throat, and I remember every second of that last moment. I couldn't scream. I couldn't breathe. Intense pressure and white stars burst behind my eyes, and pain...so much pain." She gulped a breath as if feeling Wade's thick hands around her throat. "The lights dimmed then, and I...I finally surrendered to the inevitable."

Tears brimmed in her eyes, and Gray wondered how she could possibly hold herself together when he was struggling to hold back his own tears.

"I don't remember anything else until I woke up in the cabin," she whispered, her voice quaking with emotion.

As the officer sat looking stunned and horrified, Gray stroked Sophia's back, as much for his own comfort as hers.

After a moment of choking down his emotions, he provided his part of the story, stating he'd documented everything in a journal and with his camera, from when and where he'd found Sophia to a description of her injuries and any evidence he'd collected. He ran down Silas's attack that morning, then had Sophia give the pocket watch to the officer.

"Now, that's poetic justice," Kline said. "I've heard far too many stories about this watch and the man who carried it." Suddenly, Kline looked at Gray as if remembering something important. "Miss Flynn has been with you this whole time?"

"She has."

A scowl creased Kline's forehead. "Then you lied to me when I asked if you'd seen Miss Flynn."

"Actually, I countered with a question to intentionally distract you. I'm sorry about that, Officer Kline, but Miss Flynn was under my protection. The only way to ensure her safety was to keep her whereabouts unknown until I discovered who assaulted her and had proof to put him behind bars."

"You needed to keep that from an officer of the law?" Kline asked, appearing a bit offended.

"You know as well as I that not all lawmen are law abiding or trustworthy," Gray said. "I did what needed to be done to protect Sophia."

With a slow nod, Kline seemed to accept Gray's justification. "I understand, but your decision may do more damage to Miss Flynn. There's sure to be gossip about her spending weeks in a cabin alone with you."

The startled expression on Sophia's face changed to one of mortification, and he could see that, until that moment, social mores hadn't entered her thoughts any more than they had his own. She'd been focused on healing and regaining her memory. And he'd been so focused on keeping her safe, he hadn't considered the consequences she might suffer because of his decisions.

"You and Milton Fitch are the only ones who know she was at the cabin with me," he said to Kline. "I'm sure you can convince Mr. Fitch to keep that information to himself."

"I could do that," Officer Kline said, leaning back in his chair. "But the truth will come out in Mr. Wade's trial. You know as well as I do that you can't change your story without compromising the evidence and Wade's trial."

Before Gray could comment, or assure Sophia that he would take any necessary steps to protect her, the door opened and a middle-aged man wearing a dark wool overcoat and black derby dusted with snow stepped inside. Medical bag in hand, he strode into the room and asked Officer Kline to direct him to the patient.

"I'll need to stay with the doctor while he examines Wade," Kline said, pushing to his feet. "I'll return when he's finished."

After the two men disappeared, Gray looked at Sophia whose gaze seemed fixed in the distance, as if her thoughts were far away. "Don't worry. This will all work out," he said, slipping his hand over hers where it rested on her lap. Her hand trembled, and she didn't respond. He gave her arm a light jiggle and called her name.

———

As THE OFFICER's words sank in, Sophia looked at Gray as if he were a stranger. "Is it true?" she asked, silently begging him to deny it. "Did you know my identity the entire time I was with you?"

"I'm sorry," he said, giving her arm a light squeeze.

But all she felt was a sinking feeling, as if everything inside her was dissolving and dropping away. To realize he'd known the truth while she was pouring her heart out during their talks, and on their walks, and when they found her lost shoe and the watch, and he'd let her anguish knowing how painfully desperate she felt to know her name and what happened to her. He'd even withheld the truth during the moments he'd held her and kissed her...when he'd let her believe he cared about her. The pain of his betrayal took her breath away.

"I believed you were trying to find out what happened to me, and yet the whole time you were lying to me," she said with a sad laugh. "You must have thought me a blind fool."

"Never," he said, reaching for her hand.

Lunging to her feet, she backed away, unable to bear his touch. "How could you keep the truth from me? You were right there, Gray. You saw how lost I was, yet you withheld the one thing that would have given me some comfort."

"Sophia...knowing your name without recovering your memories wouldn't have helped your situation, and it could have put you in more danger," he said, closing the distance between them. "It was my job to protect you, and that had to come first."

"You could have done your job without lying to me," she insisted. For a moment, she simply stared at him. "Decency and empathy should come first, Mr. Sullivan. Not a job."

Gray reached for her again, but she jerked away just as the door burst open, startling both of them.

"Sophia!" her father cried, rushing inside and sweeping her up in his arms. "You're really here. Thank God," he whispered again and again, rocking her in his arms as he wept. Her own tears clogged her throat as she clung to her father. To think she had forgotten the one man in her life who had never disappointed her, made her gulp back a sob.

"Where's Mama?" she asked.

"At home," he said, wiping his face on his coat sleeve. "I needed to see with my own eyes that you were really here and...I had to be certain you were all right before I told her." He cleared his throat. "I couldn't put her through any more pain."

Relieved, she gave him a hard hug. "Thank you, Papa."

When he finally released her, he spoke to Gray. "Mr. Fitch said you're the one who found Sophia and kept her safe. Is that correct?"

Gray glanced at her, then her father. "I'm sorry I couldn't tell you, Mr. Flynn. I'll never forgive myself for that cruelty, however unintended."

Confused, Sophia glanced between the men. "Do you know each other?"

Her father nodded. "I met Mr. Alexander at the plant about a month ago."

As the truth dawned on her, she felt sick inside. And angry. "This man's name is Gray Sullivan," she told her father. "He's a Pinkerton detective. Not only has he been lying to me, about everything, he has also been lying to you." She looked at Gray in disbelief. "You knew my name and where I worked, and had even met my father, yet you kept all of that from me. You could have taken me to my parents the day Officer Kline came looking for me and spared my reputation what's bound to be irreparable damage. What's worse, and utterly unforgiveable, is you let my parents suffer, wondering if I were dead. For weeks!" she said, her voice rising with each word. Tears flooded her eyes but she couldn't hold them back. It was all too much. "How could you be so cruel?" she whispered brokenly.

Tears tumbled over her lower lashes, and she turned away. Clasping her father's arm, she said, "Take me home, Papa. Officer Kline knows where to find us." She couldn't stay there another minute because every hope, every dream she'd had with Gray Sullivan, lay scattered like ashes beneath her feet. The man she thought she knew was a deceptive stranger. And she was a misguided fool.

CHAPTER SIXTEEN

Dressing for her first day back at work filled Sophia with dread. She didn't want to return to the place where her nightmare had begun. Although that terrifying incident had landed her in Gray's arms it had ended in a cruel betrayal.

Within one week of putting Silas Wade in jail, Gray and Milton Fitch had found the documents proving Wade's theft, all of it verified by Philo Holbrooke who confessed he'd been forced to do Silas's bidding. Knowing Silas was locked up and would be spending years in prison for theft and attempted murder was a relief, but it did nothing to soothe her heartache.

Knowing her boss would no longer be at the mill was a blessing, but it didn't ease her nerves over returning to work. She had to, of course. Her income, however paltry, was essential to helping support their household, and she couldn't delay returning to work any longer. So she went to the kitchen where her mother was washing baking trays.

"Those cinnamon buns smell delicious," she said, hugging her mother's thin shoulders. Her mother was a petite, dark-haired beauty who had suffered four miscarriages that left her too thin and frail. To see her working so hard worried Sophia.

"Leave the trays, Mama. I'll wash them when I get home from work."

"Nonsense," her mother replied, drying her hands on her worn apron. She pointed to a wrapped package on the counter. "Be sure to take your lunch with you."

"Thank you, Mama. I'll share it with Papa."

"He has his own lunch," her mother said, then pulled her into a tight hug that expressed relief at having her daughter back home.

Sophia felt that same relief and love for her mother and was deeply grateful to be reunited with her beloved parents, but her heartache over Gray cleaved her chest in two. "Get some rest today, and I'll see you tonight," she said, popping a kiss on her mother's cheek.

Crossing through their cramped parlor, she entered the tiny foyer and pulled on a sweater and her worn wool coat, then wound a blue knit scarf around her neck.

Just as she reached for the doorknob, someone knocked. When she opened it, she found Gray Sullivan standing on the snowy stoop. Surprised and somewhat startled by the appearance of a man she'd never expected to see again, she fumbled for words. "What do you want?" she asked, the question sounding rude and not at all friendly.

He arched one eyebrow as if shocked by her abrupt greeting. "I'm here to deliver your possessions. You left everything behind at the cabin."

"What possessions?" she asked. "I had nothing."

"I brought your clothing and the music box," he said, gesturing toward the street where a small wagon drawn by a beautiful black gelding stood.

"I can't wear boy's clothing in public, and the music box never belonged to me," she said because she could barely speak past the lump in her throat. Realizing he was only there to deliver things she didn't want, and not to see her, was crushing.

For a moment, he just looked at her. "Are you all right?" he asked, his voice low and too intimate.

Straightening her shoulders, she said, "Of course. Why would you ask?"

"I've heard things. Unkind gossip."

"About me, I suppose." At his nod, she sighed. "What did you expect?"

A frigid breeze flipped his collar up against his neck. "I didn't expect anything because I neglected to consider the ramifications of keeping you safely hidden at the cabin with me." He held her gaze. "I'm sorry about that."

"Well, I'm afraid your apology won't stop the gossip or repair my reputation."

"That's why I'm here," he said, removing his hat and holding it in one hand. "I think we should marry, Sophia."

Her jaw dropped.

"It could stop the gossip or at least change the story."

"What?" she asked on an outrush of breath.

"We should marry to salvage your reputation."

Of all the things he'd ever done or said to her, this was the most painful and demeaning. He was proposing because he felt responsible for the gossip, and this was his way of righting a wrong. There was no tenderness in his eyes, no love in his words, no promise of joy or happily-ever-after. Just duty.

A thick wad of grief lodged in her throat, and she found herself incapable of speech. Tears surged behind her lids, beading, burning, and blurring her vision. Before they could spill over her lashes, she slammed the door in his face.

With her back against the door, she gulped breath after breath, fighting back tears as she struggled to hold herself together. After all the moments they'd shared, how could he be so impersonal? So businesslike. As if marrying her was just another job.

She ached for the connection they'd shared during their time at the cabin. But that connection wasn't real.

Because it had been carefully crafted by a skilled liar, a handsome man who'd manipulated her into believing he cared about her.

It was time she faced the truth. In her desperate need for connection, she'd misinterpreted his tender ministrations and comforting manner as something deeper. But even if that were true, how could he not know how deeply she'd cared for him, and that proposing to her merely out of a sense of duty would break her heart?

Because it had. Utterly and completely.

───

WITH SILAS WADE behind bars for theft and attempted murder, Gray's job in Pine Ridge was finished. He just needed to clean out the cabin, pack his gear, then have Ben deliver him to the train station. But something was missing, left undone, incomplete.

The cabin that had once been a sanctuary had become a prison, locking Gray inside with too many memories. Everywhere he looked, he saw Sophia. Resting on her bed, sitting by the woodstove drying her hair after her bath, her skin dew-kissed and radiant, seeing her impish smile across the chessboard as she beat him at chess, her head bent over her sketchpad, her slender artist's hands making holiday decorations from berries and woodland debris, transforming a sad, misshapen pine tree into a work of art, using a stick to draw in the snow, the sound of her laughter in the cabin and in the forest, the joyful melody skipping down deer paths, the starlight in her eyes under a night sky, and the way they darkened with desire when he kissed her, and how she fit so perfectly in his arms, in his heart, in his life...

His life with Sophia was what he'd left undone, unfinished.

He'd lived more fully, more deeply, more joyfully in the few weeks he'd spent with her than he'd lived in all the years before he'd met her.

Now, the only thing left were memories that made him ache deep in his bones.

With each handmade ornament he removed from Sophia's crooked little pine tree, his sense of dread deepened. There was no going back, no saving those moments they'd shared any more than he could save the dying tree. With one single cut, one unforgivable lie, he'd set a course to an inevitable end. He'd hurt her, betrayed her, and now he was leaving her because removing himself from her life was what she wanted.

The winterberries she'd strung on thread and draped around the tree had become as dry and shriveled as his heart felt. The decorative strands of berries were spent, but the memory of Sophia making them was as sharp as the needle she'd used to string them. All he wanted was to walk out and not look back, but this mess was of his own making, and he needed to clean it up. So, one painful step after another, he took down the decorations and packed away the memories.

Two hours later, he'd finished cleaning the cabin. After a bath and a shave, he dressed for travel. His duffle was packed. The clothing he'd tried to return to Sophia had been given to Ben's family, and Sophia's music box was stored safely in a crate at the general store. He'd asked Lola Gorman to let Sophia know when she came in that he'd left the box for her. Even though she might hate him, might never forgive him, she'd loved the music box.

At the sound of a wagon pulling up out front, he took a last look around the cabin. When he'd first arrived, he'd welcomed the solitude. Now, he couldn't bear the emptiness another minute. Clutching his pack in one hand, he closed and locked the door behind him. Moving on after a job had always been an event he relished, anticipating the next new challenge, but this time it felt as if he were leaving a crucial piece of himself behind.

CHAPTER SEVENTEEN

Crane Landing was one of the few places in Maine that Gray hadn't visited or traveled through during his years as an operative. Now, he was here to reunite with his two older brothers. He hadn't seen Ashe since their delinquent father had dumped the two of them and their younger siblings Cal and River at a church fifteen years ago. It had been even longer since he'd seen Leo, and he'd never met Benny, his baby brother who was born after their family had been scattered like chaff on a hard wind.

Leo had tracked down Gray's adoptive parents a few months ago. Gray had been in Chicago on a job at that time, but Leo had reunited with their little sister, River, and left his address and a request for Gray to contact him.

Gray had planned to do so, but he and three hundred other Pinkerton Agents armed with Winchester rifles had been sent on barges, pulled by tugboats up the Monongahela River, to Homestead, Pennsylvania, to break a labor strike at the Carnegie Steel Mill. It had been one of the most violent and deadly altercations of his career, and Gray was too heartsick afterward to talk to anybody. He'd even avoided his parents, choosing to bury himself in undercover work in an attempt to forget Homestead and the men who died there. His last undercover job was at Pine Ridge where he'd met Sophia—and managed to lose the best thing in his life.

Leaning his forehead against the cold windowpane in his suite, Gray watched the ice floating in the vast Atlantic waters, clinging like lint to a shoreline that seemed to go on forever. Attractive stone cottages and fishing huts sat atop snowy bluffs. Regal two- and three-story homes created charming neighborhoods that flowed out from the town center like an outgoing tide. A diverse collection of stores and businesses, and two large inns, one of which held Gray's rented suite, ran the length of Main Street. In the distance, where Main Street met Bay Street, he could see the masts of a schooner rocking in the horseshoe bay, its sails drawn and lashed tight against the wind. Even in the grip of winter, Crane Landing was a beautiful jewel on the southern shores of Maine.

He could easily understand why Leo chose to live here with his wife, Grace, and her little brother Willy. Ashe apparently spent a good amount of time in Crane Landing, too, according to what Leo had told Gray's parents during his visit. That's why, before leaving Pine Ridge, Gray had called Crane Shipbuilding where Leo worked, and made arrangements to meet his brothers this evening at a local tavern.

It was a meeting Gray both dreaded and eagerly anticipated. Years of undercover work had trained him to manage his nerves in tense situations, which is why the tremor in his gut surprised him. He wasn't nervous. Or scared. Or even worried.

He was...emotional.

He was about to meet his big brothers...as grown men.

They would want to talk about their lives, and would ask about his. He was eager to hear their stories but knew their hardships would break his heart. He'd been lucky. His parents had provided everything a boy and his baby sister needed—except their missing siblings. Gray had already learned that Ashe had been taken in by a wealthy family, and that Leo and Benny had found a loving home and community in Fredonia, New York. He also knew Cal had been far less fortunate than the rest of them.

Memories of them as hardscrabble boys, working the fields planting and harvesting crops that never provided enough, filled Gray's mind. He remembered roughhousing with each other, trying and failing to protect each other from their father's heavy hands. But he didn't have a single memory of his brothers as adults, as men. And that's what made him emotional as he pulled on his wool coat and headed to the Crowe's Nest.

Walking a few blocks in the bracing cold helped settle his nerves and clear his head. When he arrived at the tavern, he drew in a last calming breath, then stepped inside, ready to reunite with the brothers he'd been missing all his life.

For a moment, he and two dark-haired men at the bar looked at one another. As recognition slowly sank in, the men smiled and slid off their barstools, standing to greet him. They were tall, like him, their faces familiar but without the boyish features he remembered. Wisdom, confidence, and warmth filled their eyes as they met him with handshake-hugs and pats on the back. The sound of their manly laughter resonated with the higher register of boyish giggles that lingered in Gray's memories. These men were his brothers, roots of his past, and maybe part of his future.

"Well, you're certainly not that scrawny little kid I remember," Ashe said, holding Gray at arm's length to look him over.

"Neither are you," Gray said, reminding Ashe, who was only a year older, that he'd been a scrawny kid too.

"Don't you two start with each other," Leo said, giving them a playful nudge toward the bar as if they were still kids. "Hiram!" he called, gesturing to the barkeep. "Our little brother needs a drink."

An understatement, Gray thought, as he cleared his dry throat and tightened his jittery gut. He didn't know what to do with all the emotions surging through him. Joy, regret, love, guilt, all crashed together like the roiling twain of two flooded rivers, each one vying for an outlet.

"First one is on the house," the barkeep said, welcoming Gray with a handshake and toothy grin. "What'll you have?"

"An ale, please," Gray replied, then barely had time to thank Hiram before the man placed a foaming mug in front of him, then hastened off to wait on a man farther down the bar. After taking a long draught from his mug, Gray braced one hand on the bar and released a gusty breath. "Am I really standing here with my brothers?" he asked, eliciting relieved laughter from Ashe and Leo.

"Seems like a dream," Leo said. "I can't tell you how many times I'd imagined a scene like this."

Gray had, too, until it had become too painful to think about his lost family. "The last time I called home, River shared what you'd told her when you visited them," he said, "but I'd like to know more about you two. Ashe, I know you were taken in by a wealthy family, but were they good to you?"

A laugh burst forth from both his brothers, surprising Gray.

"That's an understatement," Leo said.

"It's true," Ashe said with a nod of agreement. "I couldn't have been more fortunate. My parents are kind, generous people who have given me a life I could never have imagined."

"Another understatement," Leo said.

"I suppose that's true as well," Ashe said. "Both of my parents came from very wealthy families, so I was raised in the bosom of luxury. I grew up on a sprawling estate with a stable full of horses. I attended balls and sporting events and traveled the world with my parents and their friends, all of whom came from considerable wealth." He shrugged. "As I said, it was a life I could never have imagined."

"It must have felt like living in a dream," Gray said, trying to imagine it.

"You could say that. But dreaming, and living that dream, are very different things. The life my parents lived was so foreign to what I'd known, I felt adrift and rudderless for years," Ashe said. "I suffered chronic headaches that I now believe were a result of trying to navigate a world I didn't understand. Each day my head was stuffed full of rules on proper etiquette and behavior, of family history and our connections to other families of wealth and influence. Within weeks of my arrival, my father began training me in his merchant business that I was expected to take over one day. Trying to learn about trade routes, our ships, the supplies they carried, the ports they visited both here and abroad, the contracts we held with whom and for what merchandise, how the vessels were maintained, who captained them, how many crewmembers were needed aboard each ship, and how to nego-tiate alliances, was just the tip of a very large iceberg," he said, finishing with a hard breath. "So, yes, I was fortunate, but that life comes at a cost, too."

Gray released a low whistle. "My head hurts just hearing you talk about it. I can't imagine living it."

Ashe laughed, but Gray could see that his brother had suffered, too, and that pain and heartache do not discriminate based on one's circumstances.

He turned his attention to Leo. "River told me that you and Benny were left at an orphanage two or three years after Dad dumped us at the church."

Leo's smile faded and his eyes darkened. "Yeah, when Mom and I realized that Dad didn't take you to Aunt Betty's house, we spent months and months trying to find you all, but no one had any idea what our father had done with you. Mom was expecting with Benny and was very ill. Dad was mostly absent or drunk, so putting food on the table fell to me." Leo shook his head. "We nearly starved. Mom grew sicker and died shortly after Benny was born. I tried to care for Benny and the farm, but both were failing. When Dad told me to bundle up Benny because we were going for a ride, I knew we wouldn't be coming back." Disgust filled Leo's expression. "He dumped us at an orphanage in Dunkirk. Benny and I were there for a few weeks when a couple came to take Benny. They didn't want me, though, and I wasn't allowing anyone to split us up, so I took Benny and stole out of the orphanage."

Gray felt sick to his stomach over the tragic circumstance they'd endured because of their wastrel of a father. "Did you have a place to go?"

"Not one. I wasn't very smart back then either," Leo admitted with a wry grin. "I left in a snowstorm and had to take refuge in a greenhouse. A boy named Adam Grayson found us. His father, Duke Grayson, caught him carrying food and blankets out to us. When Adam admitted there were two orphans hiding out in the greenhouse, his dad got involved. That's when I learned Duke Grayson used to be the sheriff."

Gray released a belt of laughter. "Did he arrest you for trespassing?"

"No," Leo said, his expression softening as if recalling a fond memory. "He took us in and found us a good home. And Adam became my best friend. He lives here in Crane Landing now with his wife Rebecca and their son Finn. If you stay here long enough, I'll introduce you to them."

It hadn't crossed Gray's mind to extend his stay in Crane Landing, but he liked the idea of spending more time with his brothers.

"So what was your life like?" Leo asked. "I know you and River were taken in by the Draytons. They seemed like truly wonderful people when I met them, and it was obvious to me that you and River were loved and cared for. But how was it for you?"

It was a constant assault on his conscience. Gray loved his adoptive parents and deeply appreciated the home they'd given him, but he felt he didn't deserve either. Not when he'd left his little brother behind to fend for himself.

"It was like you said, Leo. They were good parents. They provided well for River and me. And Charleston was a good place to grow up."

They seemed to be waiting for him to say more, but he was all twisted up inside and couldn't summon the fortitude to reveal his private anguish.

"That's it?" Leo asked with a laugh. "You had wonderful parents and liked living in Charleston?"

"Well, I don't know what else to say. I went to school and worked odd jobs there until I took a job with the Pinkerton Agency."

Ashe looked at him as if considering an unanswerable question. "I can't believe you're a detective."

"Why not?" Gray asked, surprised and a little insulted by the comment.

Leo braced one elbow on the bar. "Gray was always inquisitive as a kid, analyzing and inspecting everything. I would think he possesses the perfect traits for a detective."

With one boot heel hooked on his barstool, Ashe leaned his back against the bar and angled a keen look at Gray. "What I meant is that I can't believe you worked for the largest detective agency in the country, perhaps the world, yet you couldn't find your own siblings."

The expression on Ashe's face was open and friendly. He didn't seem to be challenging Gray, but the ale in Gray's stomach churned like acid. He hadn't found them because he hadn't looked. Not after his parents failed to find Cal. The only way Gray had survived his guilt for leaving his little brother behind was to scrub his past from his memory. He'd never completely succeeded, but he'd spent most of his life diligently closing the door to his past each time it crept open.

"That's actually a good question," Leo said, angling a grin at Gray. "Were you so glad to be rid of your older brothers that you forgot about us?"

Gray forced a laugh. "Not having you two around saved me a few thrashings, I'm sure."

"Probably," Leo said. "But regardless of our epic bouts, I wish we'd have all had the chance to grow up together."

"Me, too," Ashe said, tapping his mug against Gray's. "Good to see you again, little brother."

Gray's throat was too tight to speak, so he saluted his brothers with his mug, then took a deep gulp. When he set his mug on the bar, he said, "This round is on me."

"They're all on you," Leo said, then gave a hearty belt of laughter and pulled Gray into a side-armed hug that told him they were good. His brothers were here because they wanted to reconnect with him, not because they wanted to blame him or chastise him for his shortcomings.

Ashe patted the barstool beside him. "Rest your bones, little brother, and tell us what you've been up to the last fifteen years. We're not trying to pry into your private life, just learn a bit about how you got where you are now."

So, Gray sat between his brothers and gave them a cursory history of moving south with his adoptive family, of growing up in Charleston living near the wharves and over a bakery, and he shared stories about their exuberant little sister that had them howling with laughter. He left out the misery he put his parents through over not taking Cal with them, his scathing anger each time they failed to find Cal, and ultimately his self-imposed distance from the two people who'd sacrificed so much to give him a loving home. It was easier to shift the conversation to work because that's where he'd taken on numerous personas, none of whom had left their little brother alone in the world.

"Your work sounds exciting," Ashe said, propping one ankle over his knee.

Gray agreed it was exciting, but also exhausting. "Honestly, it feels like a never-ending race, always scurrying to find evidence, trying to decipher messages in the field, relentlessly pursuing criminals and trying to shut down agitators. Frankly, I'm tired of chasing train robbers, and breaking labor disputes for wealthy industrialists who don't care a whit for the poor men and women struggling to survive in unsafe working conditions and on paltry pay." He paused and glanced at Ashe. "I'm not suggesting you're one of those wealthy snobs."

Ashe laughed. "Thank you for that. I can assure you, I'm not of that ilk."

"I can vouch for him," Leo said.

"I'm sure that kind of work can wear on a man," Ashe said. "We heard about the labor strike at Homestead. I hope you weren't there."

"Unfortunately, I was," Gray admitted with sorrow and shame.

"Good grief," Ashe said, sitting up, his expression slightly alarmed. "You're all we could think about when that mess was happening. I inquired with my contacts, but no one could tell me if you were with the agents on those river barges."

"That's precisely where I was during that mess," Gray said, remembering the onslaught of gunfire and vitriol spewed at them while he and his fellow agents were pinned down on barges.

Ashe frowned. "I asked my contacts to have men search the barges for you, but they said there was no way to get to the barges without risking their lives."

"I was there undercover, so you wouldn't have found Gray Sullivan. And had your contacts attempted such a foolhardy feat,

Ashe, it's very likely they would have been killed or badly wounded. The strikers were justifiably angry and willing to fight to the bitter end for what should have been humanely provided. To them, we were just another group of powerful men standing against them, so we were part of the problem. And those striking men and women who stood on the banks fighting for their rights knew we were sitting ducks on those barges. The local citizens had also joined the strikers, and they gathered in force on the river bank, collecting whatever weapons they could find to use against us."

"The newspaper reports made it sound like a horrific scene," Leo said. "I'm hugely relieved to see you survived."

Gray released a laugh at the understatement. "From my point of view, the scene was a living nightmare. For hours all we could hear was the crack of the muzzle loaders being fired from shore, the lead bullets pinging off the iron barges like hail. The strikers even rounded up a small cannon at one point, and dumped oil into the river in an attempt to set it, and us, afire. They were beyond reasoning with."

Leo's mug hit the bar with a hard thud. "Had I known you were on that barge, I'd have plowed through that picket line and dragged you out of there myself."

"I'd have been right there with him," Ashe said, anger flashing in his eyes.

"And you both would have been shot or beaten bloody by the crowd. I was with three hundred agents carrying Winchester rifles on those barges, and we couldn't control that mob. They threw dynamite and refused to let us land or surrender. It took five thousand militia marching into town with rifles and Gatling guns to take over the mill and place the town under martial law."

A deep furrow creased Ashe's black eyebrows. "I can't even imagine that scene."

Gray didn't have to imagine. He'd lived it. He'd suffered the beating from sticks and stones and angry fists as he and his fellow agents went ashore. In the end, several people were dead, and many more wounded.

"I don't know how you can do that job," Leo said.

For a moment, Gray didn't know either. He felt utterly exhausted at the thought of going back. "When I started with the agency, being a detective was an honorable calling," he said, "but after the disaster at Homestead, people called us thugs. I honestly can't fault them for that. I've done some good work as a detective that I'm proud of, but the job has changed, and I honestly don't know how much longer I can do it."

"Then don't," Ashe said. "If you're looking for a change, Gray, I'll hire you, or I can let my contacts know you're available for hire. You'd make a great security officer."

"Or, you could stay here and work with me at the shipyard," Leo added.

Their suggestions caught Gray by surprise. It hadn't occurred to him to quit the agency, that he could do something different with his life and live wherever he wanted. He'd always lived where his jobs had taken him, a few weeks here or a few months there, but he'd never had a home. The only place that had ever felt like home was that little cabin in Pine Ridge because Sophia had been there. The minute she left, it was just a cabin in a town like any other place he'd stayed. She hated him now, so going back wasn't an option.

But maybe staying here was. Living in Crane Landing was as good as anywhere, he supposed.

"Thanks for the offer, Ashe, but I don't want to work security anymore, and I'm not sure I have the necessary skills for building ships, Leo, but I might consider it," he said. "What would you need me to do?"

"I need someone who can manage our projects from start to finish," Leo said. "That means organizing, planning, and leading a number of teams. I need someone who can keep the work on schedule and within budget. If you can do that, the job is yours."

"When do I start?" Gray asked, knowing his work as an operative, creating plans, piecing together details, and organizing and directing teams in the pursuit of criminals gave him the skills and qualities needed for the job.

"Whenever you're ready," Leo said. "There's no rush. The job is yours if you want it."

Possibilities of taking a new direction with his life filled Gray with hope, and for the first time in his life he made a decision without carefully weighing the options. "I'll do it," he said. "I need to let my boss know I won't be coming back, and I also need to find a place to live. But as soon as that's accomplished, I can start."

"You can stay with me," Ashe said. "I have a house north of town. Now that I have trustworthy crews to run my ships, I spend a good amount of time here, but there's plenty of room if you'd like to stay."

"Plenty of room," Leo said with a laugh. "It's an estate large enough for two families."

"I would gladly trade it for your cottage," Ashe said. "I believe you're about to outgrow it, now that Grace is expecting."

"Is that so?" Gray asked in surprise.

Leo grinned. "You're both going to be an uncle in a few months."

"That's wonderful news," Gray said, giving Leo a congratulatory slap on the shoulder.

Ashe grinned. "That's why you and Grace should take my estate. But you'll have to take Gray with the house if you want it."

At Gray's look of mock offense, Leo burst out laughing and slapped Gray on the back. "Get used to it, little brother. Our heckling just means we're glad you're here."

When their laughter settled, Ashe said, "I'm rattling around the place by myself, Gray. The entire third floor is yours, if you want it."

"It sounds perfect," Gray said. But what he really wanted was to be back in that small cabin in Pine Ridge with Sophia. He wanted to turn back the clock to Christmas Eve, when he'd held her in his arms and they danced through the cabin, laughing and dreaming of a future together.

CHAPTER EIGHTEEN

Sophia and her father walked home together in the late evening after a long day of work. Two months had passed since she had returned to her job at the paper mill, and although working conditions at the mill had improved with Gray's intervention and Silas's absence, the gaping wound in her heart was raw and painful. Losing her dream with Gray felt even worse than losing her memories. She missed him in the deepest part of her soul. She wanted to forget him and his betrayal, but her heart refused to let him go.

Time and again, her father said he bore no ill will toward Gray for withholding the truth of her whereabouts, insisting she shouldn't either. Her father expressed his admiration for Gray's commitment to protecting her, even when doing so must have weighed heavily on his conscience.

Perhaps it had. Perhaps hiding the truth had been a heavy burden for Gray, but how had he watched her desperate struggle each day without offering a single crumb about her past?

"Sophia," her father said, circling her waist with one arm and giving her a light hug. "Your heartache is so big it's swallowing the sun."

"I'm sorry, Papa." She released a heavy sigh filled with guilt. "It's just been a long day."

"It's not the work causing your heartache, Sophie-girl. It's that young man you want to hate but love too much to do so."

Tears rushed to her eyes, and she blinked furiously trying to stop them from spilling over her lower lashes. "I'm just tired," she whispered, her throat too filled with grief to talk.

"That's what happens when you can't settle the conflict between your heart and your mind."

Knowing it was senseless to deny the obvious, she gave him a slight nod.

"That man you're missing saved and protected you. He put you and your safety before everything else, Sophia, and he willingly risked his life doing so. You need to decide if you want to be angry and place blame where it's not deserved, or if you want to acknowledge the love you feel for him. At some point, you need to forgive him for doing his job."

"I understand why he kept the truth from us, Papa. I know he was just doing his job, but that doesn't mean it feels any less painful."

"Sophia, it's plain as the tears on your cheeks that you love him," her father said softly. "Why didn't you say *yes* when he asked you to marry him?"

"Because he was asking out of a sense of duty," she said, feeling sick inside. "He only asked because people were gossiping about me being alone with him in the cabin. But nothing untoward happened."

"I believe that, Sophia. I know you, and there's no question that Gray is an honorable man. But do you really believe he proposed merely for the sake of protecting you from the gossips?"

"Yes, Papa." She did believe it because Gray hadn't professed his love or desire to share his life with her. His exact words were that *they should marry to protect her reputation.* "It doesn't matter now, so may we please change the subject?"

"Of course," he said, releasing her and tucking his hand in his coat pocket. "I wonder what your mother made for supper."

She shrugged because she couldn't imagine how her mother managed to create sufficient meals from their limited staples.

They headed toward the flats, an area south of the mill near the river where the mill owners had built tenement housing for the employees to rent. A sense of depression seemed to grip the place, and Sophia longed to return to the little cabin up the mountain where she and Gray had spent their days and evenings together. She missed their walks and quiet evenings playing games, talking, or reading books together.

The moments they'd shared appeared like wisps of smoke from a chimney, lingering for an instant before drifting away on a frigid wind. A vision of him in the forest calling out to her, his voice, kind, calming, promising protection...and then nothing as the world faded away. Then flashes of him leaning over her, his hands tending her wounds, his arms calming her night terrors, holding her upright, supporting her, bathing her, feeding her. Everything for her. Every day. All he'd asked in return was her trust, but she'd given him her heart.

She longed for the sound of his voice and the feel of his arms, but he was gone. The cabin they'd shared sat cold and vacant, and as empty and abandoned as she felt.

THE FRINGE of ice along the shores of Crane Landing had melted or drifted away by mid-April, but Gray's chest still felt frozen. Each day, he traversed the shipyard like a worker bee in a busy hive, clipboard in hand, tracking supplies and progress, lending a hand where needed, working hard to keep his mind and body occupied, but memories of Sophia pressed in relentlessly. At those moments, a splintering feeling in his chest, like ice cracking under pressure, would shatter his calm, stress his breathing, sink him in loneliness so deep he thought he'd drown.

Nothing, it seemed, could help. Not a new job. Not living in a new town. Not even spending time with his brothers could thaw the iceberg lodged in his chest. His brothers were certainly the best thing in his life, and he couldn't imagine where he'd be without their companionship and humor, but Gray felt frozen in place.

As he looked out the window of his flat on the third floor of Ashe's estate, he could see Adam and Rebecca Grayson arriving in a carriage shared with Leo and Grace. Ashe was hosting a small dinner before leaving for a couple of weeks to visit his parents in Saratoga. Gray suspected the party was meant for his benefit. His brothers were doing their best to help him create a new life here in Crane Landing by hosting gatherings and introducing him to their friends, people Gray liked and deeply admired. But they weren't Sophia.

Pasting on a smile to honor his brothers and show his appreciation for all they were doing, Gray descended to the main floor and joined them in the parlor.

Leo stood with his back to doorway, his black hair pulled back in a queue that hung four inches below the collar of his gray suit-coat, talking with Adam who seemed to be taunting Leo about something that had them both laughing.

"You're out of your mind, Sullivan," Adam said, giving Leo's shoulder a nudge with his fist.

Seeing the way they jested with one another made Gray a bit envious of their friendship and the strong bond they shared.

"Our man of the hour has arrived," Ashe said, raising his glass in a toast to Gray.

As a group, they all turned to face him, the men lifting their glasses, the women their tea cups. "Happy birthday," they said, their greeting lively and filled with warmth.

Dumbfounded, he stared at them. "It's, ah, not my birthday."

His comment was greeted with an uproar of laughter. "We know," Ashe said, "but we've missed so many birthdays, we figured we'd celebrate yours tonight."

It was an absurd and somewhat heartwarming gesture that made Gray laugh. "Well, then, I'm sorry to have kept you all waiting."

Leo lifted his glass. "Obviously, we didn't wait," he said, causing more laughter. "Grab a drink, little brother, then come help me win a debate with Adam."

Ashe caught Gray's arm and tugged him toward a stylish serving cart topped with crystal decanters. "Save yourself a headache and avoid their debates at all costs."

"You'd do well to listen to Ashe," Rebecca chimed in with a light laugh, her brown eyes alive with humor. She was a dark-haired beauty who seemed to adore her husband as much as he adored her.

"I would heed their advice," Grace said, glancing at Leo with such love in her blue eyes it hurt to witness it. "When these two get going, you're best to step away and enjoy the evening else-where because they could be at it all night."

"Duly noted," Gray said, pouring himself a much-needed whiskey. Standing with Ashe, he asked, "When are you going to get yourself a wife and fill this place with children?"

A belt of laughter came from his brother. "Perhaps when I find a woman more interested in me than my fortune."

Gray gawked at his brother, sobered by the reality of Ashe's plight. "I'd never once considered that having wealth could be a detriment to marriage."

"It's not a detriment to marriage," Ashe said. "There are women lined up hoping to marry me tomorrow to partake of my fortune. Having wealth is only a detriment to finding the kind of love they share." He gestured with his glass toward Leo and Grace, and to Adam and Rebecca.

"Surely, there are women out there who would love you even if you didn't have a plug nickel," Gray said, knowing his brother was a generous, handsome man with a surprising sense of humor that always attracted a great deal of female interest when they were in public.

"Ah, but that's the crux of the issue," Ashe said. "How is a wealthy man to decipher what's real?"

Gray shrugged. "Obviously, I don't know. You'll need to confer with Adam and Leo on that score. Better yet, ask Grace and Rebecca."

"Ask us what?" Grace queried, facing them, her blue velvet dress tied loosely beneath her bosom but unable to camouflage her rounding abdomen.

"We were wondering what you're going to name our niece or nephew," Ashe said, giving Gray a side-eyed look that warned him off their previous conversation.

Leo placed his hand on Grace's belly. "We're naming him Zollie if it's a boy, and Lemon if it's a girl."

Grace burst out laughing and pushed his hand away. "You are most certainly not naming our children."

With a hoot of laughter, Leo pulled her into his arms. "You are doing all the work, my darling, so it's only fair that you get the honor of naming our children."

"Well, our child certainly won't be named Zollie or Lemon."

"How about Newt or Spurgeon?" Adam asked with a conspiratorial wink to Leo. "Those are names I'm considering for our next child."

Amid laughter, Rebecca playfully twisted his ear, then grinned as he danced away with a feigned yelp.

These people were a family, Gray realized. They played and

celebrated their days and special moments together, and he suspected they shared their pain and heartaches with each other too. He was standing among friends and family, all of whom welcomed him into their world with open, loving arms, and yet, he felt as alone and adrift as an ice floe.

For a moment, he imagined having Sophia at his side, sharing the evening with them, adding her delightful sense of humor to their playful banter. She would love these people, and they would love her. A deep longing spread through him, and he realized he wanted this kind of life...with Sophia. He wanted to marry her and spend their life together in this small coastal community, raising their children among family and friends.

A feminine hand touched his forearm. "You're a bit pensive for a man celebrating his birthday. Did someone steal your balloon...or your heart?" Grace asked quietly, her smile knowing but not prying.

Although Gray had only known his sister-in-law a few weeks, he felt a special bond with her. He'd spent many hours at their cottage, sharing meals, roughhousing with her little brother, Willy, and talking late into the night with Leo. Grace floated around them like sunshine, bringing light and warmth to their household. She welcomed Gray like a brother, affectionately jesting with him but always with a gentle kindness, as if she inherently sensed he was fractured and vulnerable.

"I'm just ruminating on whether there will be cake tonight," he said.

She laughed. "We always celebrate with cake."

"Then there's nothing for me to worry about," he said.

"I wish that were true," she replied softly, her smile fading. "But there's something other than cake on your mind, and it seems to be weighing heavily on your heart."

The weight wasn't on his heart, it was on his whole being, as if he'd been encased in ice.

"At the risk of grossly overstepping, I've observed you for several weeks, and I think you're pining over a ladylove." At his startled, guilty glance, she released a small laugh. "I suspected as much, but I won't pry. Just humor me and allow me to pass along a bit of wisdom learned at the hand of your hardheaded brother. If you love this lady, do whatever it takes to win her back. If that means you have to apologize, or steal her back from another man, do it. But the most important thing, Gray, is that you must leave no doubt about your feelings for her. If you love her, you must be absolutely clear about that." She pressed her lips together and pretended to lock her mouth shut. "I'm done now," she said from the corner of her mouth, making him laugh.

"Thank you for that sisterly advice, Grace, but I'm afraid an apology won't be enough to undo the harm I caused."

"Phooey," she said, flapping a dismissive hand at him. "When I was a young girl, my grandfather told me my father was dead. I didn't learn the truth until years later, and I swore I'd never forgive him, or my father who'd abandoned me. They'd both lied to me. But I forgave them because I love them, and I know their actions, however misguided, were motivated by love for me. And as you now know, your brother kidnapped me, and we had other seemingly insurmountable issues, but I loved him even when I was angry with him. I just needed some time to cool off and sort out my feelings. But if Leo hadn't come after me, we wouldn't have married because I would never have known that he really loved me. So, Gray, if you truly love this woman, stop anguishing about whatever you or she did or whatever happened between you two, and go talk to her. Tell her how you feel about her. Don't assume she knows."

"Don't assume who knows what?" Leo asked, slipping his arm around Grace's shoulders.

"That you know how much I adore you," Grace said, then cast a wink at Gray.

"Yes, Grace was just telling me how she forgave you for kidnapping her," Gray said, redirecting the attention to his nosey brother.

"Best thing I ever did," Leo stated proudly, garnering the attention and laughter of the others.

"Let's continue this conversation over supper," Ashe said, placing his empty glass on the serving cart, then escorting them from the parlor.

As a group, they moved to the dining room where they enjoyed a delicious meal and lively conversation, then lingered for a bit of conversation in the parlor before exchanging warm good-byes at the door.

"Care for a nightcap before turning in?" Ashe asked.

"I would," Gray said, following Ashe back to the parlor. With a tired sigh, he sank onto an armchair by the fireplace, feeling the deep leather cushions hug his weary bones.

Ashe poured them a drink, then sat in the chair opposite Gray. "I hope you enjoyed your surprise birthday celebration."

Gray laughed. "It was certainly a surprise." He swirled the brandy in the wide bowl of his glass, then enjoyed the aroma before tasting it. "Wealth might pose a challenge for finding the right woman, Ashe, but it's certainly beneficial in acquiring the best liquor."

"That it is," his brother said, looking relaxed in the luxurious surroundings. Gray had observed Ashe in the more modest accommodations of Leo's cottage and noticed that his brother seemed at home there, too. It was a great relief that Ashe hadn't let his good fortune deplete his character. Gray had witnessed the lack of decency and character in too many of the wealthy industrialists who'd hired him and his fellow agents to protect their holdings. It seemed the greater their wealth, the poorer their character.

"Still thinking about that ladylove Grace was haranguing you about?" Ashe asked.

"You heard her?" Gray asked in surprise.

"Yes, but the better question, is did *you* hear her?"

Gray frowned. "What's that supposed to mean?"

"It means if you were lucky enough to find a woman you'd want to spend your life with, you'd be a fool to walk away from her."

"I did find a woman," he admitted. "Literally. In the woods."

Ashe raised his eyebrows, his interest obviously piqued. "Do tell, little brother."

Gray hesitated for a moment, then remembered he was no longer an agent with assets and secrets to protect. He was free of that world, and he was in the company of his brother, not talking with a stranger or a target. He could relax here, and he could tell Ashe the truth. And so he did. Every last detail spilled out, including how he'd fallen for Sophia, and how he'd had to betray her trust every day by withholding the one thing she needed most. "I didn't walk away, Ashe. I asked her to marry me."

Ashe released a low whistle and set his empty glass on a parlor table. "That is...one complicated story, and not what I expected to hear. I take it Sophia declined your proposal?"

Gray nodded, claws of remorse clamping down hard on his lungs. "That's when I left and came here."

Steepling his hands beneath his chin, Ashe gave a thoughtful nod. "I guess the question now is when are you going back?"

"I'd go tomorrow if I thought it would change anything, but she said she would never forgive my betrayal. I can't blame her, Ashe. It was...unforgiveable."

"Apparently, you weren't listening when Grace told you she'd only needed time to sort out her feelings to forgive Leo."

"I don't know if Sophia will ever be able to forgive me."

"You won't know unless you go back. Until then, you're just wondering and worrying and wasting time over a situation that can only be managed in person."

Staring into the dwindling fire, Gray contemplated his brother's words. The thought of seeing Sophia again filled him with hope that she might forgive him. But what if she couldn't? Walking away from her once took every ounce of fortitude he had possessed, and he'd only been able to do it for her. Walking away a second time would be...impossible.

The tip of Ashe's shoe connecting with Gray's shin made him yelp in surprise. "What was that for?"

"Because you're sitting there like a fool when you should be upstairs packing a bag."

CHAPTER NINETEEN

Sophia was at her desk making entries in an inventory ledger when the sound of tinkling bells drifted into the small office. Intrigued, she angled her ear toward the door and listened for a moment, but the usual sounds of machinery and inventory being moved and racked was absent. Only the beautiful sound of bells filled the air.

Her heart jolted at the sudden realization of what she was hearing. Pressing her hand to her chest, she spun toward the door to find Gray Sullivan standing there.

"May I have this dance?" he asked.

Stunned, she couldn't find her voice.

He extended his hand, palm up. "On three?"

"What?" she asked, utterly bewildered.

"I want to dance with you, Sophia, for the rest of our lives."

Disoriented by his unexpected appearance in the middle of her workday, she could barely think straight. "Are you working here again?"

"No. I'm a project manager for Crane Shipbuilding."

She frowned. "Are you saying you no longer work for the Pinkerton Agency?" she asked in confusion.

"Correct."

"Then why did you come back?"

He stepped into the office, captured her hands in his, and gently pulled her to stand before him. "Because it was the only direction I could go. I came back for you, Sophia. I came back to say I'm sorry I hurt you. I deeply regret that I couldn't have eased your heartache during the darkest hours of your life."

"Is that why you're here? To ask for my forgiveness?"

"Yes, and to promise that I'll never again betray your trust in me."

Her heart sank, and she pulled her hands from his grasp. He was here to ask for forgiveness, not to profess his love for her. That's exactly why she'd left his music box at the general store. Because she hadn't wanted the painful reminder that he hadn't loved her. "I know you were doing your job, Gray, but I'll never understand why you didn't just take me home to my parents. It would have spared me and my parents weeks of torment, and also avoided unpleasant gossip."

"I couldn't trust anyone," he said with a sigh.

"Not even my own parents?" she asked, utterly bewildered by his unreasonable assertion.

"It wasn't about trusting your parents. It was about keeping you safe. Do you honestly think they could have protected you had Silas Wade come knocking?"

The answer was obvious. Her father was no match for a brute like Wade. "Officer Kline could have protected me," she said.

"Sophia, I...I trusted someone once and it nearly cost a little girl her life." He rubbed his forehead as if the memory pained him. "It was my first month as an agent and I'd been sent to New York to guard the daughters of a wealthy banker. There had been a kidnapping attempt on the girls. One was eight, and the other seventeen. Within a week, I found myself completely smitten with the older daughter, Helen, who returned my affection."

Shaking his head, he said, "I was eighteen and foolish. When a local police officer showed up claiming he was there to relive me, I slipped into the garden with Helen and left her little sister, Emma, with the officer."

Anticipating what he was about to tell her, she brought her hands to her chest. "Please tell me nothing happened to that little girl."

"I wish I could," he said, raking one hand through his hair, as if reliving the stressful moment. "The man was an officer, but he was also one of three men preying on wealthy families, kidnapping their children for ransom. He used his position as a law officer to get people to trust him. He took Emma while I was dallying with Helen. I was fired from the job and from the agency, but I couldn't walk away. I spent twenty-six hours digging up clues and tracking down leads that led me to the house where they were holding the girl."

"You got her back!" Sophia blurted in relief. "Was Emma all right? Had she been harmed?"

Pain and regret stained Gray's face. "Emma hadn't been harmed, but she was traumatized. The men were loud and rough and had threatened her to keep her silent and obedient. After I returned Emma to her parents, my boss told me it took weeks for her to recover and talk again."

"You got your job back?" she asked in amazement.

"I did," he said with a solemn nod. "I'd learned a hard, painful lesson, and I'd promised the agency, and myself, that I'd never again make such a grievous mistake."

"So, that's why you didn't tell Officer Kline about me," she said, finally understanding Gray's decision not to trust anyone. It's why he hadn't put her photograph in the newspaper or asked around about her because it could have put her life in jeopardy. His lies and omissions that were such a painful betrayal were the very decisions that might have saved her.

"I'm sorry I hurt you," he said, slipping his hands over hers. "It's the last thing I ever intended."

"I know that now, and I finally understand," she said softly. "No matter how betrayed I felt by your actions, I can't hold them against you."

Relief washed across his face, and he pulled her into a hug. "Thank you," he whispered, then eased her back in his arms. "I also came to make a confession," he said solemnly.

She looked at him, wondering what more he could possibly have to confess.

He stroked her cheek with the pad of his thumb. "When I came to Pine River, I wanted to shut out the rest of the world. I was lost and empty, until I found you, Sophia. You brought humor and laughter back to my life. Despite my valiant effort to keep my distance, I simply couldn't resist you. So, I'm here to tell you that I love you."

A small gasp of surprise slipped from her mouth.

"I'm sorry I didn't say that before. You deserved so much more than a bumbling proposal that left the most important thing unsaid. I love you. I adore you. You're all I can think about." He captured her hand and she watched him go down on one knee before her. "My beautiful, resilient, Sophia, will you marry me and make me the happiest man alive?"

Speechless, heart thundering, she stared in disbelief. The moment felt dreamlike with the sound of bells tinkling in the distance and Gray holding her hand. How desperately she had longed for a moment like this, but she'd believed it would never happen.

He grinned and jiggled her hand. "Say, yes, Sophia."

Her thoughts scattered like debris in a windstorm, and she struggled for words. "Is that your music box playing in the inventory bay?"

"No, darling, it's the music box I gave to the woman I love, the one I want to spend the rest of my life with if she'll ever answer my question."

A breathless laugh escaped her. "Is this really happening? Are you truly asking me to marry you?"

"My aching knee will attest to the fact that I'm here, kneeling before the most beautiful woman I've ever met, the one I can't live without, who is torturing me by withholding her answer. Although I likely deserve this punishment, will you please show mercy to your smitten suitor?"

"Yes," she said with a half-sob, overcome with emotion for the man who'd broken her heart and was here to mend it back together with his love. "Yes, I'll marry you."

He stood and swept her into his arms, kissing her deeply, passionately. It was a joyful kiss filled with celebration. "I will spend my life striving to make you happy."

"I don't think I could be happier than I am at this moment."

"Nor could I, my love." Then, to her surprise, he twirled her in a circle that made her squeal with laughter. With another twirl, he danced her out of the office and into the expansive inventory bay where her fellow workers were paused in their labor, keeping the music box wound, waiting for them.

Before she could express her surprise, he took her through another wild, sweeping turn across the floor. Her fellow workers erupted in applause and cheers. When Gray finally brought her to a stop, she was breathless with laughter, and it took a moment to comprehend that her father was in the crowd. To realize that Gray had talked to her father before proposing to her, and that her father supported their union, brought a flood of tears to her eyes.

"None of that today," her father said, pulling her into a tight hug. "The sun is shining bright, Sophie-girl."

It was indeed. It felt as if the dark clouds that had been hanging over her head and heart had been swept away by a warm breeze, filling her world with light and love. Gray was here, and he loved her.

———

THEY MARRIED two days later in a small church with her father giving her away, her mother smiling and dabbing tears, and a few close friends present. They celebrated afterward with light snacks and beverages in the church basement.

Gray promised they would host a lively celebration when they returned to Crane Landing, but Sophia was relieved to have a simple, quiet ceremony and to know they would spend their wedding night at the cabin.

It was early evening when they finally arrived, and Gray lifted her off her feet. "It's not our house, darling, but it seems only right that this is the first threshold I carry you across."

She laughed. "I believe you did this once already."

"Yes, but you weren't my wife then."

"Nor was I conscious."

"There's that too." He popped a kiss on her lips. "Would you please open the door?"

"My pleasure," she said, grasping the door handle, then giving it a push.

As the door opened, he carried her inside.

"Oh my..." she said, completely taken aback. The little cabin that had sat empty and abandoned while Gray had been away was now filled with golden lantern light and warmth from a crackling fire in the woodstove. In place of the narrow bunk she had slept on was a bed large enough for two adults. "I take it you won't be sleeping on the floor tonight?" she asked with a laugh.

"Not a chance." He lowered her feet to the floor but kept his arms around her. "I plan to hold you in my arms all night, my love."

She placed a tender kiss on his cheek. "I can't imagine a better place to sleep, but I'm not at all tired."

"Neither am I," he said, giving her a wolfish grin that sent a thrill through her belly. "What shall we do until bedtime?"

Despite his playful banter, she knew he was measuring her response, gauging her comfort level, giving her time to ease into the intimate side of their union. She looped her arms around his neck, wanting a lifetime of love and lovemaking with him. "I'd love a hot bath."

He grinned. "Me, too. Do you think the tub is big enough for two?"

"It might be a tight squeeze but I'm willing to try. How long will it take you to fill the tub?"

"Depends on how soon you let me go."

With a laugh, she released him and stepped away. "Let's see if you can fill the tub before I finish undressing."

"Don't you dare remove a stitch of clothing, Mrs. Sullivan. That's my job."

Surprised, she propped her hands on her hips. "All right, but turnabout is fair play, Mr. Sullivan. Don't remove a single cuff link."

He released an exaggerated groan. "The waiting is going to kill me."

Her laughter rang through the cabin. "Then you'd better hurry and fill the tub."

Two DAYS AFTER THEIR WEDDING, Gray and Sophia traveled by train from Pine Ridge, Maine, to Charleston, South Carolina, where he introduced Sophia to his parents and sister. Their surprise and delight over his marriage to Sophia was evident in the warm welcome they gave her and their invitation to stay with them.

Gray gently declined, knowing he and his lovely wife needed their privacy and that his parents deserved theirs as well. With that in mind, he had booked a luxurious suite at a sprawling inn on Meeting Street, within walking distance of his parents' home and bakery. During the day while his parents worked and his sister attended school, Gray showed Sophia the city.

They spent their first two days visiting shops where he delighted in outfitting his wife in new garments from head to toe. When she balked, insisting he was being too extravagant, he assured her it was well within his means to do so. And it was. For years, he'd been well compensated for his undercover work, and without the expense of a home or family to support, he'd amassed a small fortune. Now, it was deeply satisfying to provide an easier life for Sophia, especially after her recent hardship.

The rest of the week, they spent their days taking carriage rides through Charleston. While Sophia marveled over the magnificent architecture, sprawling mansions, and expansive gardens, Gray marveled over her beauty and the shifting emotion in her eyes. They dimmed with sadness as he shared a bit of history about James Island and Fort Sumpter and the battles that had been fought around Charleston, so he took her to the harbor where sunshine melted like butter over everything. Sanderlings, plovers, and other shorebirds foraged on shore as the mighty Atlantic waters lapped at wooden docks. A bell in the distance sounded, followed by the blast of a tugboat horn, warning smaller fishing vessels to give way as they negotiated their way in and out of the harbor.

"This is spectacular," she said in a breathless whisper, her eyes wide as her gaze took in the busy scene. "When you told me about playing here as a boy, I tried to imagine this place." She shook her head. "I couldn't even comprehend the light and colors, much less the scents and sounds. This is incredibly, unimaginably beautiful."

"So are you," he said, sincerely and utterly taken with his bride.

"How can you look at me when your eyes could be feasting on all of this?" she asked, her sweeping gesture including the waterfront and the ships farther out in the harbor.

"Your question is backward, my love." He slipped his hand over hers where it rested on her lap. "The question is how could I look at anything else when all I desire to see is your beautiful face?"

She laughed and turned her palm up to lace her fingers with his. "How did I not know Detective Sullivan was hiding this romantic side?" she asked.

"Because he was undercover and very good at his job."

"Do you miss it?" she asked, her smile fading.

"A little," he said truthfully. "I miss the investigative work of solving puzzles and ferreting out details, but I don't miss the security work." Giving her hand a light squeeze, he said, "I enjoy what I'm doing at the shipyard and being reconnected with my family. Living a new and better life with you in Crane Landing is the kind of life I want, Sophia, and I hope you'll be happy there. It's a beautiful place like this," he said, gesturing to the sundrenched harbor.

"It sounds wonderful, and being there with you will be a dream come true." She pressed a chaste kiss to his cheek. "I can't imagine wanting to be anyplace else."

"Well, my love, we do have to be someplace else in about an hour," he said, checking the time on his watch. "Since it's our last night here, I hope you don't mind having supper with my family again."

"Of course not." She angled her knees slightly to face him.

"Your parents are delightful, and your sister is adorable. Truly, Gray, I'm enjoying every minute of our time here."

So was he, and it reaffirmed his decision to make a long-overdue apology to his family for not being the son and brother they deserved, and to let them know their future together would be very different.

CHAPTER TWENTY

S ophia had been in Crane Landing three weeks and it
already felt like home.

Gray's brothers and friends had drawn her into their
fold as if she were their long-lost sister. Their shared meals and
frequent family gatherings gave her a sense of community, and
one she deeply appreciated, but it also made her miss her parents.

As she sat at the dressing table in their upstairs flat of her
brother-in-law's estate, she marveled over the luxury and comfort
of her new home. The instant she met Ashe, she felt she'd gained a
dear friend. He made it clear they were welcome at his estate for
as long as they wanted to stay or, jokingly stated, until the unlikely
event he brought home a wife of his own. That had sealed their
friendship and set the tone for the evenings they all spent together
laughing and sharing stories.

Gray's parents and sister had arrived the previous day and had
spent a festive evening with them at Ashe's estate. Leo and Grace
and her little brother Willy had joined them. To see Gray
reunited with his parents and siblings filled her with gratitude that
he had these wonderful people back in his life. Learning more
about Gray's childhood and how it had affected him and his

siblings helped her understand him better. Despite their hard-ships, and in some cases their good fortune, she could see the resemblance between the brothers. They were handsome, strong, dependable men—and she felt fortunate to be married to one of them.

"Hello, beautiful," Gray said, coming into their bedroom. He was fresh out of the bathtub, droplets of water covering his torso and dripping off his hair as he stalked her with a linen tied around his waist.

"Do not get my dress wet," she said, laughing and leaping to her feet. She grabbed her dressing robe and thrust it out in front of her to stop his approach, but he moved in fast.

With a broad smile, he clasped her in a robust hug, trapping her robe between them, and lifted her off her feet. Giving her a playful twirl, he said, "I missed you entirely too much while I was at work today, and I didn't even get a proper hug when I got home."

"That's because you were filthy, Mr. Sullivan."

"Well, I've decided to quit my job because it keeps me away from you all day," he said, nuzzling her neck.

She popped a kiss on his cheek. "You can't quit because I plan to visit my parents every few weeks and you'll need to purchase my train tickets."

Easing her back in his arms, he met her eyes. "Sweetheart, you can visit them whenever you like. But before you head for the train depot, I have a surprise for you."

"You do?" she asked, loving the game he was playing with her. "Do tell!"

"You'll see this evening at our celebration dinner."

She puckered her lips in a playful pout. "Are you really going to make me wait that long?"

"Yes, love, you'll have to wait a whole thirty minutes."

Surprised at the time, she glanced at the wall clock. "Gracious! I need to dress my hair for dinner." With that, she pushed from his arms and turned toward the dressing table.

"Not so fast, Mrs. Sullivan," he said, sweeping an arm around her waist and turning her to face him. "I can't go another minute without kissing you." He drew her fully into his arms and lowered his mouth to hers.

The world tilted and wings flapped in her belly as she clung to her husband. Warm, hard muscles flexed beneath her hands as they embraced. For a moment, she considered asking him to use those muscles to carry her to their bed, but the sound of someone knocking on their door interrupted them.

"Your guests are arriving," she heard Ashe call through the door, then the sound of his footsteps faded as he moved down the wide, carpeted hallway.

Gray cast a mock scowl toward the door. "I think I'll cancel the party and keep you to myself this evening."

"You will do no such thing." She gave him a playful push. "Get dressed and stop pestering me so I can make myself presentable."

"Sophia, it's impossible for you to look more beautiful," he said, his eyes filled with sincerity and love and the promise of forever. With that, he dropped his linen on the carpet and walked away, leaving her staring open-mouthed at his bare backside.

She burst out laughing. "You are incorrigible, Mr. Sullivan."

"I know," he said, then disappeared into the adjoining room.

It took her ten minutes to contain her giggles and fix her hair.

Finally, on the arm of her handsome, incorrigible husband, she was escorted down a wide hallway to an elaborate staircase that brought them to the first floor and the ballroom where Ashe was talking to the early arrivals.

Giving her a wink, Gray said, "I hope you like your surprise," then he gestured toward the couple talking with Ashe.

When she saw her parents, she gasped and pressed her fingertips to her mouth. For a moment, she stood in the doorway, glancing between her husband and her parents who hadn't noticed their arrival. Releasing a watery laugh, she said, "I don't know how you managed this, but thank you." She hugged his arm tight against her side. "This is the best surprise ever."

"That's not the surprise, darling."

"What could possibly be more surprising than bringing my parents to our wedding celebration?"

"How about moving them to Crane Landing?"

She sighed wistfully. "That would be more than a surprise. It would be a dream come true."

"It's not a dream, sweetheart. Your parents are here to stay."

Her heart jolted and she studied her husband's face to see if he was toying with her, but he seemed sincere. "Is that true?"

He cupped her face, gazing into her eyes. "Yes, love."

"How? I mean, how is it possible? My parents couldn't even afford the train fare to get here."

"We were in need of a good maintenance man at the shipyard, so I told Leo about your father. He offered to move your parents here if your father took the job. I was going to tell you the good news last week, but your parents wanted to surprise you."

To know that her mother and father would have an easier life now, and would remain a part of hers, was something she could have only dreamed of. Somehow Gray had known how deeply she'd worried about them, how much they meant to her, and how badly she'd missed them. With tears of gratitude blurring her vision, she looked up at her husband, the man who'd stolen her heart, and whispered, "I'll never forget this moment."

"Nor will I," Gray said, gazing at his wife's beautiful face, feeling immense satisfaction that the pain in her eyes had been replaced by joy.

Now that he was reunited with his own family, he understood Sophia's need to have her parents near. Although he would always carry a wound in his heart over losing his brother Cal, Gray also carried hope that they might one day be reunited. Tonight, he would meet his little brother Benny and the people who'd given him and Leo a home. Rebecca and Adam Grayson would be attending, along with several members of the Grayson family and the Crane family who would all be arriving soon. His community was expanding in a way that left him marveling at all the changes in his life. For so long, he'd been wandering alone, untethered in a storm of emotions that battered him relentlessly, carrying him from one place to another without any relief...until he'd found Sophia. Until she'd forced him to stop, to feel, to care. Caring made him vulnerable, but she had made him realize what he'd once considered a weakness was in reality a precious gift.

As the ballroom filled with their family members and friends, Gray embraced them all, filling his new life, and his heart, with the love and friendships he'd denied himself for too long. With pride and deep devotion, he introduced his wife to their guests. Together, he and Sophia mingled, dined, and danced, and as the musicians played into the night, he drew his wife close in his arms. Gazing into her loving eyes, he knew it was she who'd rescued him. She'd tended his wounds, helped him heal, and taught him how to love again.

ABOUT WENDY LINDSTROM

Wendy Lindstrom is the RITA award-winning and *New York Times* bestselling author of the Grayson family saga, a captivating series of feel-good, emotionally powerful novels. Her books are unforgettable, heartwarming stories about enduring friendships, family bonds, and romantic relationships between strong, complex characters living in a charming small town in America.

Fans of uplifting, binge-worthy historical romance will love Miss Lindstrom's popular Grayson family series, a #1 storewide best-seller on Barnes and Noble, and a *New York Times* and *USA Today* bestselling series. Romantic Times has dubbed her "one of romance's finest writers," and readers rave about her enthralling characters and the "awesome underlying emotional power" of her work. The Grayson Brothers series is a must-read for those who love stories that uplift and warm the heart.

For more information about the author, her books, and to get the behind-the-scenes scoop at her Rustic Studio—a world much like the Grayson world—visit her website and also subscribe to her engaging newsletter where she shares personal stories about the magnificent wildlife at her Rustic Studio, her insights on writing, her tiny house obsession, landscaping her beautiful water-garden, her passion for great books, her love of martial arts, and other fun subjects.

You can also follow her on BookBub.

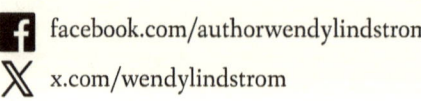

facebook.com/authorwendylindstrom

x.com/wendylindstrom

www.ingramcontent.com/pod-product-compliance
Lightning Source LLC
Chambersburg PA
CBHW050308110726
47899CB00007B/2154